THE NOMAD'S PREMONITION

GEORGES BENAY

STORY MERCHANT BOOKS
LOS ANGELES
2017

Copyright © 2017 by Georges Benay. All rights reserved.

No part of this book may be reproduced or transmitted in any form or by any means, electronic or mechanical, including photocopying, recording, or by any information storage and retrieval system, without the express written permission of the author. This is a work of fiction. Names, characters, businesses, places, events and incidents are either the products of the author's imagination or used in a fictitious manner. Any resemblance to actual persons, living or dead, or actual events is purely coincidental.

www.georgesbenay.com
www.georgesbenayphotoart.fototime.com

ISBN: 978-0-9981628-6-7

Story Merchant Books
400 S. Burnside Avenue #11B
Los Angeles, CA 90036

http://www.storymerchant.com/books.html

Cover & interior formatting by IndieDesignz.com

Also by Georges Benay

An Eric Martin Nomad Series

Nomad on the Run

A fast-paced thriller set in the beautiful and exotic Kingdom of Morocco about greed, deceit and a vicious scheme to terrorize the global financial markets…

Please turn to the back of this book for a preview.

Acclaim for Nomad on the Run

"Georges Benay's Nomad on the Run is a riveting thriller imbued with one difficult choice after another for the central character. One wrong step and all may be lost, "But when you feel a strong urge to do something, you must follow your heart. Nothing else must stand in your way, no matter what the consequences." An intriguing plotline, vivid descriptions of foreign settings, and stunning character development are just a few of the many positive aspects that Nomad on the Run offers."

Mihir Shah, Word Whispers

"Georges Benay's thriller, Nomad on the Run, is a spellbinding page-turner set in the beautiful and exotic country of Morocco...... Greed is said to be one of the seven deadly sins and Benay hits every aspect of it. In Nomad on the Run, Benay's character of Eric Martin keeps readers on the edge of their seats as he tries to unravel this web he has been caught up in."

Brittany Walters Bearden, GreatText-pectation

"Nomad on the Run is a page-turner from beginning to end..... I doubt this will be the last novel the reading public will see from Georges Benay."

Sean Liv, AllBooks Revealed

"Georges Benay has written a world-class novel and will have you reading right up to the final, cryptic message. You will enjoy the trip....a winner right out of the starting gate. He has peopled Nomad on the Run with a wide range of interesting and believable characters, and created a word canvas rich in detail...and when the reader has manoeuvred past the plot twists and reads past the roadblocks in the protagonist's path, the reward will be a story you will remember long after you read the last page."

Chuck Wadrton, author

"You will find a humane hero caught in situations that deliver realistic emotions and thrills aplenty along the way. It's a great ride with lots of wonderful scenery both internal and external. *Nomad on the Run* provides a completely engaging read for the thinking reader from beginning to end."

Stevan Jovanovich, author

THE NOMAD'S PREMONITION

In Memory of Rachel and Elias Bénay

PART ONE

"Like a nomad in the desert, he heard the wind whisper in his ear of exotic places, new adventures, and a new life. It was time for him to return to where it had all begun."

NOMAD ON THE RUN

CHAPTER 1

PARIS, FRANCE

Eric Martin's face tightened, then broke into a deep frown. He immediately recognized the signs the moment the data first appeared on the screen of his computer.

The mysterious trader was back in the market.

It should not have come as a surprise, but it did somehow. He had hoped that the trader had simply gone away—just moved on without a trace like an unresolved crime no one cared about anymore. But, that was not going to happen because the trader was akin to a bad virus that had a stranglehold on your computer. Except that in this case, it was Eric who was hooked.

He watched the deal flash across the monitor: a long series of numbers in evenly spaced columns marching along his giant LED monitor at lightning speed. A fraction of a second later another trade popped up, followed by a third, and then a fourth. Row after row the powerful computer spewed data in the blink of an eye across the length of the display monitor. There was barely enough time to transmit one transaction before the next one started to kick in. It went on for several minutes, and when it ended, three full screens were covered from top to bottom with enough figures and records to fill an entire order book.

There was nothing unusual about these buy-and-sell trades. Neither the speed of their executions, nor the size of the transactions, and certainly nothing about the counterparties were particularly noteworthy. Yet, Eric had a visceral reaction the moment the trades appeared in rapid succession on his computer. He stared a moment longer at the large screen, waiting for more data to pop up. When none showed, he swiveled his chair around and glanced at the top of his office desk. He grabbed the top printout of a huge stack of documents blanketed with computer generated facts and numbers, and closely examined the long list of figures. Line upon line, records of stock exchange transactions populated the long printout. The amount, time, and date of the trades were printed next to each buy and sell deal. The name of the counterparty—in all cases an anonymous numbered company—appeared in bold letters across the page.

What troubled Eric was not the sheer volume or frequency of the transactions that had been recorded over the past couple of months by some anonymous trader. That the trader had been very active of late was not significant in itself. After all, the bank's stocks had been flagged on every trading room around the globe since the start of the eurozone debacle.

No. Something else about the trading patterns he had observed so many times before did not feel right. There were too many coincidences. Too many improbable trades and too many good market calls.

What was really going on? He could sense the threat but could not explain it. And if this was not maddening enough, he could not get rid of the nagging feeling that someone was toying with him.

He was still deep in thought when the sharp ring tone of the phone startled him. He inhaled a deep breath, stared at the receiver for a second or two, and finally picked it up on the third ring. The booming voice of his boss, Alain Lepetit, reverberated in the room.

"Ah, good, you're still in the office."

"Yes, Alain. What can I do for you?" Eric replied curtly.

"Oh, I see you're having a bad day. Your mysterious trader is at it again?"

Eric ignored his boss's sarcastic remark. He was running out of patience with him, particularly when the issue of the trader arose. They had discussed his suspicions over and over again, and each time Alain Lepetit had dismissed his theories as pure speculation, conjecture, or plain nonsense. This time, Eric was reaching his boiling point, and he struggled with his tone.

"Alain, we really need to talk."

A silent pause at the other end of the line. Eric squeezed the receiver, expecting to hear more counter-arguments, reasons for dropping the case, or threats to fire him if he did not obey his boss. To his surprise, he heard none of these things. Instead, Alain Lepetit took an unexpected tack.

"OK let's mull over what's bothering you at dinner tonight. I'm heading for the coast on the TGV. I should arrive at half past seven this evening, why don't you join us, at say eight o'clock. Will that work for you? Chantal misses you, you know. She asked me to tell you that she is preparing your very favorite meal—roast lamb and couscous."

At the mention of Chantal, Eric pushed his dark thoughts away. "Please thank Chantal for me. And tell her that this is the best offer I have received in years."

The smile quickly vanished from his face soon after he hung up. He glanced at his reflection on the computer screen. What he saw was the face of a man torn by his past, one that had nearly cost him his life.

The last trades captured by the bank's state-of-the-art global tracking system had fired up Eric even more. *Was he blinded by the echoes of his previous dreadful experience, or was his judgment clouded by his hyperactive imagination*? He struggled with that thought for a long time, not knowing where to turn for an answer.

He was well aware of the high-speed trading systems in which computer-driven trades were made in fractions of a second. Armed with powerful algorithms, or "algos" as they were called in the industry, investment banks, hedge funds, and other securities firms could execute millions of trades in rapid-fire, buy-and-sell orders while simultaneously scanning for other opportunities in the capital and equity markets across the globe. They could spot trends across industries, public and private sectors, commodities, and currency exchange rates before the regular investors had time to blink. The high-speed, high-frequency traders always aimed at exploiting tiny price discrepancies, moving in and out in mere milliseconds, thereby rapidly reaping huge profits without leaving a trace. Rarely would they commit their firms' funds to remain invested for any length of time.

But this trader showed a very odd investment behavior. He often acted like one of those high-frequency specialists, in and out of the market in a nanosecond. The trade volumes were never excessively high, however, and the frequencies of the trades were not remarkable either. *A low-grade trader with perhaps a below average investment risk limit*, Eric thought the first time he had spotted the activities of this mysterious trader.

And then once in a while, for no apparent reason, the trader would sit on an investment for weeks at a time, sometimes even longer. The amounts of the hold investments varied, but were never exceptionally large, just like his other high-speed transactions. At times, he would sell the entire hold in one trade; at other times he would scatter the sale over several small tickets at irregular intervals.

There was nothing predictable about this trader's behavior. Except for one thing—his market calls were nearly infallible.

Eric had done a statistical analysis on the trader's transactions. The results were incredible. The trader just seemed to have a knack for making the right market decisions most of the time. The correlation was even higher for his hold investments. Seven to eight times out of ten his buy-and-sell timings were right on, always managing to reap a nice profit.

At first, Eric thought he was dealing with either a very smart market analyst or a very lucky one. But the predictive accuracies of the trades proved far too consistent to believe that smarts or luck alone had anything to do with it. *The trader must somehow have access to privileged information—an insider perhaps*, he reasoned. But in the end, he sensed something else was at play, and he did not like at all the implications.

The more Eric pondered the question, the more he felt a tightness rising from deep inside his chest. Eric was known for his logical, systematic, and thorough approach to problem solving. He had always relied on getting all the facts before making a decision. Every problem would be dissected between need-to-know and must-know data and information. He would research in depth every issue ad nauseam, consult and discuss the matter with every specialist he could get his hands on, and then he would act swiftly and decisively.

That had made him a successful investment banker in his earlier life.

But not anymore. Not since the terror he had experienced in Casablanca. Out of the ashes of that horrific experience he had learned to trust his instincts even if he could not rationally explain them. He now paid a lot more attention to his gut feelings—even if sometimes they defied common sense. The data was pointing in one direction, but his intuition was telling him something quite different. And by now his guts were blaring all kinds of warning signals at him.

He quickly glanced around his office, looking for something or someone to calm him down. He often felt that way when memories of what happened in Casablanca began pouring out of his subconscious mind. Although more than three years had passed since his whole world came crashing down on him, his mental state was still fragile. Time had not done its job. He had not healed, and all kinds of raw emotions still brewed inside him.

Eric rose from his chair, no longer able to suppress his dark thoughts. He stood in the middle of the office, forced himself to breathe normally, and took stock of his surroundings. It was not much of an office by North American standards, but this was Paris after all. He now lived and worked in the old world where space was at a premium. Nonetheless, he cherished the privacy his small office afforded him, even if his current seniority status at the bank did not justify him having such a privilege. He owed this benefit to his job function. As Director, Global Security and Internal Control ("GSIC"), at Banque du Commerce headquarters, he often came across extremely sensitive and very confidential files. Thus, the office was not only his sanctuary, it was also in a way a kind of Fort Knox, protected twenty-four hours a day, seven days a week by security guards posted outside at both ends of the hallway.

He walked to the window and stared blankly at the grey expanse in front of him. His favorite view was all but gone. The clouds hung low and heavy above the city, masking one of the most beautiful skylines in the world. Nice and the Côte d'Azur were a mere hour and a half flight from Paris, and he needed a break like never before. One last look at the city, enveloped in faint darkness, convinced him to pack up and lock his office in a hurry.

He scribbled two names on a yellow sticker, placed it on the top page of the document he had just finished reviewing, and shoved the trader's data in the safe. He then picked up the phone and asked to speak to Bartolli at Interpol. Their conversation was short and polite. Eric did most of the talking. Bartolli hummed a few times and asked all the right questions. He was as professional as they come, but Eric noticed a distinct lack of enthusiasm. Financial crimes were hard to prove, assuming you could even show that a crime had been committed. *I'm afraid our friendship is not going to be enough to get him on board*, Eric thought as he stared at the bare walls of his office.

CHAPTER 2

There is nothing more excruciating than being called first thing in the morning by an executive assistant, who then informs you that a top brass would like to see you immediately, but you don't have a clue why you are being summoned in the first place.

Alain Lepetit had received such a call the moment he walked into his office at eight o'clock Friday morning. He did not know what to make of it, and so he called in his personal assistant who, like all good PA's, worked in mysterious ways through informal channels where no secrets were safe for long. When she drew a blank, he felt his blood pressure rise a notch or two. For a moment he almost choked up, fearing that his worst nightmare was about to unfold. He knew that in the corporate world good things seldom last long. He felt good about the job he had done since they brought him back from the Canadian subsidiary to fix and strengthen the bank's internal security division. But, one could never be too careful or too certain of anything these days. What if something had slipped through the cracks? What if someone had managed to defraud the bank without his knowledge? These scary thoughts only added to his uneasiness.

And then a more frightening thought crossed his mind. *What if Eric had taken his crazy notion about the trader to the higher-ups behind his back?* It would be a kiss of death for his career at the bank. But he dismissed the idea right away, too terrified to even consider the ramifications.

"Eric would not do that; he owes me far too much," he mumbled under his breath as he walked the long corridor on his way to the elevators.

The ride up to the executive suite gave him even more time to worry about the fate that might be waiting for him on the twenty-eighth floor of Banque du

Commerce's twin tower. He hung tightly onto his attaché case as if his life depended on it, aware that the gesture was, in fact, futile. No documents could save him if someone had uncovered what he feared the most about his mission in Canada. By the time the elevator reached the executive floor, he had lost the ability to speak. A security guard and a young woman were waiting for him, posted in front of the elevator doors like two sentinels. He flashed his security pass at the guard and gave a thin smile to the pretty executive assistant. She ignored his smile and immediately ushered him to an oval-shaped reception room where at least a dozen people were already seated.

Alain Lepetit immediately sensed the charged atmosphere and the higher-than-normal level of activity swirling around him in the reception area. He knew that behind the two large, heavy oak doors at the far end of the reception area was the board room where the Executive Committee held its special sessions before meeting with the full Board of Directors. Urgent matters, sensitive and confidential issues, and important decisions were hammered out behind these massive doors by a small select group of five, sometimes six, key senior executive officers. No outside members of the Board were ever allowed in this sanctum. Hired consultants were always asked to sign a lengthy confidentiality agreement before stepping into the room, and then were required to initial a log confirming their visit before leaving the premises. Mid-level executives were hardly ever called in.

Alain Lepetit was, by now, in a state of total panic.

He observed the steady flow of "grey suits," stomping in and out of the board room, their small armies of young staff members tailing close behind with their hands full of thick and heavy file folders. Everyone seemed to be in a hurry. No one stopped to acknowledge his presence. Their faces were totally void of expression as they marched like zombies under the spell of some sort of subdued hysteria. A close encounter with the Executive Committee had that effect on everyone.

An hour, maybe more, had gone by, but he could not be sure, as he resisted looking at his watch for fear of appearing to be the worrier-type. Finally, desperate to do something—anything—he picked up a newspaper that someone had left behind on the small corner table at his side. The headline was a pleasant distraction after all the gloom and doom he had seen in the press over the summer months. The caption on the front page of the London Times trumpeted, in supersized bold letters, the great news of the day.

"World's Central Banks Act to Stabilize Financial System."

The headline immediately caught his attention, and he quickly scanned the article, enjoying the piece of good news for a change.

" .... the central banks around the globe, in a unified effort to prevent a debt

crisis in Europe from exploding, took coordinated action to ease the strains of the world's financial system. The announcement came just hours after China reduced bank reserve levels to release lending funds and boost economic growth."

His grin widened as he continued reading. *Inside the boardroom they must all be breathing a deep sigh of relief,* he reflected with delight when he had finished reading the news clip. It was not a secret that the bank had large sovereign risk exposures in all the countries most talked about in the press. Greece, Spain, Italy, and Portugal were just some of the most troublesome exposures weighing heavily on Banque du Commerce's balance sheet. Speculations about the bank's ability to survive without government support were rampant in the media. Talks of a forced merger with one of Banque du Commerce's most hated competitors made the headlines regularly. One day, Societe Generale, more commonly known as SocGen, was the identified suitor. The next day, after strong denials were issued by the bank's public relation department, BNP emerged as the more likely white knight, only to be denied that privilege the following day by another series of strongly worded statements. They were all rumors of course, but they took their toll on the morale of the bank employees—not to mention its stock price that fluctuated like a yo-yo these days. Under the circumstances, the news this morning was a welcome change, and so he believed he really had nothing to worry about.

I wonder if Eric's trader was ahead of the curve on this one? Alain Lepetit was still wearing a malicious smile when he noticed the young executive assistant standing in front of him like a Swiss guard, impeccably dressed in her blue and gold suit matching the bank's logo colors.

"Monsieur Marchand is now ready to see you," she said in a barely audible voice. Please follow me, Monsieur Lepetit."

Alain Lepetit walked into a cavernous board room. It was outrageously large, as was the oval-shaped marble conference table that virtually filled the entire room. There was no one in the room except for one small and very bald man seated in an oversized black leather chair at the far end of the table. The man was busy signing letters and communiqués that an associate was feeding him one at a time without interruption. The room still carried the scent of excitement of the good news of the day. The leather seats, perfectly lined up along all four sides of the conference table, felt warm to the touch. Alain Lepetit took a few tentative steps forward, stopped a few feet from the door, and then seemed to hesitate for a moment as if waiting for a signal from his superior.

"Come in, Alain, don't be shy. This won't take long," Marchand said without raising his head, while scribbling his initials on the documents that were being fed to him.

After a short, uncomfortable silence and a long swirl of the pen in the air, Marchand looked up to level his gaze at Alain Lepetit. "There. I'm finished. Let's talk now, Alain."

Alain Lepetit felt the large lump once again rising up in his throat, getting dangerously close to choking him. He tried to get rid of it with a cough that came out louder than he intended.

Marchand looked momentarily startled. He then smiled and asked, "Do you need a glass of water, *mon pauvre* Alain?"

"No thank you, I have been trying to fight this damned cold for a week. I'm fine now," he lied.

"You must be wondering why I called you up to see me this morning." Without giving Alain Lepetit time to respond, he went on with what he had in mind. "An opening for a country manager in Australia has just come up. Would you be interested?"

"Yes, I..."

"Good, I thought so," Marchand interrupted him. "The position is yours. You have done an excellent job for us at Internal Security. The control systems that you put in place are superior to anything I have seen at other banks. Not a single fraud committed in over three years. Not a single illegal insider trading incident since you took charge. This is a remarkable achievement that would make my colleagues across the street green with envy. Just think of all the headaches that this rogue trader gave to Socgen,. . . .what's his name?"

"Jerome Kerviel."

"Yes that's right. . . all the damage that he has caused them. He reportedly ran unauthorized positions worth about 50 billion euro and the bank took a 4.9 billion euro hit because of him. Can you believe that! A single rogue trader working in the mine for god's sake, the least sophisticated trading room in the bank. To think that he could manage to do such a thing, undetected for over two years, is mind boggling."

"It will never happen to us," Alain Lepetit said, growing in confidence.

"Don't be so sure of yourself. The check and balance systems that you have implemented are good, in fact they are very good by most standards, but they are not infallible. It's only a matter of time before someone will find a way around them. That's the only certainty that we can count on in our business. You must have forgotten about that Russian fellow who worked at Goldman."

"Sergey Aleynikov."

"Yes that's the one. Didn't he try to run away with Goldman Sachs' source codes for their proprietary high-frequency trading program?"

Alain Lepetit's heart froze. This time he was sure he would collapse and die at that very instant. Was he being 'elegantly displaced' to some far away country while the bank ran its investigation on him? Was Eric right about his suspicions about the mysterious trader after all? All of a sudden, morbid thoughts invaded his mind, clouding his brain, stifling his energy, crushing his earlier bravado. All he could manage to mutter was— "But Sir, I'm sure you're aware that he was caught before he could cause any serious problems."

Marchand stared hard at Alain Lepetit and watched his managing director of Global Security and Internal Control turn various shades of red. He gave Alain Lepetit the full dress-down stare, the one reserved to underlings who had dared challenge his judgment.

"Alain, Alain, don't be so full of yourself," he finally barked. "That's the problem with you people. That's the trap most bad managers fall into when things are going too well for them for too long. Complacency sets in, and they start believing their own lies. I thought you were better than them—with your background and first-hand experience in these matters."

He paused to catch his breath, and in a tone demanding total attention he hissed, "Have you forgotten that we had our own algorithmic trading model stolen from us four years ago? If it were not for the intervention of Interpol and your second-in-command, we would have had a disaster of catastrophic proportion on our hands."

"No, Monsieur Marchand, I have not forgotten. But thanks to our American friends, the software program has been destroyed."

"Alain, you don't need to remind me of what I already know. The problem with that way of thinking is that it ensures we'll end up in a deeper mess if we're not careful. Are you 100% sure that no other copies were ever made? Can you give me an unequivocal assurance that is, indeed, the case?"

"Yes sir. If someone had our algorithm, we would have heard about it by now. Besides, even if copies were ever made, they would be totally useless without the codes to decipher them. And as far as I know, the codes are buried forever with the man who gave his life to protect them."

"You mean Ivan Berdyek, the crazy Czech genius," Marchand cut in.

"Yes sir. He chose to sacrifice himself rather than reveal the codes to these mad men. He acted like a true hero, sacrificing his life to protect the bank."

"Or a crazy thief," snapped Marchand. "Let's not forget that nothing would have happened if he had not stolen the algo in the first place. In any case, I happen to agree with you. But you must always remain vigilant, you hear me! Where there's money, there will be people trying to steal it. And the algorithm developed by the bank is an incredibly effective money-making machine."

Marchand stopped talking for a moment to look up at the young aide standing at the door and nodded his acknowledgement.

"I have only a few minutes left before my next meeting. Let's conclude the matter at hand, shall we? We must think about a suitable replacement for you. Here is a short list of candidates that my staff put together. I would like to have your recommendation by the end of the week, and I'll give you a month to get back to me with your ideas on how to boost business in our Australian subsidiary. Got that? Any questions?"

Marchand did not bother waiting for Alain Lepetit's response. He rose from his chair and walked briskly out of the board room. The executive assistant had already started her briefing before he reached the two massive oak doors that served as gatekeepers to the most restricted room of the bank.

Left alone, Alain Lepetit felt as if the board room had transformed itself into the tiniest cell he had ever seen. He had the impression that the walls were closing in on him, and he worried that at any time now there would not be enough air to breathe. In truth, there was no room large enough in the whole world capable of containing the excitement and sheer joy he felt at the moment.

Alain Lepetit was about to realize his long awaited dream.

What he had been hoping for, for so long, was now at last within his grasp. Only one thorny problem stood in his way—but he already had a solution for that.

CHAPTER 3

The moment he walked into his office, Alain Lepetit could no longer contain his excitement. His morning coffee was ice cold where he had left it on his desk before racing up to the executive floor earlier in the day, but he did not complain about it to his assistant. He also ignored the half-dozen or so messages gathered in a neat pile beside the phone. Instead, he dialed the number of his condo in Villeneuve Loubet, where his wife Chantal spent most of the winter months since their return to Paris. She did not seem to share his enthusiasm when he told her the news about his new posting in Australia. But that did not faze him; she was from the north of France after all. He did note, however, a friendlier tone in her voice when he informed her that he was planning to invite Eric over for dinner.

"Please tell Eric that I will be preparing his favorite meal," she had said in her soft voice before hanging up.

Alain Lepetit could not believe his good luck. His lifelong dream was about to become a reality, and nothing could dampen his spirits. He fondly remembered when he first discovered the natural beauty of Australia while strolling on a sunny afternoon along *la Promenade des Anglais* in Nice. The poster, which covered the full length of the window of the travel agency, had immediately caught his attention. He was fascinated by the golden beach, the powerful surf, and in particular, the blond and very young female surfers. That image remained forever etched in his brain. And now, many years later, the opportunity to turn a dream into a reality was being offered to him.

He recalled his conversation with Marchand earlier in the morning. Australia had been dangled in front of him like a sweet to a child. His reward for a job well done, he had been told.

Alain Lepetit was no fool, however.

He understood what motivated his superiors in granting him a promotion after only a little more than three years at his current post. The Goldman Sachs affair had spooked them. The astronomical fraud of Nick Leeson—which went undetected for months and ultimately had brought down Barings—had frightened them even more. And to top it all, they had seen what happened to the unfortunate top executive rank at Societe Generale in the aftermath of the Jerome Kerviel scandal. It was not a fate that his superiors particularly relished.

Alain Lepetit knew full well that he was being promoted, or more accurately displaced, in the time honored tradition of the bank. One should not feel too comfortable in a trusted position for too long, no matter how great the job performance or the pressure of maintaining status quo. He was well aware that driven by fear, the bank executives would go to extremes to shuffle the deck as often as possible before complacency had time to settle in.

The old fool wants me out because he is afraid that I might fall asleep at the switch, Alain Lepetit thought of his boss' job offer. *But what really matters is that I'm going to get what I want. Who cares about his motivation?*

Alain Lepetit was a very proud man, some might even say vain at the core. He had no qualms in taking full credit for the achievements of his staff, whether he had anything to do with it or not. People did not like working for him for that reason. But no one could ever deny his exceptional organizational skills. He had a real flair for spotting exceptional talents, not just gifted employees but the absolute ideal candidates to fill the most demanding vacancies. The quick turnaround he had achieved when he took over the leadership of the moribund Internal Security Division had solidified his reputation in the bank. He had immediately cleaned house and brought in the best analytical brains from the bank's control and audit departments across the globe. He sought analysts possessing a rare combination of strong statistical background and unbridled creativity. And to inspire his staff, he quickly realized that he would also need a second in command who did not feel constrained by rules and regulations. He knew he would need to recruit an intelligent, imaginative, and tenacious rebel to complement his team of technically savvy analysts.

And so he immediately thought of Eric Martin, who had once worked for him as the head of the Toronto office. They had parted ways when Eric had decided to join a small investment bank in Casablanca. That experience had turned out to be a huge mistake—one that had nearly cost Eric his life. Left for dead at the bottom of the Mediterranean, Eric had been rescued in the nick of time by the American Special Forces. He was the only survivor. The terrorists had all been killed, their bodies scattered over the ocean floor, and with them the stolen algorithm forever buried in the sand. Alain Lepetit had found Eric barely alive in a military hospital in Toulouse. He had endured a horrific nightmare and was lost and in need of support and guidance more than ever. That's when Alain Lepetit approached Eric with his job offer—an offer he knew Eric could hardly afford to refuse.

For three years the Control and Internal Security Division performed marvelously well under Alain Lepetit's leadership. The new security systems were monitored like hawks by his team and turned out to be a virtual juggernaut against any attempt to defraud the bank. Above all, he was particularly pleased that he had found a way to entice Eric to join the group. He was by far his best recruit. Despite a few rebellious incidents along the way, Eric had been instrumental in keeping the staff alert, always ahead of the learning curve, and constantly challenged to think outside the box.

Satisfied with himself, Alain Lepetit glanced at his reflection on the monitor of his computer and broke into a wide grin. "You're a very lucky, good-looking fellow," he mouthed while brushing off a strand of hair from his face. He had retained his youthful appearance and a twinkle in his eye despite his twenty something years at the bank. He had also been fortunate to have been born into an old family blessed with wealth and a good name in a country where affluence, pedigree, and tradition meant everything. His good family-standing had gained him access to the prestigious, French National School of Administration, more commonly known as ENA, even if the results of his entrance exams were far below average. Armed with the much sought-after diploma, he was set for life—virtually guaranteed a rapid and successful career path in any public or private French organization.

He was only twenty-four when he joined the Inspection Department of Banque du Commerce, a sort of internal audit with a much broader mandate than its North American counterparts. The inspection reviews dealt with such issues as strategy, adequacy, and quality of the staff, as well as the appropriateness of the mandates ascribed to the subsidiaries. Although the job was not particularly stimulating and not very demanding, a good performance in the Inspection Department was considered a stamp of approval for an executive position at the bank.

After two good audits and a mere year and a half in the Inspection Department, Alain Lepetit's career began its meteoric rise. He was given a succession of appointments with a vast array of ever increasing responsibilities in the bank, beginning in Hong Kong, then Singapore, London, Seoul, and finally back to Paris where he was placed in charge of a global product line. Eight years later he was posted in New York, where he assumed various senior management functions over a five year period, culminating in his appointment as Deputy Managing Director for the Americas Division. In 2007, he was nominated Country Manager and President of the Canadian operations. That's when his troubles started.

"In Montreal, I'm a big fish in a small pond," he often used to brag to his colleagues in New York. At first, he dedicated all his energy and attention to reshaping the Canadian subsidiary. He began by strengthening the Toronto office with a focus on financial institutions, the automotive and telecom sectors, then setting up shop in Calgary to capture the booming oil and gas industry. In Montreal, he hired the best market analysts and foreign exchange traders to augment the already formidable equity desk. All went well according to plan for a couple of years. Growth, profit, and return on equity increased by leaps and bounds. The big boys in New York were throwing envious glances at him. Senior executives in Paris congratulated themselves on their wise choice of country head for the Canadian subsidiary. And his wife seemed to have settled down in her routine, finally accepting the fact that winters were dreadfully cold in the Province of Quebec.

But then he allowed the success to get to his head, and his roving eyes went in overdrive.

Blond, young, athletic—with a smile flashing at you like a strobe light—the poster girl summer-trainee was too good to resist.

Why did she have to lie about her age and keep that child, for Christ's sakes? She was just a child herself.

It took him a very long time to get out of Montreal and get a new posting elsewhere. He hated the thought of going back to headquarters where he would be another mid-level executive among hundreds of other equally insignificant executives in the big scheme of things. But he finally accepted the challenge offered to him, knowing that it was the only way to escape from what could turn out to be a total disaster for his career.

But that was the past and now a bright future lay ahead of him. He had paid his dues, and Australia would soon be his reward. He paused to look at the list of candidates on the documents marked 'strictly confidential' that Marchand had given him. Four names were listed in alphabetical order, along with a brief description of the candidates' current responsibilities. His mind was already made up. His successor would have to be malleable, so qualifications were secondary. He examined each name for a while, drawing on his vast memory banks. It did not take him long to recognize every name, and he was not surprised that they had made the short list. He deliberated for a moment longer and then circled the third name. He then placed a question mark against the first name and crossed out Eric Martin from the list. *Now,* he thought, *I better spend some time devising a winning strategy for the Australian subsidiary,* and his mind went automatically to Canada.

The high-pitched tone of his desk-phone nudged him out of his train of thought. He picked up the receiver on the fourth ring, silently cursing the caller who had dared disturb him.

"Monsieur Lepetit, did you convince Eric to stop poking around into matters that do not concern him?"

Every muscle on Alain Lepetit's face tightened at the hollow metallic sound of the voice echoing in his ear. His mind reeled in every direction, panic set in, and his throat contracted so much that he could barely breathe, let alone speak. The call was a rude awakening—a dreaded reminder that all was not well behind the carefully crafted facade.

"Not yet, but I'm working on it," he finally managed to blurt out, in a whining voice.

"For your own sake, you better stop wasting my time Monsieur Lepetit."

"Please bear with me for a little while longer. I think I have found a way to make him stop."

"You had better be very convincing, Monsieur Lepetit. It is in your best interest to get it done quickly; my patience is running out. You must understand, I can no longer promise you that your little escapade in Montreal can be kept secret for very long. She is a very pretty girl and so, so young. Raising that baby alone—well it is very, very expensive—poor girl, she can hardly afford the rent. She is desperate, and I'm afraid that I would have to step in to help her if you don't do as I say."

Fear stuck Alain Lepetit's heart like an arrow. He felt a sharp, searing, twisting pain penetrating his chest from front to back. *Damn it, why now,* he wanted to scream. He swallowed hard against the bitter taste rising in his mouth and somehow managed to muster a semblance of composure. In a voice knotted with fear, he whimpered, "You won't need to call me anymore; Eric will not bother you ever again."

"Good. We understand each other then."

The line clicked dead.

CHAPTER 4

NICE, CÔTE D'AZURE, FRANCE

A golden sun resting on the edge of the Mediterranean welcomed Eric when he landed at Nice Côte d'Azure Airport. He felt the warm, moist breeze lightly stroking his face as he stepped out of the congested Terminal 1. It was late afternoon, and people were in shorts and T-shirts. The foul weather in Paris was just a distant memory.

Eric took a quick look at the rental car sign pointing in the direction of a narrow pedestrian bridge across the road. He wiped the sweat from his face, removed his jacket, and started to walk briskly. The back of his shirt was drenched when he entered the ultra-modern building made of glass and steel, which housed more than a dozen car rental agencies under one roof. The air conditioning blowing at full blast took him by surprise. Something else surprised him even more. And it was not just the ultra modern premises either. The waiting area was jam-packed, and to his dismay rental cars were in short supply.

Eric eyed the crowd with quiet exasperation. He hesitated for a moment, considered his options, and made up his mind by choosing the SIXT kiosk. The rental agency advertised the most expensive daily rates, but the line was the shortest. He took the only compact car available. The SIXT representative showed him a picture of the car, apologizing profusely for its condition. Eric barely glanced at the image of the Ford Focus with its well worn status of deep scratches and dents prominently displayed on the front and back end of the vehicle. The shocking lime green color of the rental car did not faze him either. He simply asked for the key and headed for the underground elevators.

It took him a long time to locate his car in the enormous multi-level garage. Vehicles were lined up in rental agency order, but no one had bothered to tell him where the SIXT cars were parked. He walked the entire length of the parking lots on at least four different floors looking for his rental car. On each floor it was the same—the white parking numbers painted on the concrete floor always ended before he could find the number he was looking for. He was about to give up and head back to the front desk, when he finally spotted the Ford Focus hidden behind a massive Mercedes SUV.

The condition of the engine matched the beat-up state of the car's exterior. The small engine of the Focus choked at least three times before he was able to pull out of the garage. The car also had a tendency to veer to the left, which made the driving even more challenging. He by-passed the A8 autoroute exit at the roundabout and drove along the old Route Nationale 7 for a short distance, only to make a rapid U-turn at the first opportunity to catch his favorite coastal road. He was heading for Antibes. Known as Antipolis in the antiquity that literally meant "the city across," the picturesque city was situated across from Nice, roughly halfway to Cannes. It was a city favored by English and Australian tourists because of its world class marina. But to Eric, Antibes had a more personal significance. It held a special place in his heart that would remain with him forever.

The city across the bay was where the Martin clan had established the family home.

Eric loved the drive along the coastline with its beaches bordering the road on the left and rows of seaside cafes streaming along the passenger side on his right. The winding road had a soothing effect on him. It filled his mind with echoes of better days when everything seemed so simple and perfect. Career, girlfriends, the illusionary pursuit of happiness, and Canada had changed all of that. His nomadic restlessness had led him to many exotic destinations. But that never stopped him from longing for the place where his family had planted its roots.

The pebble beaches were deserted at this time of the year, abandoned by the hordes of tourists that trampled their shores during the summer months. The empty shower stalls stood tall, bordering the narrow road like gangly scarecrows in the wind. The vast Mediterranean seashore seemed desolate for as far as one could see, except for a few rare fishermen gathering up their gear on the side of the road. Eric drove in peace, letting the emptiness and silence replenish his soul —a much needed reprieve after the mayhem of Paris.

He turned off the coastal road and drove the car up a steep street in the direction of *La Fontone*. The family home was located at the very end of a cul-de-sac populated on either side by rows of villas with red clay roofs. He parked the car in front of the iron gate and peeked inside the property. A hired hand was busy trimming the cedar hedge in the back and did not notice Eric observing him. The grounds were immaculate—the way his father would have liked them. The almond trees were heavy with stonefruits. Another cause for joy, he thought. He smiled a contented smile and filled his lungs with the orange-scented air.

"Bonjour Jean Pierre."

"Oh, Monsieur Martin, you frightened me. I was not expecting you. Why didn't you tell me that you were coming? I would have prepared the house for you."

"This is an impromptu visit, Jean Pierre. I'm only staying for the night. How are things in Antibes, my friend?"

Jean Pierre wiped his hands on the side of his jeans, an old habit he had acquired over the years when he was about to greet someone he felt important. He then pulled a heavy set of keys from his back pocket and headed for the gate, grinning from ear to ear. As soon as he unlocked the heavy metal gate he came forward to greet Eric with outstretched arms. There was much warmth in the gardener's strong embrace. He had always liked Eric for the way he treated him like a member of the family.

He held on tight in Eric's arms as a rush of sadness suddenly broke over him. Eric's question had touched a sensitive chord, and he was struggling with the answer. He paused for a moment, fighting off tears, and swallowed hard before speaking again.

"Life here is not the same now that your parents are gone. The Bertrands sold their house and moved to Biot two years ago. Madame Pelletier passed away this summer, and her husband couldn't wait to get away. And Giselle. . . you remember Giselle? Well, Giselle dumped her fiancé and moved in with a girlfriend in Juan-les-Pins. She is with another woman, Monsieur Martin. Who could have believed that she would do such a thing. As you can see, there have been lots of changes since your last visit. But what's sad is that no one seems to care about their neighbors anymore. Everyone seems too busy, too self-absorbed. We are like invisible ghosts, mere shadows on the walls. No one sees us; no one pays attention to us."

Eric laid a hand on Jean Pierre's shoulder. The gesture was meant to be comforting, but he was not sure that it carried the warmth and support he wanted to convey. He, too, had lost his bearings somehow, somewhere, in some faraway place.

He now barely managed to get by, living a day to day existence that seemed devoid of real purpose. He had lost more than a lover and his best friend in Casablanca. The very essence of his raison d'être had been taken away from him. Three years had gone by with nothing to show and nothing to hope for. The fear of not ever getting back his sense of self had suppressed his zest for life. As he listened to Jean Pierre, he felt like a shadow forever running away from sunlight.

Once inside the house, his first thought was to open wide all the wooden shutters and let the sun bring back life to the dark tomb that had become the family villa. He found his bedroom on the second floor the same way he had left it when he went to college in Montréal. Old pictures of himself and his brother wearing various team uniforms still adorned the walls. His high school graduation picture sat in a cheap metal frame on the night table by his bedside, and the same towering stacks of old books were gathering dust on a bookshelf above his bed. Nothing had changed. It looked as if someone did not want things to change and had wrapped the entire room in some sort of time capsule.

He stripped naked and pushed open the bathroom door. Moments later, he screamed as the cold water streaming out of the shower spout poured over his bare skin. *Nothing ever changes here,* he laughed out loud as he washed the soap off his shivering body. A change of clothes, freshly shaven, and feeling somehow revitalized, he was now ready for Alain Lepetit and his charming wife.

Marina Baie des Anges was a huge residential complex consisting of four massive buildings that looked like giant cruise ships circling each other; sheltered at its heart was a small but bustling marina. Alain Lepetit had bought a large, two bedroom suite with a magnificent ocean view when he was posted in London, thinking that it would be an ideal place to relax and recoup during his infrequent down times. He was not a sailor, but always had a fascination for the sea and would sit on his terrace for hours at a time gazing at the sleek yachts and tall sailboats glimmering in the sun in the small, private harbor below. He relished the time he spent alone on the terrace letting his mind ride the gentle surf and wander freely on the azure sea.

Eric found Chantal waiting for him at the doorway of her apartment when he stepped out of the elevator. She kissed him on the right cheek, lightly brushing her lips over his lips as she slowly tilted her head to give him another kiss on the left cheek.

"It's so kind of you to come and visit us," Chantal said in the Provençal accent she now favored.

"Thank you so much for inviting me. I'm so glad to see you again, Chantal. You look absolutely ravishing."

A faint blush painted her face, and still holding on to Eric's hand, she led him inside the spacious residence.

"Come in, please. Alain is waiting for you in his favorite spot."

At that instant her husband appeared on cue at the far end of the apartment, gesturing at Eric to come over and join him on the terrace. He was holding a glass full of a milky-white substance on ice, and asked Eric if he wanted one.

Eric declined the Pernod, preferring instead the Cinzano that Chantal had already prepared for him.

The view from the terrace was remarkable. Nice on the left, Cap d'Antibes on the right, and Cannes a faint silhouette etched on a golden Mediterranean on fire. Wearing a pale blue polo shirt, khaki pants, and white *espadrille*, Alain Lepetit had transformed himself into a typical resident of the French Riviera.

"Dinner will be ready in about twenty minutes. Enjoy yourselves in the meantime, but please, no business talk until after we have all finished our meal. Right, Alain?" Chantal punctuated her last words with a pointed nod while staring at her husband.

Alain Lepetit rolled his eyes and turned to Eric with an annoyed grin on his face. "When did you get here, old boy?"

"A couple of hours ago. I stopped over at our house in Antibes before heading up for Villeneuve Loubet."

"Good. Tell you what: let's follow Chantal's good advice and hold on to our discussion until we have finished eating the delicious meal that she prepared especially for you." He paused for an instant, and then added something sounding more like a tease than an afterthought, "I know that you have something important on your mind, but I think you're going to be very, very pleasantly surprised with what I'm going to tell you."

Alain Lepetit knew exactly what he was doing. His last words had the desired effect on Eric. He noticed it immediately in the slight, and barely visible, twitch on Eric's eyelids.

Eric was clearly intrigued. Over the years, the two men had learned to trust each other beyond the typical office matters that preoccupied them daily. They had grown close to one another when they both worked in Canada—Alain Lepetit as the Country Manager and President of the Canadian Operations, and Eric as the Head of the Toronto office. Their private chats had evolved over time to more personal issues. They felt comfortable enough with each other to discuss their very personal aspirations and secret life ambitions, their views on what was really going on around the bank and what it meant not to be totally in control of their chosen career paths. At times they would even allow themselves to openly discuss what their life would have been like if only they could have pursued their dreams.

A kind of sacred trust had developed between the two men that went far beyond the demand of their functions at the bank. They always entered into these discussions cautiously of course, both men fearing full exposure as a sign of weakness—a sure kiss of death in the corporate world—but what they shared over the years created a certain sense of camaraderie that could not be easily shaken.

Eric glanced sideways at Alain Lepetit and saw the satisfied grin stretching his lips from ear to ear. Something was clearly afoot, and he did not need any sixth sense to tell him that his boss was toying with him.

Dinner was a splendid affair. Chantal, always the wonderful hostess, lavished attention on her guest. Alain Lepetit, looking more relaxed than usual, kept on pouring wine from his everlasting supply of Chateauneuf du Pape. The conversation was light, pleasant, and non-consequential. Chantal was pleased and appeared satisfied that the dinner was going well, absent of the usual tensions between husband and wife.

After dinner, the two men settled in comfortably on the terrace. They kept quiet for a long while, eyeing each other like chess players, not wanting to be the one to make the first move. Eric knew the power of patience and just kept on grinning at Alain Lepetit. Once in a while, they would exchange a questioning glance but did not utter a word, pretending to enjoy the fresh ocean breeze.

At long last it was Alain Lepetit who broke the ice, but with a question, and not with his promised news. "Alright, Eric, tell me what's on your mind?"

"Nothing new, really. As you know, I have been following the deal patterns of my trader for some time now."

Alain interrupted Eric with an exasperated sigh, "So what did you find out this time that's so special?"

"Well, I had our staff run a correlation analysis on the data."

"You did what?"

"I ran…"

Alain Lepetit was furious. He clenched his fists and stared hard at Eric, his eyes bulging. His voice was a shout when he finally spoke. "I never authorized you to use my staff for this crazy idea of yours."

"Calm down Alain. You have not heard the full story yet."

"I can hardly wait to hear what other farfetched scheme you have come up with."

"As a matter of fact, what I found out would interest you very much. The data was absolutely unbelievable. This guy is either the luckiest man in the world, or he has worked out an incredible system that can beat the odds at will. His market calls are almost always bang on. He seems to know exactly when to buy and when to sell without fail."

"So, he is very lucky. So what?"

"The problem is that I don't believe that luck alone has anything to do with it."

"Alright," Alain Lepetit said, looking visibly irritated. "So what's his story? What's your theory? Is someone on the inside giving him tips?"

"No, I don't think so. The trades are too fast and furious—there is no time to feed him any meaningful info."

"Are we strictly dealing with an internal issue then?"

"Possibly, but not likely. Most internal frauds involving the bank's own equity securities do not follow this pattern. It's too dangerous. Also, insiders' trades are usually event occurrences timed around major announcements. And the amounts involved are typically not large, so as not to attract attention. The insider who wants to commit a fraud has one main concern and one overriding objective—he does not want anyone to think that an insider is on the take, and he wants to stay below the radar of audit."

Alain Lepetit shook his head. He had a satisfied grin on his face. Something Eric said had somehow changed his mood. He let a few seconds pass, leveled his gaze at Eric, and then went for the jugular with a barely audible voice. "Let me see if I get the picture. Someone is actively trading on the bank's stock and that, normally, is a good thing. He happens to make the right calls more often than not, but he is not an employee of the bank and he does not get his info from an insider. Right so far?"

"Right."

"So why the hell are you wasting your time and mine by the same token? Our job, if you have forgotten, is to catch the bad guys working at the bank. Protecting and safeguarding the bank from internal frauds is what we are being paid to do. "

Eric went silent. Several thoughts raced through his mind, some less kind than others. After a moment, he exhaled slowly, fighting the rising temptation to tell his boss to take his job and shove it up his ass. *Yes, Alain Lepetit was correct in pointing out the weakness of his case. The empirical evidence pointed to an outsider, and the worse thing about it was that on the surface there was nothing apparently illegal in what the trader was doing.* But Eric could not forget the nagging feeling inside of him that kept on sending him those damn warning signals. He could not rationally explain it; he just knew that something was wrong. And he was not about to let it go without getting to the bottom of it. His mind was made up when he said, "This is something I must do. If you don't authorize me to pursue it, I would have no other alternative but to go after this guy on my own."

"You're not going to do that again to me!" Alain Lepetit shouted, losing his temper once again. "This was not the way this conversation was supposed to end," he let out, totally flustered.

Alarmed by the commotion, Chantal ran to the terrace to see what was going on. By now the two men had their backs turned on each other, lost in their own anger and staring at the black empty space hanging over the sea.

Chantal glared at her husband disapprovingly. "What's going on here? Are you fighting like little boys again?"

"You're not going to believe this, Chantal. Eric wants to quit on me again. And this time, like the last time, when I need him the most."

"Is that true Eric?"

"Well, not exactly. What I asked for is some leeway to investigate a matter."

Alain Lepetit interjected, "A matter that does not concern us!"

"Did you tell Eric the good news?" Chantal said, wanting to calm down her husband.

"He didn't give me a chance. But now that you mention it, let me tell him and see if that will put some sense into him."

Alain Lepetit inhaled deeply, letting his anger slowly dissipate as he gave his wife an ' I'm fine' nod.

"I have been asked to head the Australian subsidiary," he began telling Eric, "and I would like you to join me as my second in command." He started to say something else and then decided to let it go, preferring to hear Eric's reaction instead.

Eric looked surprised and elated at the same time.

"This is fantastic news, Alain. I'm so happy for you. You have been talking about going to Australia for so long; I never thought it would ever happen in your life time. Congratulations, no one deserves it more than you."

"Thank you, that's very kind of you. But what about my offer Eric? You have never been happy in the job here. It's not hard to see it. You're not fooling anyone, you know. Investment banking is in your blood, and I'm offering you the opportunity to get back to where you really belong, to what would make you really happy."

"Yes I know; you're right Alain. I'm not a bloody detective—never was, never will be—but what's going on with this trader is really bothering me. You're most probably right about it. There is most likely nothing there. But it's out there, and that's what is annoying me. Tell you what I'm going to do. Give me a couple of days to think about your very generous offer. I promise you I will give it serious consideration."

"Good. Do that. But in the meantime, I do not want you to track the activity of this trader, talk to anyone about him, do any investigative work, or even think, dream, ruminate or bitch about him. That's an order Eric."

"You drive a tough bargain, Alain."

Alain Lepetit nodded his agreement, a wry smile creasing his lower lip.

CHAPTER 5

Antibes, French Riviera

The rental car would not start. Twice Eric turned the ignition key and pumped on the gas pedal, and each time the engine died after barely a half-turn. He slammed his fists on the steering wheel so hard he almost broke his knuckles. The evening had not gone as he had planned, and the fact that the damn vehicle refused to co-operate was pushing him over the edge.

Earlier in the day, Eric had accepted Alain Lepetit's dinner invitation in his home on the coast in *Marina Baie des Anges*. He had much to discuss with his boss, but mostly he wanted to simply ask for an allocation of staff resources and some time to work on his investigation. He was, perhaps, overconfident that he would get his way. After all, Alain Lepetit had always given in to his requests in the past. But the discussion did not turn out the way he had envisioned it. He fell into a trap carefully laid out by his boss, and a bitter taste rose in his mouth when realized that he had been played like a child.

After dinner, Alain had dangled a sweet carrot in front of Eric in the form of an incredible job opportunity. But the offer came with a very explicit condition, a condition that Eric was not prepared to fulfill. Alain demanded that Eric dropped his investigation immediately." That's an order, Eric" he had said.

Eric recognized that he had been outmaneuvered by a skilful man. And if that was not infuriating enough, the fact that he saw it all coming—the sweet talk, the delicious dinner (his favorite couscous meal,) the fine wine, and then to cap it all off, the dress down at the end of the evening—but did nothing about it, was even more than shocking to him. He knew that the whole charade could have been avoided if he had been more forceful at the outset. He realized that he should have stood firm on his demand to pursue his investigation, followed through on his threat to quit the bank otherwise, and not appear to give in to Alain Lepetit's scheming job offer. He had many options in his arsenal, but ultimately he elected not to counter attack. For some reason, he had let his guard down and made the unforgivable mistake of underestimating his boss. And now he was furious at the world, furious at the circumstances that led him to this unpalatable situation, furious at himself for not walking out as soon as he realized that Alain Lepetit had another agenda in mind.

Eric was never cut out for the job in the Global Security and Internal Security Division of the bank. While he possessed a brilliant analytical mind (which served him well as a detective and a watchdog,) he was at his best when plowing through financial statements and devising creative solutions for a myriad of corporate issues. Where most saw impediments and stumbling blocks, he saw only challenges and opportunities. It was a cliché perhaps, but Eric's reputation had been built on his incredible knack to get to the root cause of any financial problem and come out with the most innovative solution before anyone, including his clients' CFOs, had even thought of it. No deal was ever too difficult for him. Competition just raised the bar and made him want the deal even more. He excelled in the intense negotiations that were part of the regular demands of a good investment banker. The rush that he felt each time he closed a transaction fuelled his hunger for more. And he was always on the lookout for more thrills. Once a friend had told him, "Investment bankers are no different than drug addicts." That definition fitted Eric like a glove. Ultimately however, it was the financial rewards that came with the job that kept him hooked, and along with them, all the other fine pleasures that life had to offer.

But something snapped inside of him a few years ago. It affected his work, his judgment, and his passion for life. He had no idea whether he still possessed any of the qualities that were his trademark. He knew only one thing—if he stayed in this lousy job any longer he would certainly turn into one of the living dead that populated the entire bank.

He thought again about the job offer that Alain Lepetit had made to him earlier in the evening. *After all, perhaps it is what I need.* He could not discount the idea that it was a chance for him to get back into what he knew best and enjoyed the most. An opportunity to get away from this drudging work that was eating at him every day. And down deep he knew that it meant even more: a chance, and perhaps his last one, to bury once and for all what was troubling him so much.

Eric turned the ignition a third time and did not step on the gas pedal, fearing he might have flooded the engine with his earlier attempts. The small four cylinder engine turned once. . . twice. . . and then, with a loud bang, finally kicked in. He was so excited that the rental car had finally responded to his command, that he did not feel the vibration of the Blackberry inside of his pocket. But the little black smart phone with the berry stylized symbol on the back would not stop shaking, and he finally pulled it out of its casing, more than annoyed at the intrusion. He did not recognize the phone number displayed on the small screen and was tempted to let it ring until his voice mail took care of it. He changed his mind at the last second.

"Monsieur Martin. Monsieur Eric Martin?"

"Yes, this is him."

"Monsieur Martin I would like to meet with you as soon as possible. Are you free now?"

"I'm sorry, but I don't know who you are, and it's kind of late for a meeting don't you think?"

"Oh I'm sorry, I did not introduce myself. I'm special agent Stephanie Brulé, Interpol; I just flew in from Lyon to see you. Monsieur Bartolli has asked me to meet you as soon as possible."

At the mention of Bartolli, the whole tone in Eric's voice changed. "Where do you want to meet Stephanie?"

"Do you know where Fort Carré is?"

"Antibes is like my second home."

"Good, then please meet me there in twenty minutes."

Eric swerved off the coastal road and turned into a public parking lot at the foot of a hill crested by a gigantic fortress. Overlooking the Saint-Roch peninsula, Fort Carré stood guard over Port Vauban and the neck of land beyond. Once a military post with four fortified arrow-headed bastions, the fort had been turned into a tourist attraction at the turn of the century. But during the off season and at night, the fort was mostly a desolated place.

An ideal place for a romantic escapade, smirked Eric, as he got out of the car to stare at the fortification looming high above him. It was very dark, and he stumbled a couple of times as he made his ascent along the narrow path leading up to the top of the hill. It took him a good twenty minutes to reach the fort, and he was slightly out of breath when he pushed open the heavy, iron-studded door. He then crossed the wooden bridge that led into the fort itself. At the far end, he found a small courtyard surrounded by barracks that once housed the garrison. Against the wall facing the seaside, there was a small circular chapel that had been recently restored. Next to the chapel he found the narrow passage giving way to a steep flight of stairs that corkscrewed upward to the ramparts. When he reached the top of the stairway, he leaned against the stone parapet and glanced around looking for Stephanie.

Fort Carré was not an inviting place at night. Shadowy, cold, desolate, and eerily quiet, the old fortress was a ghastly site in the dark. The murmur of the wind along the thick walls added to the uneasiness that Eric felt intensifying with each passing minute. Little by little, doubt began to fill his mind, and he started to question the wisdom of agreeing to a meeting in a place that looked ghostly-abandoned in the middle of the night.

All of a sudden, he felt a sharp, searing pain in his hand. Something had hit him from behind. Startled, he turned around to look behind him. There was nothing but darkness and silence. Moments later, a stone splinter ricocheted off the thick rampart and almost hit him in the face. This time his senses came alive, and a ripple of fear swept across his face. Someone was using him for target practice.

He glanced up and down the stairway but never saw the two burly men who tore at him from the shadows. He fell to the ground in pain from a kick in the kidneys and a violent blow on the head. One assailant had him pinned down on the ground with a knee to his chest, while the other man grabbed him by the hair, violently pulling his head back. The second assailant was holding a knife with the tip of the blade pointed at his left eye.

"Keep your nose out of our business," the man snarled in Eric's ear. The knife came down fast and furious and drew blood from Eric's cheekbone, barely missing his left eye.

Eric screamed a loud, guttural howl borne out of primal fear. His heart froze and his mind took him to some faraway place. Memories of a dark alley in the Medina of Casablanca came flooding back. Three years had passed, yet he could still feel the terror and recall the dark thoughts rushing through his mind under the assassin's knife. It was all so vivid. It was happening all over again. He was a prisoner of his past and no amount of struggle could free him from that dreadful nightmare.

A loud bang startled Eric's attackers. They both sprang to their feet—standing at the ready, their eyes scanning the darkness, and their senses on high alert. Another loud shot, and the assailant standing close to the edge of the rampart flipped over the railing—a bullet lodged in his chest. His partner did not flinch, holding onto his gun at chest-level in front of him. In slow, careful, barely noticeable steps he started to step back toward the stairway. With his eyes constantly darting from side to side, he stopped at the top of the stairs. The flash of a gun armed with a silencer pierced the night twice, chasing some shadowy figure ahead. When silence came in response, he turned and stepped down and disappeared into the darkness.

Eric's supine body lay motionless on the cold stone floor. Under the shock of the assault, his heart missed a beat or two and made it difficult for him to breathe. He remained sprawled on the ground, making a quick assessment of his injury. He let some time go by while remaining vigilant for any sign of his assailants. He scanned his surroundings expecting another assault at any time. That went on for awhile until he was fully satisfied no danger was lurking in the dark. He jumped up to his feet and bolted for the stairway. Bounding down the stairs, his feet landing hard on every step, he almost missed the narrow passage that led to the bridge and the heavy wooden door.

He ran and ran, sucking hard on every breath and drawing on every ounce of energy left in his body. Twice he stumbled on the steep dirt trail, scrapping the inside of his hands, and hurting his kneecaps, and twice he got up immediately, ignoring the excruciating pain. The muscles in his thighs and calves screamed for him to stop, but still he ran faster and faster. He bolted forward, breathing laboriously, his arms pumping in the air, the soles of his shoes beating hard on the gravel.

Unarmed and fearful of an ambush at the bottom of the hill, he staggered his way to the rental car in the empty parking lot. Near exhaustion, he leaned against the door for support. His head started to spin and he bent over, wheezing, panting, and clutching his knees to draw as much air into his lungs as possible. The headlights of a lone car passing by reminded him that it was not safe to remain for too long in that deserted place. Gritting his teeth in pain, he somehow found the strength to yank the car door open and climb in. He hit the clutch, turned the ignition key, heard the engine kick in at the first turn, and gunned the gas pedal. The engine roared, and he took off, leaving behind him a cloud of dust.

He drove at high speed, wanting to put as much distance as possible between himself and Fort Carré. He finally put an end to his mad flight and parked the vehicle on the side of the road under a sign indicating: Nice Côte d'Azur Aéroport 500 meters. He stared at his white knuckles for a moment and exhaled a long and deep breath. Cars were zooming by him—some honking, others flashing their headlights. He ignored them all and turned off the ignition. He leaned his head against the steering wheel and let his mind slowly dissolve the tension he felt throughout his body He could not remember how long he remained in that state, staring blankly at empty space while mentally processing what the ambush in Fort Carré was all about. *My God, I must be right about the trader.*

The ping of his Blackberry startled him.

"Are you alright?" Stephanie asked.

"Where the hell were you? I almost got killed up there waiting for you!"

"I know, I was there too," Stephanie replied, sensing the tension in Eric's voice.

"So why didn't you do something to help?"

"I did."

"The hell you did!"

"Look Eric, when I tell you I was there helping you, you're going to believe me and you're going to trust me. Otherwise this conversation is over!"

Eric's silence was the only response.

After a long pause, Stephanie said, "Good, now listen to me carefully. I noticed two men following you up the path, so I stayed hidden in the bushes to see what they were up to. When I finally reached the fort they were on top of you, and I took care of them. So now answer my question, "Are you able to drive?"

"You took care of them, really?"

"Yes, I did; why do you sound so surprised?"

"Oh, nothing. It's just that...."

"Just that what? I shot one of them. He is probably dead, his body lying somewhere at the bottom of the fort, if you must know. Now would you please answer my question. Can you drive?"

"What do you I think I've been doing for the past half-hour?" Eric replied.

"Well in that case, please meet me in fifteen minutes at the port of Antibes. There is a little bistro facing the statue of the *Nomade*."

"I will be there; just make sure you don't miss our appointment this time!" Eric shouted, unable to control the strain in his voice.

CHAPTER 6

Port Vauban, Antibes, Cote d'Azur

Stephanie Brulé arrived at the rendez-vous point in Port Vauban ten minutes early, and made good use of her time. Standing by the giant white statue of a man looking out at the horizon beyond the sea, she glanced around, paying special attention to the people roaming in the square on the upper deck of the old fortified port. They were mostly tourists and a few young lovers looking for a quiet place. *No threats here,* she thought.

 She slowly walked over to the side of the wall facing the marina. From that vantage point she had a great view of all the super yachts lined up like sardines in the largest yachting harbor of Europe. The yachts were mostly empty except for the muscular security men dressed in black and standing guard at the top of the immaculate gangways. She recognized the names of a few yachts from her research back in the office at Interpol headquarters and knew them as Russian and Middle Eastern owned, for the most part. She stopped for a moment to admire the biggest and sleekest looking ship, and wondered about its real ownership that was listed in the official records as a Russian steel magnate. *At least that's what the papers say about the owner,* she mused with a knowing smile.

 She looked for things out of the ordinary knowing that was where she would most likely find signs of danger: an open umbrella on a sunny day, a newspaper held too close to the face, dark glasses in the middle of the night, or someone too quick to look away. Anything that did not belong or looked suspicious would be picked up immediately by her sharp eyes. Satisfied with her walkabout, she turned her back to the wall and slowly proceeded to the middle of the square. She glanced one more time up at the giant hollow statue that was dwarfing her. *It is strange,* she thought, *why the artist would call this statue "Le Nomade." What is the significance of all the letters that make up the hollow shell of this faceless, half kneeling man who seems to be getting ready to jump in the water?* There was probably no logical explanation for the symbolism of this art piece, but she liked to muse about such things. It was like a game for her—a mind game that she often played when something else was bothering her.

But now was not the time to let her mind wander. Out of the corner of her eye she caught two policemen climbing the stairs and heading her way. She looked up at the statue, pretending to be another curious sightseer, but her senses remained sharp and alert. The policemen walked past, chatting away and paying no special attention to her. She remained rooted by the statue until they finished their round and left the square moments later. She breathed easier; the shooting in Fort Carré had not yet been reported. She would take care of the paper work later, once she had all the facts. Her inspection tour completed, she walked over to the bistro where she would be meeting Eric.

The bistro was noisy and smelled of beer and cheap wine. She picked the last table in the back with a view of the sea. With a smile permanently glued on her face, she looked like another tourist passing time. While placing her order, a Perrier on ice with a lime twist to top it, she took the opportunity to give the establishment a rapid glance over. The tables were mostly occupied by English speaking patrons and sailors, whom she judged to be Australian and British from their uniforms of khaki Bermuda shorts and white Polo shirts. They were young, energetic, and eager to have a good time. No one paid any attention to her, and for that she was thankful.

Eric appeared in the center of the square on time. She frowned when she first saw him. He looked disheveled, with blood on his face and pants torn at the knees. He seemed impatient and edgy, shifting his head from side to side, apprehensively staring in all directions at the same time. *A walking billboard inviting suspicion and unwarranted attention,* she thought, as she observed him from a distance. She did not give him the signal right away, and continued to watch him a little longer to make sure that no one had followed him.

All along, Stephanie continued appraising Eric, testing her first impressions of him against the profile she had read in the file, looking for clues that would explain the reasons for the relentless drive that had almost got him killed in

Morocco—anything that would justify her boss's high regard for this man. She did not find him particularly handsome. Of average height and stature, she judged him to be slightly less than six feet tall. She was sure that many women would find him charming, and perhaps even possessing a certain sexual appeal, *in a rough-looking way*. But there was something striking in his eyes—they sparked with intelligence and intensity, noticeable even at a distance. He smiled, with more a lopsided grin, when he spotted her waving at him. Stephanie was now convinced that Eric was a mystery that needed to be unraveled.

"Eric," she simply said, as she came forward to greet him with a firm handshake.

Eric nodded glumly. "Well, I guess you know who I am. Now would mind telling me who you are?"

"Stephanie Brulé. Monsieur Bartolli has told me a lot about you. He admires you very much you know."

"Oh yeah, what did he say?"

"For one, he can't stop talking about what you did in Morocco. How you almost single-handedly prevented a huge market calamity from happening. How you fought hard to convince the authorities to take action despite all their skepticism. How an entire terrorist organization was wiped out because of you."

"Enough. Enough, already; it's just more of Bartolli's nonsense. I'd rather like to talk about what happened tonight. So what can you tell me?"

Stephanie was not surprised by Eric's reaction to the praise that she had thrown at him. It was expected. The profile she had read on the plane was full of descriptive terms like impatient, little tolerance for incompetence and self-serving flattery, and an iron-willed determination bordering on obsession. But she had to see it with her own eyes, and was rather pleased with the results. She crossed her legs and brushed an invisible piece of lint off her pants. She remained quiet, hiding her satisfaction behind a faint smile. After a long pause, she pulled out a handkerchief from her bag and said, "Here, clean the blood from your face."

Eric did as he was told, feeling somewhat at a disadvantage sitting before this woman wearing an enigmatic smile. If he had been a photographer he would have enjoyed a subject like her—high cheekbones, almond-shaped green eyes, and a sensuous mouth with ample lips that curved slightly at the corner. But it was also a face that emanated intensity, an abundance of energy, and absolute self-control. He started to say something, but thought better of it and just stared back at Stephanie.

"I'm sorry I could not have been there to stop them earlier," Stephanie said, sensing Eric's unease.

"Where were you when I was assaulted?"

"Oh I was there alright. I saw what they did to your face, and I shot one of them. The other goon escaped before I had a chance to shoot him."

"But why didn't you come and help me right away after the attack?"

"I didn't think that you were too badly hurt, so I ran after the other thug."

Eric appeared somewhat satisfied with the response, but so many questions were reeling through his mind all at once. He wanted to know if she had caught up with the assailant, what he had told her, and whether it was safe for him to be here anymore. But upon reflection, he asked a question that caught Stephanie off guard.

"Why did Bartolli send you instead of coming here to meet me himself?"

"I don't know. You're going to have to ask him that question yourself," she shrugged, and then added, her tone now sharper, "Why don't you tell me more about your mysterious trader?"

"Why? Do you think there is a connection with what happened to me tonight?"

"I don't know yet if that's the case. But I do know one thing, Monsieur Martin—you must have pissed off someone real bad for them to want to scare you that way."

Eric pondered the response for a moment. He hadn't yet told her what the man said before jabbing him in the face with the knife. It was an old habit of his from his days in investment banking, when he would hold back vital information from the negotiation table until he was absolutely certain that the information could not be used to leverage a better deal out of him. Stephanie had probably saved his life, and for that action alone he should be grateful and trust her totally. But like Alain Lepetit, earlier in the evening, he did not get the feeling that she really believed him. The mocking tone she used when she asked about his mysterious trader did not win her much favor at all in his eyes. *Is she merely going through the motions to please her boss, or is she here because, like me, she truly thinks that something is not above board with the trader?* Then he thought of Bartolli. The Interpol agent had been the only man who had believed him from the get go, and had been even more upset than Eric when they failed to catch the terrorist group alive in Casablanca. Such a man would never send anyone on a mission on his behalf if he did not totally trust that person.

"You don't need to second-guess their actions anymore. There is definitely a connection," Eric said with conviction.

"Really? And how did you come to this conclusion?"

"They told me that much when they grabbed me."

This was Stephanie's second surprise of the evening, and she could not help wondering what other piece of important information Eric was holding back from her. So she asked him, in no uncertain terms, to tell her everything he knew, suspected, or sensed about the trader and his market activities. Otherwise, she would instruct Bartolli and Interpol to drop the case immediately.

This time Eric did not hesitate, and told Stephanie in minute detail every piece of data he had gathered on the trader over the past three months. He also told her that from old records he had retrieved from the bank's system, he had been able to trace the suspicious trades as far back as eighteen months ago. He admitted that his misgivings were rooted solely on his gut instinct, except for the fact that the data could not lie about the unbelievable accuracy of the market calls. He estimated that in that short period of time, the trader must have earned roughly at least a couple million euro by trading the bank stocks alone. "And who knows which other financial institutions he was also targeting with his system?" he said in conclusion.

"When can I see the data?"

"Right now," Eric replied as he pulled his Blackberry from his pocket.

Stephanie gave Eric a second glance-over. She was impressed by the precision and thoroughness of Eric's briefing. It was, indeed, a very interesting story full of intrigue and possibilities, but there was nothing in it that could explain the threats and the assault of this evening. *We must be missing an important piece of information,* she surmised with an expression that could not mask her deep unease.

Mistaking her silence for another stalling tactic, Eric brusquely asked, "So what do you suggest we do now? What are our next steps?"

"Nothing, as far as you are concerned; just go back to Paris and continue doing what you have been doing at the bank. Leave the investigation and everything else about this matter to us."

"You don't really mean that?"

"Yes Eric, this time you're going to listen to me. You were very lucky in Morocco, don't tempt fate again; it might be a fatal mistake this time around."

"You don't get it, do you? I'm tired of running away—don't you understand? I want my life back. There is something about this thing that tells me that I must deal with it myself. Otherwise, there won't be any peace for me. So please, help me. Work with me to get to the bottom of it."

"It's not something I would recommend to my superiors, but I promise you, I will relay your request to them."

Eric threw Stephanie a twisted smile by way of a response.

CHAPTER 7

INTERPOL HEADQUARTERS, LYON, FRANCE

Success does not always breed happiness. Rewards may have an unintended effect if they are not wanted or desired. Seated at his desk, Bartolli was painfully aware of these maxims while leafing through a stack of paperwork. Field reports, inter-agency briefings, department budgets, proposals and recommendations from various standing committees; the list went on and on with the mass of paperwork he had to deal with every day at the office. Always diligent, he carefully read every report that was sent to him, marking every document with either one of two annotations—FU and a date for follow up, or TF, meaning: send document to file. The other half of his work day was filled with endless meetings that he felt accomplished little or nothing of real value for the organization. Nonetheless, his attendance record was stellar. Bartolli had never missed a meeting in his three years on the job, even if it meant that he would be bored to death.

As Director, Financial and High-Tech Crime Division, Bartolli was at the peak of his career, having joined Interpol some twenty years ago. He fondly remembered his early years in the organization when, as a young field agent, he would roam the globe to assist national police forces. It was a time full of adventure and exotic destinations. A time when success came easily and failures were quickly forgotten.

In those early years, Interpol was mostly neglected by its member countries and lacked the resources it needed to become an effective international crime fighting force. But that did not stop Bartolli. He quickly built a network of police officers, agents, and informants in all the hot spots across the globe, never hesitating to throw in favors and rewards, or reverting to one arm-twisting tactic or another to get what he wanted. He was not above using a powerful combo of blackmail and veiled threats when cooperation was not forthcoming. His case load was always full, his reports were thorough and extremely well documented, and he would work like a workhorse until all the cases that had been assigned to him were solved. But it was his unorthodox investigative methods and incredible success ratio in solving cross-border crimes that set him most apart from all the other Interpol agents.

Then came September 11th. The world stopped for a moment and then spun in the opposite direction. Security became everyone's obsession, and Interpol regained its luster. With a sudden large influx of funds, Interpol reclaimed its *raison d'être* as a pivotal crime fighting organization in the global war against terrorism. Newer and faster computers were purchased. The network of National Central Bureaus was expanded and modernized across all of its member countries. The police force was significantly increased, and agents were better trained in the use of cutting-edge, investigative technology. Bartolli made the most of this new environment, and his career took off in leaps and bounds. As a special agent, a liaison officer, then later as a team leader, Bartolli was recognized by his peers as one of the true founders of the electronic financial crime unit. He was often consulted, and ultimately always called upon to tackle the most difficult cases. About three years ago, his success in the field brought him the ultimate reward—Head of Interpol Financial and High-Tech Crime Division—responsible for operational police support services to its one hundred and eighty-six state members worldwide.

When the Secretary General of Interpol awarded Bartolli his promotion, he told him that this was, "Our way of thanking you for your loyal and excellent service in the force." Bartolli had beamed proudly.

It did not take him very long, however, to find out that there would be many aspects about his current job that he would dislike very much. He understood the need for the function and duty up to a point, but wished them on someone else. Loyal to the core, he never complained about the job to anyone, preferring instead to draw his sole pleasure from one of his other designated responsibilities. Due to the highly specialized nature of the Finance and High-Tech Division, the budget for the training and development of new recruits fell directly under his purview. And so, against all standard procedures, he took it upon himself to personally select and oversee the training of a few 'high potential' candidates. Over the years, he proudly followed the successful careers of several of his special recruits. Many stayed and progressed fruitfully in the organization, some left to join other police forces where their careers also flourished. None, however, were more talented and successful than Stephanie Brulé.

Stephanie had joined the force shortly after graduating from a mid-level university. Nothing in her curriculum, grades at school, teachers' notes on her achievements, or letters of recommendations, revealed any special talent for police work. "A very average student best suited for manual technical school," one teacher wrote on her graduation report card. During her interview with Interpol, she even admitted candidly to an incredulous recruiting officer that she had no idea what financial crimes were all about. Her main interest was police investigation work, a passion she had apparently developed while watching the French version of Law & Order on television.

And passion for investigation—she had plenty to spare. She aced the three police examination tests that were given to her during the interview process and completed the field undercover exercises in record times. Nothing seemed to escape her. She thrived on complex situations, simplifying them into their core components at laser speed and accuracy. She had the uncanny ability to pick the most innocuous detail that would thread her highly inquisitive mind right to the culprit. And surprisingly, she showed a very special aptitude in her tests for anything to do with financial crimes.

At the request of Bartolli, Stephanie Brulé was offered only one position at Interpol, which she refused at first. But when she realized that none other would be forthcoming, she reluctantly accepted the job offer to join Interpol Financial and High-Tech Crime Division.

Shortly after completing her formal police training at the top of her class, she was sent to HEC business school to complete her education in high finance. She breezed through the three year program in eighteen months and eagerly rejoined Interpol HQ in Lyon, France to start what she aptly described as *what she was meant to do all her life.*

"*Bonjour grand ours,*" Stephanie cheered as she walked into Bartolli's office.

Bartolli looked up under his thick lenses and saw his favorite special agent heading towards him with open arms. A stocky man with a thick neck and a crew cut nesting his square head, Bartolli deserved his nick name of 'big bear.' He raised one hand to stop Stephanie in her tracks and said, "Why is it that when I send you on a mission you never do as you're told?"

Stephanie looked at him incredulously. "What do you mean? You sent me to take care of Eric Martin, and I did just that."

"No one asked you to start a war. The local police are going nuts in Antibes looking for the criminal that killed a tourist."

"A tourist my ass! This guy was a well-trained hit man. Judging by the way he and his partner followed Eric, took care of business, and how his partner managed to disappear into the night without a trace, I would say that we are dealing with pros."

"I see, but did you have to kill him?"

"I did not kill him. He fell over the ramparts and broke his neck."

"Same difference; the police report showed that he had been shot in the chest."

By now, Stephanie looked exasperated and was rapidly reaching her breaking point. Her boss was not acting fairly towards her, and she was about to let him know. With a strained voice, she tore into him. "Alright, they looked like they were about to slice open your dear friend's throat from ear to ear, so I shot one of them to wound him. Was it my fault if he lost his balance and fell twenty feet below? What was I supposed to do, turn my back on Eric and tell you that I couldn't help him because I might hurt one of his attackers?"

Bartolli broke into a wide grin, which made Stephanie even more furious.

"You bastard; you are pulling my leg, aren't you?"

"No, I was just following protocol. Under the circumstances, you know what I'm supposed to say for the record and for the report that I'm going to have to file to cover your ass."

"Leave my ass out of this, you pig!"

Bartolli grinned widely.

"Alright, now that we have settled the official version, off the record what can you tell really happened?"

Stephanie shook her head in disbelief. "I can't believe you did that. And what's even more incredible, I can't believe I fell for it."

They exchanged glances and both broke into a loud laugh. Stephanie gave Bartolli another dirty look and then resumed her report, taking on a more serious tone.

"One of the men ran away, and I could not catch up with him. I found the other one lying at the bottom of the ramparts. He had no identification on him, but he made one big mistake. He had his plane ticket stub inside his coat pocket."

"Interesting, and what did you find out from the ticket stub?"

"A lot of very useful things: first—that he was carrying the stub for a couple of days; second—that he was on a plane that landed in Paris; and thirdly, what is probably the most interesting piece of information—he flew in from Istanbul."

"A Turk national?" Bartolli asked.

"Probably. He definitely looked Middle Eastern."

"And what can you tell me about Eric?"

"Well, he is very intense, just as you described him to me. He is restless and looks like someone looking for a cause. You know, *a banker with a conscience*, or something like that. I noticed something different about him as well. There is a fire burning inside of him, that's for sure, and he is determined to go after the trader all by himself if he has to. But I don't have a clue what's really motivating him. He mentioned something about intuition, a gut feeling, a hunch, these sort of things, but he offered no clear explanation as to why he thinks that there is something illegal going on behind the trades, except, as he said, that he wants his life back."

"Alright, that's very interesting. But what do you really think about the whole thing?"

"Someone is definitely not happy with him poking around their business. In my opinion, he is on to something."

"In that case, we better get on with it ourselves before he gets into trouble once again."

Bartolli pressed the intercom button and asked his assistant to bring special agent Jules Betton in his office right away.

Stephanie winced and Bartolli recognized the look on her face for what it was—annoyance, with more than a trace of disdain.

"He is the best in the business. We need him if we want to get to the bottom of this affair quickly," Bartolli said, as Jules Betton walked in unannounced.

"You want to see me, Boss?"

Jules Betton was a tall, wiry man with extraordinarily long arms that dangled awkwardly at his side as he walked. Brown hair, brown eyes, and wearing a brown shirt with brown pants and matching brown socks, he was not a man who liked to experiment with fashion. His only exception was his black leather shoes that he polished every day before going to work. He had joined Interpol about the same time as Bartolli, to work as an internal analyst, but unlike his boss, never left the office for field work. His strength was his ferret-like ability to dig out information from the most guarded computer databases. He was like a musician in a trance, playing on his keyboard for hours without interruption, sensing every breakthrough in the system before the computer firewalls had a chance to stop him. "Pure poetry in motion," an analyst once described Jules Betton's hacking skills.

Bartolli paused briefly, fixing his eyes on Jules Betton to acknowledge the raw genius of the man standing in front of him. With more authority in his voice than was necessary, he finally answered the question, "I would like you to drop everything you're working on and take on this new project immediately. You will be working with Stephanie, and for the time being, no one besides the three of us will know what the project is all about. Got that?"

"That's cool, Boss," Jules Betton replied, his lips taking on an awkward twist as he glanced sideways at Stephanie.

He is in love with her, immediately thought Bartolli. *But then, who in the force is not?*

"Good. Now, both of you get on with it; and please, close the door behind you. I have lots of work to do.

Alone in his office, Bartolli glanced at the stack of documents that seemed to have grown in size since the morning. They were waiting for him just like Eric had been waiting for him in front of an office building surrounded by the Moroccan police. The police raid he had orchestrated had not gone well. In fact, it had been a total fiasco. The terrorists were long gone when they arrived, tipped off by an informant. The office that served as a front for their illegal activities was stripped bare and left empty of anyone and anything. They had vanished in the middle of the night without leaving a trace of their ever having been present in town. Bartolli knew that he had missed his only realistic chance of ever catching the terrorists dead *or* alive.

Eric was beside himself when he heard the news. He was the portrait of distress, frustration, resentment, and anger all wrapped up into one bundle. There was nothing Bartolli could have done or said to Eric that would have made it easier for him to accept the fact that they had been beaten by a more cunning enemy. He remembered counseling Eric to go back to his condo in Toronto and forget all about having been involved in this affair, and not truly believing in his own advice. Failure was not something Bartolli accepted easily, either. And so they both struggled with their lives ever since. Eric never went back to Toronto, accepting instead a job in Paris with his former boss. Bartolli left field work shortly after and grudgingly accepted the promotion that was offered to him as a crowning achievement for his successful career as a special agent. The Moroccan case was mentioned at the ceremony at the time of his appointment, to his embarrassment and disbelief. He knew he had been lucky and owed a huge debt of gratitude to the CIA. The terrorist cell had been obliterated in the end by an American special unit. He had found out about it after the raid, and was not even aware of the CIA's interest in the case.

It was with a heart full of doubt and regret that he grabbed the first document on top of the pile. He knew that he would never forget his only black mark on an otherwise spotless record. After a short pause and with a heavy sigh, he began reading the report, drawing some comfort in the knowledge that at the very least, he had appointed his two best agents on Eric's new case.

Stephanie walked out of the office in a hurry, with Jules Betton trailing behind, barely able to keep up with her. She had the determined look that she often wore on her face when an important case had been assigned to her. But this time, her facial expression had another streak. She was annoyed that Bartolli had deemed it necessary to tag along another agent, even if she understood the reasons. But then, she was a professional and finally decided not to let her ego get in the way. She stopped in front of her office door to look at Jules Betton running to catch up, arms flying in all directions. She gave him one of the stares that she was famous for. It froze him dead in his tracks. He hesitated, looked around on either side, and then behind, unsure of himself. He finally decided that he was, indeed, the recipient of her gaze, and meekly asked: "We're partners, right?"

"Don't get the wrong idea. Concentrate on finding out who is behind the numbered companies responsible for the trades, and I will take care of the rest."

Jules Betton looked down at the reflection of his face on his polished black shoes and cleared his throat. "I see. A full partnership is not what you want."

Stephanie abruptly turned her back and headed straight into her office. "I don't have time for this. I will send you the data."

She slammed the door, leaving Jules Betton on the outside trying to decide whether to run back to Bartolli and complain about Stephanie's behavior or do what he was told. After much hesitation, he thought it was best to get to work immediately. Like Bartolli, he knew that the job took precedence over personal feelings. Besides, he was certain that Stephanie would soon see the light. It was only a matter of time before she would realize that she needed him more than he needed her. *She'll come to me begging for my help and attention,* Jules Betton mouthed at the closed door.

CHAPTER 8

Paris, France

Eric lay in bed wide awake, feeling somewhat uneasy about the day ahead of him. The room was buried in darkness, waiting for the sun to rise above the left bank of the River Seine. He was fidgety and agitated most nights. That was par for the course since his return to Paris. The nightmarish images that plagued his sleep stuck with him all the time like painful reminders of his past life. They were the consequences of a series of bad decisions he had made when he believed himself infallible because of his success as an investment banker. He should have known that nothing about his life experience could have prepared him for the tragedy that awaited him in Casablanca. The betrayals, the lies, the diabolical schemes, the murders were not part of any investment banker repertoire. He thought he was following his calling when he jumped on the first plane headed for his ancestral land. *A journey in his homeland to reconnect with his roots.* That's what he believed he had done. But then his oversized ego kept on blinding him every step of the way. And now his life was in tatters. Ridden with guilt and remorse, he saw no way out of this nightmare that haunted him every night.

But something felt different this time out. The dreams were more intense and haunting than usual. He was more restless and tormented than he ever felt before. A new conflict had invaded his troubled mind, and he was at loss on how to deal with it. A fantastic job offer had been hurled at him a day earlier. It was an attractive proposal full of interesting opportunities and rewarding challenges. It could even give him a way out of the hell he was stuck in, and even perhaps ease, somewhat, the pain that was troubling him. But it would also have meant giving up on his quest for the truth, burying it deep down in his soul forever, and most definitely never being able to find total peace of mind.

As he tossed in bed, he struggled with two equally unpalatable choices and cursed out loud what fate had thrown at him once again. He brushed back his long hair with his left hand, and then ran his fingers along his face. When he touched the bleeding wound on his cheek, everything suddenly became clear to him. He jolted out of bed, having found the answer to his dilemma. *I never had a real choice.*

He walked across the bedroom to the window and gazed at the city of light making its morning calls. The silhouette of Notre Dame shaped the far background of his view, and on a clear day, if he stretched his legs and neck far enough over the railing of his tiny balcony, he could make out the tip of the Eiffel tower rising above the tree line. Loud noises in the street below caught his attention. Shopkeepers were already busy cleaning the front porches of their establishments or unloading merchandise for the day's business ahead.

Eric stood stark naked in front of his window for what seemed like an eternity, just staring at the city life below bustling with energy. That too was part of his daily ritual from which he could always draw some comfort. A spark of curiosity for life was left in him, albeit feeble.

The apartment was sparsely furnished in the Japanese style that he preferred—uncluttered, functional, and clean. He had found this small apartment while strolling along the left bank in the Latin Quarter on the third day after his arrival in Paris from Toulouse, where he had been convalescing after his dramatic rescue from the bottom of the sea off the coast of Gibraltar. The apartment could not be found on any recommended lists that the bank provided to all expatriates as part of their welcome and orientation packages. But that suited Eric just fine. He had no desire to reconnect with his North American colleagues. He wanted to break from his investment banking past, thinking that it would make the transition into his new life easier. After a while, he realized that his isolation served only to dull his existence even more, and gave his mind more reasons to think about the things that haunted him in his sleep every night.

It was time for him to get ready for the office. After a quick shower, in a bathroom no bigger than the smallest closet of his condo in Toronto, he grabbed a fresh set of clothes and his faithful Blackberry, then headed down to his favorite *patisserie* at the corner of the street.

"An Americano for the Canadian," the owner of the establishment immediately called, out as Eric took a seat at the small round table closest to the bar. The owner's wife welcomed him with a handful of morning papers and two croissants. Eric had become a man of habits, something he had always loathed in his previous life.

He quickly scanned the headlines of the newspapers. They were full of news about the demise of the euro and a new treaty that could solve Europe's crippling debt crisis. He was amused to see the difference in the Anglo and the French morning press in the way they were treating the big news of the day. The Times and the other English newspapers focused on the new deal signed in Brussels that morning that could save the euro from an almost certain disaster. *The deal could turn the raging euro crisis into a deeper crisis,* was the view expressed by most in the English speaking press. The French papers, on the other hand, had a totally different take on the news. While recognizing the importance of the treaty, they chose to emphasize the political implications behind the deal by noting that only Britain remained opposed. *Sarkozy has succeeded in doing what even the great Napoleon could not achieve—isolate Britain,* a popular French newspaper blared on its front page. *The European and the French economies could collapse under crippling debt loads, yet scoring political points seemed more important to them. It was, after all, an election year,* Eric thought in amazement.

The RER station was a short walk from the French pastry shop where Eric ate his breakfast every morning. He stepped on a fast-moving escalator that took him two levels underground, below the crowded Parisian Metro. At the station he purchased a return ticket to *La Defense* and walked over to *Ligne A,* where he embarked seconds later on a slowly approaching train. Just when the train was about to leave the station, two men with dark complexions jumped on and stood at the far end of the car, facing Eric. Squeezed between a man reading his newspaper and another passenger smelling of garlic, Eric failed to notice the two men who had followed him. He was preoccupied by something he had to do and wanted to get to his office as fast as possible.

In keeping with his morning routine, he stopped in front of *La Grande Arche* and stood in awe at the sheer size of the monument which had been erected at the center of the ultra-modern complex of glass skyscrapers. The complex itself had been built as a testament to France's triumphal restoration to an economic powerhouse after the wars. It housed the headquarters of many of France's best known companies, as well as the twin towers that lodged the main office of Banque du Commerce. His thoughts went to the morning news, and he wondered sadly if France would be able to maintain its economic status for very long if the euro zone were to collapse under the crippling weight of the debt of its member states. More to the point, Eric knew that France could no longer hide the fact that it has the biggest debt and deficit ratios among the euro zone's highly rated countries, and its banks were dangerously exposed to southern Europe, the epicenter of the financial crisis. The old world was in danger of breaking up, and by some ironic twist his life had suddenly taken a new turn. Fate had spoken to him once again, and he knew that it had to be answered.

He felt the strong wind whirling around, telling him that it was time to move on. Turning his sight to the far distance ahead of him, he briefly watched L'Arc de Triomphe making a valiant effort to free itself of the heavy morning fog. Having completed his morning ritual, it was time for him to head for the office where he knew important business would need to be taken care of.

His assistant followed closely in his steps carrying a large folder and several orange slips in her hands. She placed the file folder on his desk and handed him the orange slips on which she had inscribed in her elegant script the names and phone numbers of persons who had called.

"Jeannette told me that Monsieur Lepetit would like to see you as soon as you come in," she said while looking intently at Eric's face. She paused for a moment, widening her eyes, horrified by what she had seen. She covered her gaping mouth with her hand staring at the blood seeping through the bandage under Eric's eye, and finally blurted out: "Oh my God, what happened to your face?"

"Oh that," Eric replied as he nonchalantly touched the bandage. "I just cut myself shaving this morning. It's nothing serious."

But the expression on her face did not change, and Eric knew that she did not believe him. He hid the bandage with his hand and quickly diverted her attention. " That will be all, Madame. I have tons of work to do today, and I do not want to be disturbed. Please tell Jeanette I will come over in one hour to see the boss."

He turned his back to his assistant and without waiting for her to leave his office, he headed for the safe where he kept the trader's data. He rapidly perused the documents, stopping only to underline in red the names of six numbered companies. A quick look at the computer screen reassured him that the trader had been inactive over the weekend. Satisfied, he finally picked up the phone and dialed a long distance number in Montreal. His younger brother Paul immediately answered the phone.

"I can't believe it's you, big brother. When was the last time you called?"

"I'm sorry, but I have been kind of busy lately."

It was a poor excuse, and Paul took it for what it was. Communication between the siblings had never been easy. While the brothers were close when they were growing up in Morocco, they had quickly drifted apart as soon as the family moved to Montreal. Their father was a free spirit entrepreneur who was always on the lookout for opportunities. When the king of Morocco asked that France end its protective regime over his kingdom, most settlers and other French expatriates immediately headed back to the homeland. But that was not what Eric's father had in mind. He took a quick look at the giant globe in his living room and decided that the 'new world' was the real land of opportunity. Without giving the matter any further thought, he informed his wife of his decision, convinced that Canada would be a better place to start a new life.

In the beginning, both Eric and Paul were extremely unhappy with the move. They felt like they had been uprooted and dumped in a frozen land without friends and relatives for support. Their first impression of Montreal was that of a gigantic, sterile village, extremely cold in the winter, hot and humid in the summer, and populated by strange people who always seemed to avoid making eye contact.

Like Casablanca, Montreal was a city where a great divide existed. At the heart of town laid the border line that carved out the metropolis into two distinct societies. There were no fences, no walls, and no border guards, yet the existence of a real split between the two founding cultures could not be denied. The division was fueled by differing ethnicity, language, and religion—all very powerful wedges. Nowhere else in the country was the partition more evident than in Montreal. And what was even more shocking to the two young brothers, was the inability and/or unwillingness of anyone to extend a warm and friendly hand to the neighbors across the street.

One half of the city of Montreal spoke English, although most of the residents in that part of town were not necessarily of English descent. The people who lived in the east end spoke predominantly Québécois, a blend of old French and English. Somehow the inhabitants of Montreal seemed to have found a way, however uncomfortable, to coexist next to one another without feeling the need to share this corner of land. Faced with a choice that was imposed on them, Eric and Paul immediately went into survival mode and found their adopted identities at opposite ends of the English and French Canadian divide.

While they were both successful in their chosen careers, not surprisingly they also followed totally different routes to get there. Paul married young, soon after graduating from law school at *Université de Montréal*, and followed the well proven path to a successful law career—a wife and two children, a pillar in the local community, a large network of friends and acquaintances, and a law practice built on trust, hard work and loyalty. Silverstone was the first and only law firm that ever employed him.

Instilled with a strong work ethic that first generation immigrants always seemed to be beset with, Paul pursued his law career with great zeal and vigor, often at the expense of his home life. He was a good provider and an adoring father, but unfortunately, his career got in the way, and his relationship with his wife suffered as a consequence.

Eric was cut from a different cloth. Driven by success but not a slave to it, he perceived his career as a means of achieving the very best for himself. He was two years older than Paul, had never been married—having never found the time or right partner—and had far too many love relationships than he cared to remember. He attended business school at McGill University, where he graduated at the top of his class with an MBA. He too worked hard, but unlike his younger sibling, always managed to find the time to play hard. He never settled on any one job or firm for long, often leapfrogging from one institution to another, wherever a better opportunity presented itself. By his standards, his employment at Banque du Commerce was the only exception, and the fact that it was a French financial institution made it twice as ironic.

Eric could hear Paul fidgeting at the other end of the line. Eric knew that like a typical lawyer, his brother would spend too much time trying to second guess what the phone call was all about rather than ask him directly. He decided that patience would work best for his purpose, and thus waited quietly for Paul's response. His reward came shortly after.

"Well, I shouldn't be complaining; at least you took time from your busy schedule to call me," Paul finally said. Then he quickly added like a second thought, "I'm fine; and you?"

While Eric noted the edgy sarcasm, he also detected something else in his brother's voice. A veiled sadness was barely noticeable, but it was there nonetheless.

"I'm OK, but you can't hide anything from me, little brother. What's wrong?"

"Well, it finally happened. Louise and I have split up."

"I'm sorry to hear that. What happened? How are the girls taking it?"

"It's been a long time coming. I didn't leave her, if you want to know. She is the one who walked out. The girls, well the girls took it hard at first, but they quickly found out how to push the guilt buttons when they want something. Don't worry about them; they will be fine, Eric."

"And how about you? Any chance of working things out with Louise?"

"No way; besides, I'm seeing someone."

Paul stopped—hesitating for a moment—unsure whether he should tell Eric anything more. He waited a while, hoping that Eric would make it easy for him by asking him the obvious question. When only silence came back by way of response, he reluctantly continued, "Do you remember Tracy who works at Fielding & Fielding?"

Eric gasped. "You mean that big blond with the big mouth and equally big....you know what I mean. You must be kidding, Paul! She is at least twenty years younger than you; and besides, she is a lousy lawyer. You said so yourself."

"Easy big brother. There is only a twelve year difference; and besides, you didn't call me to talk about my personal life. So just tell me what you want, and let's get it over with."

Eric knew right away that he had gone too far. Paul had never been comfortable discussing anything that did not relate directly to work or politics. It must have taken a lot out of him to reveal that much about his personal life, even if Eric was his brother. "You're right. I shouldn't be meddling in your private life. I'm sorry. I'm sure you know what's best for you. Just take care of yourself—and the girls," Eric replied tactfully.

"Thanks, I appreciate the thought, but you still have not told me why you called me."

"I need a favor."

The words echoed like alarm bells in the two brothers' head. Neither Paul nor Eric had spoken to each other for a long time, yet they both made the same connection right away to the last time Eric had made the same request. Eric had once relied on one of the private investigation agencies used by Paul's law firm to research the background of his former associates. The agency was extremely well connected with government security agencies around the globe. They employed a large and very reliable network of agents and highly placed informants. Their reports were thorough and insightful. The information was always corroborated by two, and sometimes three, independent sources and could always be relied upon in court. Their reach was phenomenal; there was nothing they would not or could not investigate, and above all, they respected confidentiality. While very expensive, the flip side of the coin was that their investigations always produced results—except in one very unfortunate instance.

The investigation agency had drawn a complete blank when asked to check the background of one of Eric's former associates. Despite their formidable resources, they had not been able to find any information, any record, or any hint of information on the senior partner of the investment bank boutique that employed him in Casablanca. They checked and rechecked the database of all their sources—in the U.S, in Asia, in Europe—and each time they came up with absolutely nothing. The man simply did not exist as far as the official and unofficial records were concerned.

Paul was painfully aware that the failure to uncover the true identity of one of the principals that employed Eric had almost cost his brother's life. Eric had never mentioned it again. And if Paul had asked, Eric would have held him totally blameless. He knew perfectly well that he had no one to fault for what happened in Morocco but himself alone. Yet, there was an element of lingering guilt that would not go away in Paul's mind. So when Eric asked for another favor in the same way he had done three years earlier, there was more that a tremor in his voice when he finally replied, after much hesitation, "What can I do for you?"

"Not much really. I would like to find out who is behind a handful of numbered companies. I'm convinced they have the same owner or a group of owners in common, and if you can't find out who they are, I would settle for their country of origin."

"That should not be too difficult. Send me what you have," Paul said, breathing somewhat easier now that he knew the nature of the request.

"It's on its way to you," Eric replied while clicking the send button of his computer.

"Please, reassure me Eric. You're not in some sort of trouble like the last time?"

"Relax Paul; I'm doing an investigation on behalf of Banque du Commerce. That's my job now, you know."

"Alright, then give me a couple of days and I will get back to you with the name of the owner or syndicate who controls these companies. It shouldn't be that difficult."

"Don't count on it Paul."

Eric hung up, feeling somewhat satisfied with himself. He had told Paul a half truth, but his brother had left him with no other alternative. Paul would have balked at getting the information if he had known what was really behind the request.

Eric searched for a name in his contact database, quickly found what he was looking for, and dialed another long distance number. This time it was his financial advisor in Toronto who answered the phone. He knew of no one that was better plugged-in with the investment community than Charles Timble. A former investment banker like himself, Charles had decided to make good use of the experience and knowledge he had acquired while working for more than twenty years at Credit Suisse. One day after his retirement party, he showed up at Nesbitt Burns and told the executive in charge that he was, "Ready to share the benefit of his knowledge with anyone who might be interested." He was hired on the spot and his first client was Eric.

When Charles picked up the phone, he wasted no time in warning Eric about the looming Euro crisis.

"I spent the better part of the past three weeks breaking down my clients' portfolios for them. Everyone wants to get out of Europe. And you know what? I don't blame them in the least. It's the only smart thing to do under the circumstances. The situation in Europe is a real mess. Everyone is talking about the heavy debt load and the lack of economic growth across Europe, but they are all forgetting about their pension obligations. They are staggering. It's a real time bomb! Did you know that state-funded pension obligations in two-thirds of the European Union nations are about five times higher than their combined gross debt? Even Germany is guilty of the same excess. According to Mercer, the state pension obligations in Germany are three times the size of their economy. And get this: the average French pension benefit is sixty-three percent of the national average wage!"

Charles paused briefly for effect, and then continued, "Where did they think they were going to get the money to fund these generous pension plans? Economic growth? I don't think so, not in the foreseeable future anyway. More debt? If they believe that, I would love to have some of the same stuff they've been smoking over there."

Charles started to clear his throat and had to stop to catch his breath. He coughed twice and suddenly began to laugh, realizing how silly he must have sounded over the phone telling these things to someone living in Paris.

"But I'm venting here, old boy," he finally said, once he recovered his composure. "Pardon me Eric. I'm sure you have heard it all before. What can I do for you, my friend?"

"Well, not much really. I just wanted to pick your brain a bit."

"Shoot. I'm all ears."

"I agree with you; this mess has been their doing all along. They have created a totally unsustainable situation for themselves. Unless Europe decides to bite the bullet and agrees to make some serious structural changes, which in all likelihood will mean cutting down on benefits and possibly lowering the living standards for a while, we're looking at a potential meltdown of the world's second biggest economic bloc after the U.S. But I did not call you to debate the EU crisis. What interests me is to find out who is benefiting from the situation. Have you heard of anyone who is actively trading on euro securities and is exhibiting an unbelievable winning streak?"

Charles broke into a loud laugh that rapidly turned into another short coughing spat. "Well you're not going to believe me when I tell you who is making a killing out of this mess."

Eric was all ears, as though entranced by the mere possibility that his trader had been picked up by Charles' vast network. He closed his eyes to better concentrate on what valuable piece of information his financial advisor was about to reveal to him.

"Custody Banks. You know—these old boring banks that make their money by holding and administering securities for others. Can you believe that Mellon Bank, JP Morgan, State Bank, and even Equilend are all making huge short-selling profits these days? The more volatile the Euro zone crisis, the more money it seems they are reaping in."

"I see," Eric said simply, trying to hide his disappointment, "but what I'm looking for is a high-speed trader that seems to always be on the winning side of the transactions he is involved with. Someone who seems to be able to anticipate, better than anyone else, market trends, and is always making the right bet."

"Eric, if you know of someone that possesses such a perfect crystal ball, please tell him to call me right away."

"I will Charles. But please, take this request seriously and make some quiet enquiries around your people. Will you?"

"Sure thing. Count on me Eric."

Eric did not let his financial advisor's light-hearted comments bother him too much. He had another phone call to make; one he hoped would be more productive. He never made the call, however, as David Luchatel beat him to it.

He had met David Luchatel at a bank security conference in Zurich. The conference was an excuse for overworked and somewhat repressed bankers to let loose and party wildly after hours. Little real work was ever done at these offsites, but the conferences had one redeeming feature that Eric found very useful for his job—not an opportunity for networking, as the conference brochures advertised, but a chance to gather useful, competitive intelligence during the off hours. Indeed, Eric found more information about what other banks were secretly working on in the three nights and two days that he spent in Zurich than he would have been able to do through the regular and formal interbank meetings. He knew that only a very tiny percentage of all the banks fraud cases ever made the headlines. Banks were run by conservative and cautious executives. Scandals were to be avoided at all cost, and the public's right to know was overshadowed by the fear that the bank's funds might be perceived as not being adequately protected.

Whether it was the alcohol that was consumed in great quantity or the fact that they were far away from their suffocating work environments, the bankers attending the Zurich bank security conference seemed more relaxed and willing to unreservedly talk about their bank's most guarded secrets. A sort of trading bazaar was quickly set up the first night of the conference, where a free exchange of information took place. Bankers would sit down in various dim corners of the local pubs where they played a kind of a truth game—you tell me your secret and I will tell you mine.

The object of their little game was not to uncover the latest massive fraud case kept hidden from the public's eye. It was cleverer than that. The real purpose was to uncover the ways and means in which internal financial crimes took place at other banks, the modus operandi of rogue traders, and the system inadequacies and failures to detect them. The information would be exchanged, lessons would be absorbed, remedial actions implemented, security systems upgraded, and all the bankers attending the conference would go back to their home offices that much smarter.

David Luchatel had approached Eric with a fraud case he was investigating at his bank, BNP Paribas. He thought there was more to this scam than a greedy and disgruntled employee trying to make some extra money for himself before jumping ship to another financial institution. He suspected collusion with market traders at other banks, and Banque du Commerce was high on his list. Eric agreed to co-operate in the investigation and kept in contact with David Luchatel long after the case was closed, without ever finding any accomplices.

It was now Eric's turn to seek a favor from his colleague at BNP Paribas. He had sent him the list of the numbered companies and asked him to check for any suspect data following a similar trading pattern at BNP Paribas. David called to let him know that he had uncovered some interesting information. They agreed to meet at Café de la Paix to discuss the matter over lunch.

Eric hung up the phone on a high note. *A breakthrough might be in the offering*, he thought, feeling particularly pleased with himself. He cleaned his desk and made sure to lock up the documents in the safe before closing the door of his office behind him.

"I'm off to lunch," he said as he walked by his administrative assistant, who appeared flustered by the news.

"But Monsieur Lepetit is expecting you," she barely managed to say before Eric stepped out into the hallway rushing for the elevators.

"Please tell him I will come over to see him after lunch. I may have some important information to share with him," he shouted as the door of the elevator was sliding shut with a muffled hiss.

He had a sudden change of heart and stopped the door with his right hand. "Strike that." he yelled. "Just inform him I would like to see him at the end of the day."

The administrative assistant looked at him in disbelief. Eric smiled at her. He had the self-assured look of someone about to strike a good deal.

CHAPTER 9

David Luchatel strolled along the streets of Paris like a true Parisian. Sour face, nose in the air, a Givenchy scarf wrapped too tightly around the neck, he walked briskly down Boulevard Haussemann swearing under his breath at everyone blocking his way. He was not late for his appointment or in any particular hurry. Café de la Paix was virtually around the corner, a mere ten-minute walk away, and he had more than half an hour to kill. He just looked and acted the part, as if Paris had been his birthplace.

David raised the collar of his grey raincoat, which concealed the fact that he was not French. In fact, in spite of his appearance and feigned mannerisms, there was nothing French about him either by birth, nationality, or bloodline. He owed his last name to a great-grandfather Russian émigré who was so fed up with the way people were mangling his name that one day he decided to adopt as his own the first name he saw advertised on the window of a bread store. By an unlikely coincidence, the store keeper was French and her name was Lucie Chatel. As the story goes, everyone believed that the old man was saying Luchatel when he was asked for his name.

Born and raised in Chicago, David Luchatel was considered by everyone to be your typical mid-westerner. He played baseball in grade school, basketball in high school, and football while attending Chicago State University. Watching hockey on television was his favorite pastime, even though it pained him every time the Chicago Blackhawks missed the playoffs at the end of every season. Married to his college sweetheart, he quietly pursued an uneventful banking career, first at Bear Stearns before its demise, then at JP Morgan Chase, until he got his big break when he joined BNP Paribas.

His first position at Bear Stearns was a low paying job as a junior analyst in the Capital Market division. Eighteen months later, at the urging of his wife, he moved on to JP Morgan to work in the audit department. He would have stayed there for the rest of his working life if it were not for his wife's constant reminders that they needed a bigger home with their third child on the way. Feeling the pressure, he finally contacted a headhunter who, thinking that he was a French national, told him about a job opportunity of a life time with an important French bank that was expanding its network throughout the United States. "I have a great job for you—you're the perfect candidate," he remembered the headhunter telling him.

No one believed David during the interviews when he said that he was not of French origins. "Don't worry, in the international division we all speak and work in English," the bank recruiter had said to reassure him when he was presented the job offer.

His experience working at the audit department of BNP Paribas proved to be very valuable, and he quickly progressed to a junior-level managerial position. One day, his supervisor told him that with a name like Luchatel, all he had to do was to learn French and his career in the bank would flourish. "I heard that headquarters were looking for bilingual candidates with international experience," his supervisor confided in him during one of his job performance evaluations. David did what he was counseled to do. He always followed the advice of his supervisor. He purchased a complete Rosetta Stone software package to learn French after work, and one year later he was awarded with his big break. At least that was the way his wife first described his new posting in Paris.

Judith Luchatel was thrilled by the news. "Imagine all the art galleries, le Louvre, L'Opera, the Eiffel tower, les Champs Elysée, and the shopping, oh my God!" she squealed to her girlfriend over the telephone. "And yes, we will tour all over Europe during the summer months," she quickly added, barely able to contain her excitement. Like her husband, Judith loved her new life in the first three years of their stay in Paris. They did all the things they had set out to do back in Chicago. Cuddling in bed at night, they would reminisce about how much their life had changed since their big move to *La Ville-Lumière*.

Then the daily grind set in, and they rapidly discovered that the life of an expat was not what it was purported to be after all. More was expected of David at work, and everyone made sure to remind Judith that she was an outsider living on borrowed time, even when she tried to get rid of her American accent. So instead of roaming across Europe during the summer months, they started spending their holidays back home, touring California, Arizona, and Colorado, where David would stuff himself with huge hamburgers and *real* French fries drowned in a ton of ketchup.

Six years later, he was still working at BNP Paribas in Paris. He was well liked by his superiors. In their minds, he was the right person for the job. Above all, they appreciated him because he was not at all like the other 'arrogant loud-mouthed American expatriates' who were brought to Paris to gain exposure at the bank's headquarters. David was quiet, diligent, and obedient to the point of being almost subservient, and they very much liked these qualities at the home office. He never dared raise the issue of going back home to anyone, and readily signed the three-year renewal contract without question or any thought of negotiating new terms and conditions. David Luchatel was not a man about to draw any attention to himself. He was like a shy chameleon, always looking for a way to blend into his surroundings.

The waiter rushed to meet David and pointed at a table on the sidewalk at the front of Café de la Paix, then quickly changed his mind when he recognized David's familiar face. David was promptly seated in a corner facing the grand Opera House. The table was reserved for the regular patrons and was shielded from the fumes of the mid-day traffic by a glass partition. It was a small privilege that David had managed to acquire over the years, and he never failed to use it to impress his friends visiting him from abroad. He picked up the menu that was handed to him and placed it on the small round table without looking at it. With a silent nod he signaled to the waiter that he would wait for his guest to arrive.

Eric showed up a few minutes later and immediately picked up the hand signal of the waiter pointing in the direction of where David was seated.

"Right on time; how are you Eric?" David warmly welcomed his colleague.

"Great. I feel great," Eric replied, with perhaps too much enthusiasm.

"Let's order then and eat first. We can talk after."

"It's fine with me, but I know how much you're always in a hurry. Are you sure you have enough time?"

"Yes, you're right," David replied, instinctively looking at his watch." Let's talk about our investigation while we eat. But I have to tell you something first before I forget. Judith came up with this wonderful idea. I told you about her girlfriend who works at the embassy. Well, Judith thought it might be a good idea if......." David noticed the glare in Eric's eyes and stopped right away in mid-sentence. He never finished what he was about to say. What he did not notice though, was that Eric had also made a mental note that he had personalized the matter they were about to discuss by referring to it as *our investigation*.

Eric took a huge bite out of his sandwich and helped swallow the food with a gulp of his Stella. He shook his head twice, and David took it as his cue to change the subject and talk about what they had come to discuss in the first place.

"I'm afraid I have some good news and lots of bad news," he said, waiting for Eric's approval to continue. Eric remained silent, his eyes only revealing his intense curiosity.

"Well, let me start with the bad news then," David continued after a short pause. "I looked into our trading records and found absolutely no trace of anyone doing what you described. So I called a few colleagues in New York and they too came back empty handed. So I started thinking maybe your trader is not limiting his activity to financial institutions. What if he is also targeting other industries?"

"Good thinking. And what did you find when you broadened your inquiry?" Eric immediately interjected.

"I'm sorry Eric, but I'm afraid that too was a big waste of time."

Eric nodded glumly. He started to think that perhaps Alain Lepetit was right about the whole matter after all. There was nothing there but his hyper-active imagination grasping after some illusionary scam. But then he remembered that David had also said that he had some good news, and sounding more frustrated than hopeful he blurted out, "Enough with the bad news David. What's the good news?"

David gave Eric a teasing smile. "I think what I'm about to tell you is going to interest you very much." He took another sip of his beer and wiped his mouth with the back of his hand. Lowering his voice to a whisper, he went on to say, "After New York, I thought that I was approaching the problem the wrong way. Instead of looking at stock trades exhibiting a similar pattern as what's been occurring at your bank, I wondered what would happen if I ignored the pattern altogether and simply searched for a match with the numbered companies. So I made one more call to Zurich, and bingo! I got a hit right away."

"Really?" Eric bellowed.

"Yes, that's right. UBS and Credit Suisse have seen a couple of the numbered companies on their books. But that's not all. Surprisingly, they told me that three numbered companies not on your list were also making regular high-speed trades that, although they did not exhibit the same characteristics, were suspiciously on the money more often than not. So I immediately proceeded to make another phone call to my best buddy working in Frankfurt. And guess what? Deutsche bank and Commertzbank have also recorded trades bearing some of the same numbered companies on your list. And what's even more interesting, the trades were never higher than 1,000 shares at a time and always seemed to work in favor of the investors. The only difference is that the transactions didn't show up as rapid fire like you described, but more like a short seller at work. It would seem that your mysterious trader has a European bank centric preference. What do you think of that?"

Eric pondered what David had just told him for a moment. So far he had not heard anything that necessarily pointed to any illegal activity beyond the fact that Banque du Commerce was not the only bank stock that interested this so-called mysterious electronic trader. The fact that the trader always seemed able to pick the right time to buy or sell bank shares was puzzling though. Eric touched the bandage on his face and looked David squarely in the eyes.

"David, please be extremely careful when you investigate this matter. I'm still not convinced that we are dealing with an internal fraud case. There are too many things that don't seem to fit. The number of banks involved for instance, the lack of similar trading patterns from one bank to another, and the difference in the counterparties must also be taken into account. The only thing we know for sure at this point is that someone is making a killing out of trading in bank stocks. So, let's first concentrate on finding out who is hiding behind these numbered companies from official records. Don't try to dig anymore than that without consulting with me first."

"You got it. I have to be honest with you, Eric. I had some doubts about your case when you first approached me, but now you have got me hooked. I will get back to you as soon as I have something. Rest assured I will be careful."

Eric was about to reply when he noticed the flashing red light on his BlackBerry telling him that he had a new e-mail. It was a short note from Stephanie Brulé.

Eric,
Interpol is taking your case. I'm the officer in charge of the investigation and our best analyst is digging into the data.
Stay put and go about your business as usual.
Best,
Stephanie

Eric made a mental note to thank Bartolli the next time they met. He glanced at David getting ready to leave the café and briefly debated whether to tell him to drop the whole matter altogether, then thought better of it, seeing the eagerness in his colleague's face. Like Eric, the case had truly caught David's imagination. But his reasons for wanting to work on it were totally different than Eric's. David loved mysteries. They occupied his mind and made his daily life more palatable. Eric was motivated by a totally different set of circumstances. He was drawn to the mysterious electronic trader by an invisible and powerful force from the past. There was nothing rational about it.

He shook David's hand, reminding him once again not to do anything foolish, and watched him for a moment hurrying down the boulevard with his head held high and his nose in the air. David had taken the mantle of a Parisian as he headed back to his office.

Eric's personal assistant was virtually camped at the doorstep of his office when he arrived shortly after 2:00 pm. She looked very agitated and not at all pleased that she had missed her regular lunch date with her friend.

"Monsieur Lepetit is looking for you. I told him that you went to lunch, and he asked me to call you back immediately. I know how much you dislike being disturbed during your lunch time so I didn't call you. In the meantime, he's been asking for you every fifteen minutes," the assistant screeched in her high-pitch voice that seemed to raise a notch higher every time she was under stress.

"It's alright; give me a minute to check my messages and I will be on my way to see him."

But his show of co-operation did not seem to appease his personal assistant. Looking even more flustered, she handed him an orange slip and said, "Also, this gentleman has phoned you four times this morning. He left this number for you to call him back. He said that, "He possesses the information you're looking for," and asked me to repeat the message back to him twice as if I was incapable of taking notes. Who does he think I am—some air-head bimbo or something?"

Eric grabbed the note and immediately headed for the phone in his office. "Please close the door behind you," he instructed his assistant in a tone that incited her frustration even more.

The man had a slight accent that Eric could not place. He spoke in a low voice and in short bursts, as if he were afraid to say too much. "Well, you must be a very busy person, Monsieur Martin. I have been calling you all morning."

"Why don't you start by telling me who you are?"

"Who I am is not important. What's important is the information I would like to share with you."

"And what can be so important that you felt the need to call me four times?"

"You are curious to know who is speed-trading your bank stocks, no?"

"Lots of people are investing in the bank. What's so special about that?"

"I see, you have decided to be cute about it. Let me be more clear. A bunch of numbered companies are making millions trading on your bank, and you want to know who is behind it. How am I doing so far Monsieur Martin?"

"Go on, I could be interested."

"But you are very interested. You're not fooling anyone, you know. Why are you insisting on playing that game?"

"Alright, I will admit that much. What can you tell me about it?"

"Not so fast. This is not something I can reveal over the phone. You never know who might be listening."

"Where would you like to meet then?"

"In Istanbul."

"Why Istanbul? Why not here in Paris?"

"Let's put it this way, Monsieur Martin. Certain circumstances make it very difficult for me to travel anywhere outside of Turkey. The only place I can meet you is in Istanbul. So if you want the information, catch the first flight to Istanbul, and I promise you will not be disappointed."

"How do I know you're telling me the truth?"

"You don't. But unfortunately for you, you don't have much of a choice; this is the only way you can find what you're looking for."

Eric lowered the phone away from his ear and exhaled slowly. Several thoughts raced through his mind as he fought a rising suspicion. He needed a moment of reflection, a time to assess, ponder, and reflect on the opportune, but highly unusual, offer of assistance. The man on the other end of the line was holding back much information, the least of which was why he was willing to tell him anything, let alone disclose the name of the mysterious trader. He had a decision to make, and so little information on which to rely. *What I have got to lose anyway?*" he mumbled under his breath after a short deliberation.

"I will be staying at the Conrad Istanbul," he informed the man on the phone.

"Good, I will call you in two days. Have a nice trip."

Eric hung up thinking that he had no time to waste. But before embarking on this journey, he knew that something else important had to be taken care of. He swiveled his chair around to face his computer and typed a short email addressed to Alain Lepetit.

CHAPTER 10

The ornate executive dining room on the eighth floor of Banque du Commerce was jam packed with important clients. Half-hidden by a large red velvet drape, Alain Lepetit stood at the doorway scanning every face in the room, not believing his eyes. Table after table, clients and bankers alike looked happy and in a great party mood. The atmosphere in the room was charged with high octane energy. It was indeed an incredible scene made more extraordinary by the fact that all of Europe was on the brink of economic collapse. Greece was about to implode, threatening to engulf with it the entire euro zone into a bottomless black hole, yet the dining room was full of laughter and happy faces. It seemed as if the entire corporate elite of France had agreed to gather in one place, and just pretend that everything was fine in the world.

Alain Lepetit sighed.

There was not a single seat available and he felt left out. "What's going on?" he asked the waiter who was rushing back to the kitchen, carrying a stack of dirty dishes.

"Have you not heard the news, sir? You know, the new treaty struck in Brussels to save the euro?"

"Yes of course," Alain Lepetit replied, cursing under his breath that he had not kept up with the morning news. He studied the room a second time, scrutinizing every face even more closely, hoping that he would find someone to tag along. He quickly realized that it was a big waste of time. He had no clients to speak of, given the nature of his job at the bank. With an air of resignation, he shrugged his shoulders and turned his back to leave. He was about to enter the elevator, which was delivering yet another fresh load of new happy faces, when he heard someone calling his name from the far end of the hallway. It was the maitre d' running after him, slightly out of breath and barely able to hold on to a stash of leather-bound menus.

"Monsieur Lepetit. Please wait, Monsieur Lepetit. Monsieur Marchand would like you to join him for lunch."

All is not lost, thought Alain Lepetit as he turned to follow the maitre d' leading him promptly to Marchand's table. As he marched across the dining room, all smiles for everyone, he could feel the stares of the bankers piercing his body like laser beams. He immediately recognized what was behind the deliberate glares that his colleagues were throwing at him. It was something he had experienced many times before during his long banking career. His smile turned into a wide grin when he reached the middle of the dining room. He was a key player in a corporate domino game that was about to start. His promotion had triggered a chain reaction, and the rumor mill was whirring in high gear by now. International jobs were in great demand, and everyone had a favor to ask or a deal to make—new jobs would be available, IOUs would be cashed in, favors would be granted, and job-swaps would be entertained. And Alain Lepetit was at the epicenter of this job bazaar that had been unleashed by his appointment in Australia. Overnight, he had become a power broker, a role that he particularly relished and had always made a point of leveraging to its maximum potential.

Marchand was having lunch with the CEO's of Alcatel and France Telecom and a couple of other guests that Alain Lepetit did not recognize. He thanked his boss for the invitation and shook the hand of everyone at the table before settling into his chair, his smile never leaving his lips. He listened to the small-talk and the back-and-forth exchanges of viewpoints on how to permanently resolve the euro crisis, not daring to contribute anything more than a nod of the head and a smile here and there to signify that he was paying close attention to the conversation, which of course he was not. He was not very comfortable sharing a table with a senior executive of the bank, feeling somewhat ill-at-ease with the way the impromptu lunch invitation had come about. A quick sideways glance at Marchand told nothing more about his boss's surprising gesture. Marchand was not known for his benevolence or kindness towards his subordinates. He belonged to the old school of management, where it is professed that fear alone commands respect and guarantees results. *Why have I been asked to join in?* Alain Lepetit was now really worried.

He did not have to wait long for the answer.

"How are you making out with our little project?" Marchand muffled under his napkin in between two bites of food.

Alain Lepetit blew a huge sigh of relief.

"I'm making good progress on the staffing side. I have already identified a broad list of good candidates for the various key positions. I must give more thought to the business strategy portion of the assignment before I can complete the personnel recommendations. I should have a good idea on how the org chart should shape up in a week's time."

"Not good enough. I'm meeting with Human Resources tomorrow afternoon and I must have your staff recommendations before then. Australia is a real gem in waiting; it's like a rough diamond that needs to be cut and polished. It requires steady and experienced hands to handle it. I trust you have selected the right people to second you for this important mission. And we must not forget your replacement here in Paris. I don't have to tell you about the vital importance of that job. I must have your entire org chart and your recommendation for your replacement by 7:00 a.m. tomorrow morning at the very latest."

Alain Lepetit studied the face of the bank executive, feeling suddenly trapped in a situation where he saw no escape. He never felt very comfortable dealing with Marchand even at the best of times, and now the pressure had been turned a couple more notches. What he had been asked to produce in an unrealistic time frame was beyond belief. He stared down at his plate, picking at the food that by now had lost all of its appeal, and cursed his growing insecurity. He dared not look up, preferring instead to mull over the dark thoughts that always seemed to surface when feeling stressed or under pressure. *Why do powerful people always feel the need to show off their power? Why do they constantly need to remind themselves that they are omnipotent?* He wanted to shout at Marchand, but didn't. Instead, he reverted to his automatic coping mechanism by kowtowing in self-defense.

"You will have my staff recommendations first thing tomorrow morning," Alain Lepetit meekly uttered in between two painful sighs.

"Good. I look forward to seeing who you came up with. I trust your profitability development strategy for the Australian subsidiary will be on my desk by the end of the week as well."

Alain Lepetit gasped in total panic. This last request was so far over the top that he was left momentarily speechless. And this time, he could not avoid the glare in Marchand's eyes demanding an immediate response. He stumbled on his words, and after several false starts, finally managed to rearrange his thoughts in some sort of logical order.

"Yes sir, you can count on me. It'll be ready for your review on time, as requested," he muttered under his breath, knowing full well that it would take him at least a month of hard work to research and put together a half-decent business plan.

The conversation around the dining table had died down quickly by the time coffee and dessert arrived. A couple of clients looked at their watches and Alain Lepetit took the signal as his cue to excuse himself. A banker at the back of the room gave him a hesitant wave, with his index finger pointed at his mouth while holding his thump up towards his ear. Alan Lepetit acknowledged the phone request with a discreet nod of the head before stepping out of the dining room.

"I've a very important business to take care of immediately, and I don't want to be disturbed," Alain Lepetit barked at his assistant as he entered his office. He then pulled the candidate list from under a stack of documents piled up on a credenza next to his desk, and briefly examined the names that were circled in red. He nodded his approval at the selection, and then proceeded to add a couple of names from memory. Those were people he had worked with throughout his international banking career. He knew these men well. They all had a proven track record and were very discreet. But above all, they all possessed two redeeming qualities that were absolutely essential as far as he was concerned: they were loyal and reliable.

Eric's name came up underlined with a thick red pen. Another name had been handwritten in the margin. It was Alain Lepetit's handpicked candidate for his current job as Managing Director, Global Security and Internal Control. He checked the name of his replacement and briefly pondered his choice of Eric as his second in command in Australia. His wife had approved his decision, and he always respected her opinion. Satisfied, he began typing the staffing recommendations, aware that the list was incomplete. *That will be Eric's first assignment*, he concluded, as he buzzed his assistant. "Please tell Eric that I want to see him right away."

Next on his to-do list was the strategy paper that was due in four days. He knew that he had not been given enough time to put together a well thought-out and comprehensive plan. All he had to guide him in this task was a three year old inspection report that focused more on operational deficiencies than on marketing strategy. Apprehension coupled with suspicion began to fill his mind. *Why the rush? Am I being set up for failure?* After much deliberation, he finally found a way to convince himself that this was all part of a test. "I must show him what I'm capable of," he murmured to himself, pleased with his self-serving observation.

He cleared his mind and started to think about what he could do in the short time that he had to write an insightful strategy paper. His first thought turned to his last international post, and he rapidly realized that his experience in Canada could prove very valuable. Similarities between the two countries were striking. They both were commodity-based and largely export-driven economies. As well, they both were located at the cusp of vast markets. Whereas Canada sat on top of the giant U.S. market for its products and services, Australia was a natural doorway to Asia. And so, guided by his successful experience with the Canadian subsidiary, Alain Lepetit quickly identified four product lines that would surely also work well in Australia. Export finance, trade finance, asset securitization, and mining finance were a good start. As a second phase, he thought of advisory services in the mining and food and beverages sectors to complement an already well-established broad spectrum of traditional product lines. Borrowing from Marchand's description of Australia at lunch, he typed in the title of his strategy paper:

Australia—A Diamond In The Rough,
A Strategy to Exploit a Hidden Gem

The outline of the strategy paper began to congeal in his mind, but he was well aware that he still lacked most of the basic data. He knew that Marchand would never be satisfied with just broad guidelines and soft targets. He would want specific and quantifiable goals and objectives, and well-defined resources to achieve them. In short, the strategy had to be defensible with iron-clad facts and figures, or else it would be rejected by the Board and dire consequences would certainly be the outcome as far as Alain Lepetit's career was concerned. He was about to pick up the phone to call Eric for help, when the ring tone beat him to it.

"Well, well Alain, you're hiding something from me?" the head of the Audit and Inspection Division chuckled on the phone.

"Not at all, I was about to call you to tell you about it, but lunch with Marchand got in the way."

"Yes, I know. I was told of your private lunch affair with the boss."

"Not so private, as I'm sure your spies up there must have also told you."

"So when were you thinking about asking me for a full audit of the Australian subsidiary?"

Alain Lepetit grimaced, once again feeling the weight of the mammoth task ahead of him. "Not in the near future, unless you can produce your report by Friday," he said after a short pause.

The head of the Audit and Inspection Division broke into a loud laugh. "I see; the old fox is back to his old tricks. He sure knows how to put the squeeze on his people."

Alain Lepetit was in no mood to waste any more time. He had heard enough and was clearly exasperated by now.

"Alright. Did you call me to help me or to bug me?" he blurted on the phone.

After a long moment of silence, and when he felt he had regained full control of his temper, he resumed speaking in a gentler tone. "I have your last staff report on the Australian operations. The problem with it is that it's out of date and it contains precious little information on how to boost business in the region."

"Yes I know, but we had to delete the entire business development section."

"Why in the hell did you do that?" Alain Lepetit asked, barely able to contain the shock in his voice.

"On order from above."

By now Alain Lepetit was totally beside himself, and his voice was a shout when he said, "Who and why, for crying out loud?"

"Marchand, and the reason is simple. He wanted to protect one of his special protégées who made a mess out of things down under."

After a long, uncomfortable pause, Alain Lepetit finally asked, "Where is the section of the report that has been deleted?"

"We had to destroy every single copy, my old friend, on order of you-know-who."

Alain Lepetit gasped.

"Calm down Alain. The news is not as bad as it sounds. Luckily for you, the *chef de mission* has a phenomenal memory and maybe a few personal notes lying here and there that he might be willing to share with you. If you want, I can ask Jean Francois to pay you a visit."

This time Alain Lepetit was pleased with the response and, no longer caring to hide his eagerness, blurted out, "Please tell him that I would like to see him immediately to discuss his candidacy for a position in Australia."

The telephone conversation ended on the right note, and the two bankers were pleased at how well they had handled this delicate matter. A deal had been struck and favors exchanged in the best banking tradition. Alain Lepetit breathed out a long sigh of relief and was almost cheerful when he hung up the phone.

He clicked on the Word icon on his computer and opened the file that contained the draft staffing recommendation. The document which flashed on the screen seconds later had eight names listed in descending order of seniority, with Eric Martin's name and position appearing just below his own. He scrolled down the list and carefully mulled over each name, drawing from memory the candidate he considered to be the weakest. It was not an easy task. He knew the men well, having forged close relationships with each one of them over the years. He recognized that loyalty was a hard thing to earn and, by all accounts, they had all proven their trustworthiness to him. After much hesitation, he finally settled on the third name and clicked the delete button. Jean Francois would be a good CFO, he thought, while adding the name of the inspector to the list.

Although his conversation with the head of the Audit and Inspection Division had been somewhat guarded—not surprising, given the sensitive nature of the subject matter—there was no doubt in Alain Lepetit's mind about the value of the information he was about to receive. He was confident that the inspector would bring with him a wealth of information on what had gone wrong with the Australian subsidiary and what was needed to rectify the problems. He had seen his reports and had always been impressed with the quality of his work. Satisfied with the last change he made on the staffing recommendation, he felt that all he had to do now was to relax and wait for Jean Francois to show up.

Once again, however, the ring tone of the phone disturbed his agenda. He pressed the speakerphone and heard the voice with a hollow metallic echo crackling on the line.

"Monsieur Lepetit, you have disappointed me once again.'

Alain Lepetit's heart froze in mid-beat. "What do you mean? I took care of Eric. He will not be bothering you again," he said, his voice shredded with fear.

"Really? Then please tell us what you think he's been doing all morning?"

"I don't know. I have not been able to reach him yet, but I can assure you that I have done everything you asked me to do."

"Well, I'm sorry to inform you that you were not very convincing. It did not work, Monsieur Lepetit. I'm afraid that this leaves us with no other option."

Alain Lepetit pressed his fingers on the side of his head and held his breath as long as he could. He felt his pulse rise up to a dangerous level and barely managed to choke a response that he hoped would satisfy his interlocutor. "Please, let me try again. I will find a way to convince him this time. I promise you."

A loud laugh echoed in the office. Alain Lepetit rushed to turn down the volume of the speakerphone, but feared that it might have been too late. He broke out in sweat, afraid that his assistant sitting across the hall from his office might have heard the conversation and was probably wondering what was going on. He slammed shut the door of his office, just in case, and started to plead his case one more time, when the voice cut in on the speakerphone.

"And I suppose you're going to tell me that I should trust you. Please, tell me why I should believe you this time, Monsieur Lepetit? You had your chance.

Now. . .before you die of a heart attack, let me tell you what we're going to do. We're going to take care of Eric ourselves, and you are going to wait for our instructions when you arrive in Sydney to take on your new function. You will do whatever we ask of you. From now on, you'll take your marching orders from us. Is that clear?"

The speakerphone buzzed for a second and the phone line went dead.

Alain Lepetit buried his head in his hands and pressed as hard as he could, trying to squeeze the last words he had heard out of his brain. He had an uncontrollable urge to bang his head on his desk so hard that somehow it would wipe out any memory of that conversation. *I might as well quit the bank and kiss my career goodbye.* But all he was capable of doing was to blame Eric for his failings and scream at the top of his voice "***ERIC***.... **ERIC** what have you done to me*?*"

His assistant burst into the office and stood at the doorway with a terrified look on her face. She knew about her boss's occasional fits of anger, but nothing had prepared her for what she was witnessing. Alain Lepetit had hurled the phone, the notepads, the files, and everything else he could get his hands on, against the walls of his office. His eyes were bloodshot, his fists tight as a vise, as he stood in the middle of the room looking for more things to hurl around in a fit of rage.

The poor assistant was sure that her boss had gone totally mad.

"Monsieur Lepetit, please calm down. You can't solve anything by acting that way."

Alain Lepetit glared at his assistant, who was standing cowed in fear near the door ready to bail out at the first sign of danger.

"I told you that I want to see Eric in my office. Why is he not here?" Alain Lepetit screamed at her.

The assistant retracted to the outside edge of the doorway." I have been calling his assistant all morning," she sheepishly replied. "She just called me back to let me know that he left the office an hour ago."

"What do you mean he left the office? Where did he go? Has anyone told him that I want to see him right away?"

"Oh yes, Monsieur Lepetit. His assistant assured me that she gave him my messages. She also said that he sent you an email."

"What? What email?" Alain Lepetit bawled as he turned to check his computer.

Alain,
It is with sincere regret that I must decline your kind offer to join you in Australia. My last job in Casablanca has left me with much unfinished business. I now realize that unless I deal once and for all with the memories that are haunting

me, I'll never be able to move on with my life. I must get to the bottom of this affair with the high speed electronic trader. It is something I must do now, and I know that I would be acting against your wishes if I pursue it while working for you at the bank. So please accept this email as my letter of resignation, effective immediately.

Best regards,
Eric
Ps Best of luck to you and Chantal in Australia. Let providence work its magic. And who knows, our paths may cross again.

Alain Lepetit's lips quivered. His face was flushed red in anger as he screeched Eric's name at his stunned assistant. No one answered. The assistant had stormed out of the office, concerned for her safety. He was left staring at the monitor of his computer, not believing his eyes.

"It's a nightmare," he roared at the screen.

CHAPTER 11

The man with skin the color of dark olives looked at his watch for the third time, but paid little attention to the needles marking the time. He was not in any hurry, late for an appointment, or waiting for anyone. In fact, time was not relevant to what he was doing. This was just a habit. Something he had acquired while fighting along with his Kurdish brothers against the blood-thirsty hordes of Saddam Hussein's army in northern Iraq. Something he used to do often back then with a cell phone in hand, while observing the enemy hidden on the side of a dirt road, and waiting for the right moment to trigger the improvised explosive device. It was one of those mindless gestures that had stuck with him all these years, owing its origins more out of a need for comfort and reassurance in times of danger than because of a real need to know how much time had elapsed. A kind of quirk that reminded him that he was still alive and in possession of all his limbs and faculties.

He glanced at the grey stone building across the street and let his eyes wander briefly toward the window on the second floor. He had been observing the same window for the past three hours without any interruption or distraction. But something had caught his eye this time, and he nudged his companion sitting beside him. He pointed at what looked like the shadow of a man gazing at the mostly deserted street below. He stared at his companion, seeking acknowledgement that he had done well by spotting their target right away.

The reaction of Hogir's comrade was slow and purposely nonchalant. He barely bothered to lift his head, buried deep in his newspaper, to take a quick glimpse at the window where a thin, translucent, cotton curtain was fluttering in the early morning breeze. He simply smiled at Hogir, and then resumed reading his paper. Nothing in his outward behavior showed that he had any special interest as to what might be happening on the other side of the street. To an untrained observer, he was simply sharing an early coffee break with a friend before heading out for the office.

Hogir was not fooled by his companion's apparent lack of interest, however. He noticed that he had not bothered flipping the page of the newspaper the entire time they had been sitting together inside the pastry shop across from Eric's apartment building. He had no doubt that nothing could escape his comrade's acute sense of awareness of his surroundings. He saw the way his partner had ever-so-slightly tightened his hold of the newspaper moments before Eric's shadow swept across the window of his living room. In fact, he was certain that he had felt Eric's presence before his silhouette could be observed from the street below. It was a special skill that never failed to impress everyone back home and made Karzan the best team leader they ever had in their terrorist organization. Hogir was even more in awe now that he had personally witnessed Karzan's special premonition gift, and felt honored that he had been selected to accompany him on this important mission.

The shadow moved away from the window. Hogir worked the sleep from his shoulders and sipped another drop of black coffee from his cup without taking his eyes off the second floor of the building across the street. He would never admit it to anyone, but the long wait throughout the night had tired him. The red eye flight from Istanbul the day earlier had also contributed to his weariness, even if he fought hard to overcome it. He had been sent to Paris on an urgent basis to replace a comrade who had met an untimely death in Antibes. It was not an ideal situation for a first mission abroad, but Hogir was determined to make the best of it. He would be ready and would not hesitate when the time came to strike decisively. He was battle hardened; his training had prepared him well.

The death of a companion on a mission in a foreign land came as a shock to all the members of the group. Everyone was alarmed by the news, and the leadership in particular was worried that somehow the identity of the dead man could be traced back to them. But when Karzan confirmed that he had personally made certain that no one was carrying any identity papers while working in the field, the mood of doom and gloom that had affected everyone vanished like magic. The green light to resume the mission was given shortly after. The decision was hotly contested, however. The commandant and the foreign woman had argued angrily about the objective of the operation, neither wanting to back down for fear of appearing weak. In the end, the solid reputation of Karzan alone had carried the day.

Without warning, Karzan dropped the newspaper on the table, pushing it aside in one sweeping motion of his hand, as if he wanted to get rid of a pestering fly. His neck stiffened and his senses came alive while he focused his attention on the massive wooden door at the entrance of the apartment building. Hogir noticed the change in Karzan's demeanor, and immediately responded in kind. No one would escape his watchful eyes.

Moments later the heavy door swung open and Eric appeared carrying a light, overnight leather bag in his right hand. He remained standing in front of his building for a moment, his eyes surveying the length of the street like a man wary of his surroundings. After a while, he pulled up the collar of his black leather jacket to fight off a cold chill that seemed to have suddenly affected him. He then took a step in the direction of the small pastry shop across the street that sent a small tremor along Hogir's spine. He stopped at the edge of the sidewalk, hesitated briefly, then appeared to make up his mind and remained where he was standing.

Karzan watched Eric intently, ready to spring into action at the first opportunity. There were lots of things he wanted to do to the man who had caused the death of a friend and comrade in arms. He struggled to keep his personal feelings in check, but vowed to get even someday. "There will be plenty of time for revenge," he swore under his breath, while signaling Hogir to take care of the tab. In the meantime, he was determined to obey his orders without question or second thought. His parents had chosen well when they named him Karzan, which meant 'professional' in their Kurdish dialect.

Eric heard the roar of the engine before he saw the taxi making its way around the corner. He raised his hand and the grey Peugeot screeched to a sudden halt. He threw his bag in the backseat and hopped in the taxi, which then took off right away. Across the street, Karzan wasted no time. He pulled a set of keys from his pocket and gave it to Hogir.

"Here take the wheel; I have a phone call to make," Karzan said while rushing out of the pastry shop with Hogir trailing close behind.

As soon as they got into their car, Karzan reached for his coat pocket and this time pulled out his iPhone. He scanned the screen with his index finger and settled on a name.

"Eric is on the move. He just got into a taxi, and if I had to guess, I would say that he is heading straight for the airport."

"Don't guess, and don't lose sight of him!" The female voice on the phone carried the harshness of someone used to giving orders.

Karzan bit his lower lip hard, drawing blood into his mouth. He resented the tone and the manner in which he had been spoken to. It was hard enough for him to accept being told what to do, but a foreigner, and a woman at that, made matters even harder for him to swallow.

Hogir glanced at Karzan's taunt face and guessed right away what was upsetting his partner. He was about to say something, but the stare from Karzan immediately silenced him.

Karzan ground his teeth, took a couple of deep breaths, and with his mouth pasted on the iPhone he finally managed to mumble a few words in response, "We're glued to his tail. He will not escape us."

"Good. Do that and don't screw up like the last time in Antibes."

Karzan clicked the smart phone dead, not bothering to reply. "There is no sense arguing with a bitch who does not have a clue as to what it takes to work in the field," he hissed under his breath, just loud enough for Hogir to hear.

For five days he had been watching Eric. He had followed him across France to his villa in Antibes. He waited patiently in the parking lot while Eric was having dinner with Alain Lepetit in Villeneuve Loubet. He had even visited his apartment in Paris to plant a small digital transmitter while he was at work. Not for one instant had he let Eric out of his sight. And that had cost him dearly because of a black devil of a woman who had intervened in Antibes. His mission had now become a personal affair. *I don't need to be reminded by anyone how to do my business*, Karzan thought, while staring at the car ahead.

Karzan shoved the iPhone back in his side pocket, and made a quick assessment of their current situation. The traffic was light—mostly delivery trucks, taxis and motorbikes. Hogir had kept their black Citroen at a safe distance behind Eric's taxi, keeping up with the flow of traffic so as not to attract any attention. He glanced ahead and noticed that the taxi had unexpectedly swirved to the right to catch the highway ramp. The large panel above the road indicated that they were heading for Charles de Gaulle airport.

"Step on the gas; we don't want to lose them," barked Karzan.

"I'm on them. Don't worry. I have them in my sight," replied Hogir, noticeably disturbed by the abrupt change in direction.

They followed the taxi up the ramp and continued their chase at high speed. The traffic on the highway was much heavier, and this time, Hogir was having problems keeping up the chase. Hogir could sense Karzan's impatience growing by the minute. It made him nervous, and he fought the urge to glance at his watch.

They reached the airport twenty minutes later and slowed down to a crawl, looking for Eric's taxi. The airport terminal was congested. Rows of black limousines, grey and white taxis, and passenger vans bearing the logos of the best hotel in Paris, were fighting for the few available parking spots to quickly unload their passengers. They circled the crammed parking lot a couple of times, but found no trace of Eric's taxi. Tension was building inside the car. A stretch limousine pulled out on the right side, and Karzan's neck stiffened. He sensed something, and asked Hogir to turn back.

Hogir was the first to spot Eric's parked taxi, half-hidden between two vans. Breathing easier, he pointed in the direction of the taxi, "There they are; what do you want me to do?"

"Drop me off here. Find a parking space and look for me inside the airport."

The taxi driver had parked his car in front of the terminal entrance A8. Karzan approached the vehicle from behind and stood on the side concealed by the large van. He watched Eric hand the driver a 100 euro note and leave for the terminal in such a hurry he didn't bother with the change. Karzan kept pace with Eric, only to be stunned moments later when he realized what was ahead. He picked up his iPhone and lightly tapped with his index finger on the name displayed on the screen.

"Our friend is on his way to Istanbul,' he said in the Kurmanji-Kurdish dialect.

"Are you sure?" his commander asked.

"Well, he is standing in front of the Turkish Airline terminal waiting to check in for the 9:00 am flight to Istanbul."

The commander went silent.

Karzan held his iPhone close against his right ear. He could hear his commander's heavy breathing. Obviously this trip had not been expected, and he was wondering what Eric was up to. From the corner of his eye, he spotted Hogir walking briskly in his direction. He waved him off immediately, not wanting to take any chance with Eric being so close.

The commander finally spoke, with a voice that carried much tension, "Are you absolutely certain that he is on that flight?"

"Yes, he just received his boarding pass, and he is now heading for security."

"Get on that plane. We must know who he is meeting in Istanbul."

"What's wrong, Abdullah?" Karzan asked, calling his commander by his first name as a sign of close friendship.

"I'm afraid that we may have a traitor among us."

The words pierced Karzan's ears as surely as a bullet would find its place in the traitor's head. The fear that someone would betray them was always there in the back of his mind, ever since the time their unit had been caught in an ambush and decimated by one of Saddam's elite commandos in northern Iraq. Ten good men had been mowed down by machine gun fire. At nightfall, their beheaded bodies were thrown onto the dirt road in the main village square for everyone to see, but not touch. The bodies laid there for weeks on end. No one dared to move the corpses and give the men a decent burial in the little plot of land on the outskirts of the village. The entire village was gripped by a fear that was more paralyzing than death.

Karzan and Abdullah were the only two survivors of that massacre. On that fateful day, Karzan's special premonition gift had saved their lives, and a bond of steel was forever forged between the two freedom fighters, now described as terrorists.

"Don't worry about Eric. He is not going anywhere without me," Karzan replied with firmness.

Abdullah remained silent

So Karzan found the words that Abdulla wanted to hear, "Let me know once you have found the traitor and I will personally take care of him. *Khwahafeez*, goodbye for now my friend."

PART TWO

"I hope for nothing.
  I fear nothing.
    I am free."

NIKOS KAZANTZAKIS

CHAPTER 12

Istanbul, Turkey

The Turkish Airlines' airbus banked its wings above the azure Marmara Sea, making its final approach to Atatürk airport. Eric had a seat overlooking the right wing of the plane, and for the first time since their rapid descent he was able to catch a clear view of the majestic city below: Istanbul, the capital of three empires, once known as Constantinople or the "city of World's Desire." In the far distance, he could see its seven hills rising above the horizon, each of them adorned by a massive mosque with a golden dome and tall, rocket-like minarets pointed at the heavens. Then all of a sudden, the Bosphorus emerged out of the corner of his eye. He watched in awe at the golden sun that glistened like little diamonds over the deep blue waters of the strait that divides the old imperial city at its heart.

Istanbul had been the capital city of the Byzantine and the Ottoman empires for thousands of years. That honor was bestowed to Ankara in the 1920s at the urging of the founder of the modern Turkish Republic, Mustapha Kemal—better known as Atatürk. But Eric knew that the old majestic dame had not lost any of its magical powers, despite having been plucked out of its throne in modern times. He was fairly familiar with Istanbul, a fascinating city he had visited on a number of occasions when he worked as an investment banker in Toronto. He often wondered what attracted him to this city that bridged two continents and stirred visions of Sultans, harems, and magnificent palaces. Yet, he also knew Istanbul as a unique place in the world where sharp differences between old traditions and the modern world managed to co-exist in apparent harmony. A place where pronounced contrasts between eastern values and western lifestyles have found a way to commingle for years without tension, envy, or resentment. He had roamed the streets of the city at peace with itself, where young girls were often seen in stilettos and miniskirts, holding the hand of their mothers wearing traditional *şalvars* trousers and *başörtüsü* head coverings. He found incredible the ease in which the inhabitants were able to marry the rich history of their ancient city, deeply rooted in Asia Minor and the Middle-East, with the ambition of a country that aspired to become a modern European secular state.

Eric could think of only one other place in the world where he had once felt the same emotional connection and warm attachment. Not that the two cities had much in common in terms of scenery, people, or tolerance towards other cultures. His feelings for Casablanca were equally strong because he had found solace and happiness in the city that once represented the outermost western frontier of the mighty Ottoman Empire. But now the fondness he had once felt for the city of white houses no longer held a special place in his heart. That feeling had vanished somewhere in the depth of the ocean.

Would Istanbul be another disappointment, he wondered?

As Eric observed the magnificent skyline of Istanbul, he could not help but feel uneasy about his motivation for rushing to this part of the world in the first place. Was it the vague promise of a man on the phone who alleged to know about the people behind the mysterious high-speed electronic trades? In the big scheme of things, why was it so important for him to find out the identity of the trader? Could it be a trap? A way to snare him from his relative safety in Paris? But he also saw another side to his predicament. What if the caller was telling him the truth and he did find out that he was right to suspect the activities of the trader all along? What would he do with the information anyway?

His thoughts were a tangle of uneasiness, conflicting thoughts, and self- doubt.

He shifted in his seat, ill at ease with himself and no longer confident about the mission or even his motivation. He gazed down at the golden Bosphorus, but his eyes saw only a vast, empty space. The airline stewardess said something about putting his seatbelt on. He heard the words but did not seem to comprehend their meaning. Frustrated by his apparent lack of co-operation, the passenger seated next to him grabbed the seatbelt and shoved it into his hand, pointing his index finger at the buckle. Eric stared blankly at the man.

Without any warning, the jet engines roared in reverse. The plane shook violently, and he finally snapped out of his trance. He glanced over at the airline stewardess, nodded his acknowledgement, buckled his seatbelt, and ignored the anxious passenger to his left. The plane jerked up and down as the tires hit the runway. The man beside him gasped, but Eric paid no attention. His mind had already drifted elsewhere, preoccupied by a central thought that stuck like glue and would not come undone.

Why did I allow the whole matter about the trader to become so personal? He grumbled.

It all became clear to him the moment the customs officer stamped the entry visa on his passport and collected the visa fee of forty five euro. Strangely enough, the revelation did not come to him as a great surprise. It was there all this time, hidden somewhere in the back of his brain, ready to jump into his conscious mind when the time was right. And it was personal alright, just like the time he had decided to put his life in the hands of providence one fateful night in the *Mellah* of Casablanca. His inner voice had spoken to him back then and he simply accepted the call at face value. It was a personal decision, made for personal reasons that required no further justification. It was just something he felt compelled to do, pure and simple.

That same gut-wrenching feeling had hit him hard the instant the trader's transactions first appeared on his monitor—with trades that flashed like a lightning bolt on his computer screen and yanked his stomach, twisting it from the inside with such force that he remained transfixed in his seat not knowing what got into him.

And now he realized that it was meant to be that way. He had received another calling that needed to be answered, leaving him with no other choice but to deal with it if he wanted the pain to go away.

Eric marched resolutely out of the terminal, looking for a taxi to take him to his hotel. His mind was clear. His path unambiguous.

He believed in what he had to do.

Conrad Istanbul hotel was a massive structure perched high on top of a hill overlooking the Bosphorus and the Asian side of Istanbul. Located in the Besiktas neighborhood at close proximity to the Dolmabahçe Palace and a mere five minutes from Istanbul Lufti Kirdar Convention & Exhibition Centre, the hotel was a favorite of visiting dignitaries and business executives. Thus, security at the hotel was, by necessity, very tight.

Eric passed by four men dressed in identical red and black uniforms who looked more like security guards than valets. They did not seem to pay much attention to him, but he knew that he had been watched discretely the moment they saw him heading for the front entrance of the hotel. One of the men was carrying a large, oval-shaped mirror attached at the end of a long handlebar. Eric stopped for a moment to observe the man checking the underside of a vehicle parked on the ramp leading down to the underground parking. The other three men eyed him suspiciously when he made his final approach to the revolving doors made of thick glass. They made their stares obvious, as if to imply that they would be ready for him if he caused any trouble. Eric knew the game well and the three men finally broke into smiles when he mouthed, with a nod of the head, *merhaba*, a polite hello in Turkish.

Once inside the lobby of the hotel, he dropped his small carry-on bag onto a conveyor belt before passing through another archway that hid a metal detector. He gave the lobby a quick panoramic glance-over while the athletic-looking guard was busy checking his luggage. The lobby was as he remembered it—cavernous, opulent, bright, colorful, and buzzing with attendants in blue uniforms. In short, the reception hall was meant to impress with its spiral staircase, giant gold dome, soaring pink granite columns, gigantic arched alcoves, and the mandatory waterfall as a center piece. And it certainly had that effect on Eric.

He armed himself with patience as he approached the reception desk, passport in hand. He anticipated having to deal with a whole list of intrusive questions about the purpose of his visit to Turkey, the length of his stay at the hotel, and perhaps even a long form or two to fill in. But he was pleasantly surprised when the receptionist gave him the electronic key to his room with only a cursory look at his passport and a polite request to sign at the bottom of the guest card. *A nice improvement,* Eric thought with an appreciative smile as he thanked the young, dark-haired, blue-eyed receptionist. He grabbed his bag and declined the assistance of the valet standing close behind him. He then proceeded to hurry down the hallway to catch the elevator, having spotted a large group of Australian tourists also heading that way. They were all wearing Insight Vacations tags, and he knew by experience that, like most tour groups, they had acquired a herd mentality and would all try to squeeze into the same elevator at the same time with their bulky luggage.

In contrast to the lavishness of the reception hall, his room was small and functional. No doubt designed to accommodate the fussiest businessman with its office desk, ample supply of notepads and pens, three phones, oversized flat TV screen, and internet Wi-Fi connection. Eric took one quick look around the room and immediately began to strip naked, heading straight for the shower. Without thinking, he had automatically reverted to his long and well-practiced ritual—an old habit he had acquired on his many business trips as an investment banker. A revitalized body, a clean shave, and a fresh set of clothes was how he always used to prepare himself for all business meetings after a flight. Whether it was a short or a long haul, it mattered not. As far as Eric was concerned, all business appointments were equally important and required the same level of preparation.

Eric knew that his rendezvous with a perfect stranger was not to be treated lightly either. The information could be explosive. The negotiations would therefore be intense. Danger could be lurking, like it had in Antibes. And no one needed to remind him that he had to be at his very best. Too much was at stake.

His transformation to a well-traveled businessman was complete and convincing. Totally rejuvenated by the long, steaming-hot shower, Eric stood in the middle of the hotel room feeling like he did in the good old days. His mind was sharp, focused, and most importantly, wiped clear of all the clutter and other side-distractions that seemed to have plagued him in Paris. The time spent in the back office of the Banque du Commerce, GSIC Division, busily chasing elusive internal frauds, was a thing of the past. He had closed the last chapter of that suspended non-existence when he submitted his resignation before taking off to Istanbul. There were no lingering regrets. On the contrary, he felt good about having broken the ties to a job that was at best to him, more of a way of passing time, and at worse, an excuse to bury his head in the sand. Besides, he had always known that he was never really cut out for that kind of work and should have walked away the moment Alain Lepetit had offered him the post.

He checked himself in the closet mirror and felt like a liberated man for the first time in a long time. It had taken him forever to get to that point. Three years to be precise. But he now looked at the future with hope and conviction.

His pre-meeting preparation ritual complete, he reached for his Blackberry and turned it back on. After the usual short, musical chime, a long series of emails and messages reeled on the small screen like a racing car trying to make up for the lost time spent at the pit stop. Alain Lepetit had sent several emails but nothing else caught Eric's attention. His contact had not called, but that was to be expected. He had flown to Istanbul a day early.

Now is the time to learn to be patient, he chided himself, as he stared at his reflection for a second time in the full length mirror.

But his good intention lasted less time than a heartbeat before the phone rang. He stared at the white phone on the desk, his hand slowly reaching for the receiver, willing himself to be patient. He could hear his own heavy breathing over the loud chime. On the second ring, he gave up, no longer able to resist his growing curiosity. He grabbed the receiver with his right hand, pressed it tightly against his ear, and after a curt greeting, listened carefully to the voice of a man who spoke English with a heavy foreign accent. It was the front desk informing him that his guest had arrived and was waiting for him at the Summit Bar.

"Who did you say is waiting for me?" he asked, his voice betraying his anxiety.

"Mrs. Stephanopoulos enquired if you had checked in, and asked that you meet her at the Summit Bar on the 14th floor."

"Are you sure that she asked for me?"

"Yes, Mister Martin, the lady called several times earlier and seemed to know that you would be checking in at the Conrad."

Eric hung up, alight with anticipation. *Could it be that my informant is a woman after all? But the call was not supposed to come until tomorrow. Why the sudden change in plan?* He pondered the matter for a beat and quickly surmised that there was only one way to find out.

His patience quickly ran out once again as he waited in the corridor for the elevator. He hit the call button several times, but that did not make a difference. The elevators seemed to have a mind of their own. *So much for my resolution,* he muttered under his breath.

When the door of the elevator hissed open, there was another unpleasant surprise waiting for him. A second wave of visitors from Australia had arrived. They were packed like sardines, and the way they glared at Eric left no doubt what they wanted, or did *not* want, to be more precise. *Forget about getting in,* their stares warned him. But that did not deter Eric. He was not going to wait a minute longer for the next ride up, and so he began to shove, squeeze, and somehow carve out enough space between two tall Australians with their protruding beer bellies and oversized safari hats that kept scratching his face throughout the elevator ride.

"Just hold on to your breath mate," one of the giant Australians pressed against his backside counseled him. Eric could barely breathe, let alone tell the fellow what he really thought of his ordeal.

The Summit Bar with its breathtaking views of the Bosphorus and Istanbul's unique cityscape, was a very popular meeting place in town. At any time of the day, it was always packed with local businessmen, tourists, and other visitors hunting for trade deals in Turkey. Eric gave the bar a quick scan. "This is an excellent place for a private chat; one can easily blend into the crowd and no one would know that a meeting is taking place," Eric mumbled under his breath.

The Australians herded as a pack at the entrance of the bar, waiting to be seated. They looked like a disgruntled bunch of very thirsty patrons. There was not a single table available, and they seemed at a loss about what to do next, not wanting to venture outside the hotel on their first night in the city. Eric elbowed his way to the front of the group in order to gain a better view of what was going on inside. He first checked the bar where an early 'happy hour' was already in full swing, and then turned his attention to the dining section that was set in the back against a row of large bay windows. He looked for anyone seated alone. There was no single woman, and no one made eye contact with him.

He stepped in, heading for the bar, and then appeared to hesitate for an instant, hoping to lure his visitor to make the first move. But no one took the bait. He was about to retreat and rejoin the Australians still waiting at the entrance of the establishment, when he noticed a waiter making his way from the back of the establishment. The waiter ignored the Australians who, by then, were more peeved than thirsty, and instead greeted Eric.

"Thank you, I'm looking for Mrs. Stephanopoulos," Eric said.

The waiter looked like he had been expecting him and immediately asked Eric to follow him, leaving behind a boisterous group that had become even more vocal in expressing their displeasure. The waiter guided Eric through a sea of people, leading him to the rooftop terrace where a wild bunch of partygoers had gathered. In a corner, hidden by a group of three men busy chatting up a pretty girl, a musician was playing a Beatles tune on a keyboard. The lyrics to the song *Yesterday* came into the girl's mind and she began to sing in a language that Eric did not recognize. One by one, the three men with the girl picked up the tune and soon after everyone on the terrace was singing along in a harmonious mix of foreign languages.

The pretty girl noticed Eric staring at her and gave him an inviting wave to join in the song. But Eric had something else in mind. He surveyed the full length of the terrace, hoping to catch a glimpse of the woman that had asked to meet him. Unfortunately, a wall of people blocked his view and he glanced up at the waiter looking for assistance. The waiter pointed his finger at the far end of the rooftop terrace in a corner sheltered by a glass partition. "Your guest is waiting for you over there," he said.

The woman rose from her chair the moment she saw Eric heading for her. She stood with her arms at her side, waiting to greet him. Her face was obscured by a pair of large dark sunglasses and a long silk scarf wrapped high around her long neck. A light breeze startled her, swirling her shoulder-length jet black hair across her face. She lifted her sunglasses over her head, holding them with both hands as a headdress to pin her hair away from her face. Eric's feet froze on the spot, his eyes locked on the striking woman standing in front of him.

She smiled first.

CHAPTER 13

First she smiled with her arms held wide open at the ready for an embrace that did not come right away.

"Oh my God! Is that really you, Laura?"

"Of course it's me, silly you. You're not dreaming, Eric."

Then they burst out laughing, a loud mix of joy and exhilaration. It was a deep raw laughter that left them both gasping for air. It overwhelmed them with unbridled excitement, like two former lovers reunited for the first time after a long separation. They were not supposed to feel that way about each other anymore—of that they were certain. Their relationship had ended and they went their separate ways following their final lover's quarrel.

They stood mere inches apart, not knowing what to do next. They looked like two statues frozen in time, a mere rendition of their true selves. He took a small step back, holding his gaze on Laura, not trusting his emotions, somewhat fazed by a strong dose of uneasiness that suddenly erupted in his heart. She appraised him, biting her lips, eyes unwavering, wrestling with her thoughts, and fretfully wanting to give in to her first impulse. Finally, it was Laura who broke the spell, and she embraced Eric with outstretched arms. The warmth of the body he had once longed for every minute of his life, overcame any trace of resistance that lingered in the very fibers of his soul. And they held tight onto each other for a very long time, rekindling the fondness they once shared for one another.

"But what are you doing here? How did you find me?" Eric asked when he finally recovered from the surprise.

Laura kept on smiling. She was truly enjoying the moment. It was just like she had imagined it would be, and she was determined to take her time to savor every last drop and make the moment last as long as possible. So she decided to string Eric along a while longer. Her lips broke into a mischievous smile when she vaguely replied, "I have my spies."

"Oh come on. Who told you I was here? And come to think of it, what are you doing in Istanbul?"

"I live here."

"You live in Istanbul? Laura, please stop teasing me. What are you really doing here?" Eric asked, meeting her smile with a grin of his own.

"Well, I might as well tell you now since apparently you no longer work at the bank. Chantal Lepetit and I have kept in touch all of this time. She is a wonderful woman, you know. She is the one who told me where to find you because she was worried about you. And by the way, if you really wanted to keep this trip a secret, you should not have asked your assistant to book the flight and make the hotel arrangements for you."

Eric brushed off the last remarks, knowing that it was the way Laura liked to poke at him—mixing truths with half-truths when she wanted to keep him guessing. *Alain must have put her up to this,* he thought. He did not want to play the game anymore, and so he decided to confront her right away.

"I see, so what can you tell me about the speed trader?"

"What speed trader? What are you talking about?" Laura puzzled.

"You're telling me that you did not come here to tell me about the trader?"

"No, of course not. I don't have a clue what you're talking about. All I know is that Chantal contacted me when she found out that you were heading for Istanbul. She said that it was an incredible and wonderful coincidence—something that fate has surely placed in our path—one of these rare, predestined events that should not be ignored. She went on and on with all that new wave mumbo jumbo. To tell you the truth, I got the feeling that she wanted to be here herself."

"But that does not explain what you're doing in Istanbul," Eric curtly replied, trying to manage the skepticism in his voice.

He was not entirely successful and Laura picked up quickly on his change of tone. Although she was hurt by the way Eric was now treating her, she did not flare up like she would have done in the past. Something about the way her former lover was looking at her told her to tread carefully with him. There was a hardness that she did not recognize. Chantal had warned her about him. "He is not the same man you once knew. He has suffered terribly. His soul is raked with deep scars that have not yet healed," she had confided to her over the phone.

Laura's heart had too been broken, and she could relate to what Eric must have gone through. Her reaction was, at first, a brave attempt at self-control. Fighting hard to control the swell of emotions rising fast inside of her, she held on to her breath for as long as she could. That was the best she could do to prevent her from choking in tears and blurting out all the things she had sworn to herself to never speak about to anyone. She stared hard at Eric, digging into his mind, letting her eyes communicate all the pain she had buried deep inside of her for so long. But she still held on to her words, not trusting her voice, and slowly lowered her eyes to gaze at the gold ring on her finger, seeking strength and comfort in the symbol of eternal love.

When she finally spoke, her voice took on a harsher tone than she intended. All her efforts at self-control were of no avail in the end. The pain she felt had turned into a need to hurt back. It was her nature after all, a compulsive reaction that, despite all her willpower, was still beyond her control. The only way she knew how to protect herself. It was something about herself that she had worked so hard to change, or to at least mollify somewhat. But in the end, she had only partially succeeded.

"Well after you dumped me..." She started saying, but stopped in mid-sentence right away when she noticed Eric's stare turning quickly into a fierce scowl. *This was no time for retribution.* That was not how she wanted her first encounter with her former lover to turn out. Her mind was a tingle of mixed feelings at odds with one another, but this time, this time for the first time in her life, she was more determined than ever to have the upper hand over her compulsive need to strike back.

"After you left me to go to Morocco alone," she went on in a gentler voice, after a long pensive pause, "I was devastated, lost, and angry. At first, I blamed you for everything—your selfishness, your arrogance, your lack of empathy, your ready-made excuses—all of it. It was your fault that things did not work out between us. I stayed away from my family for a very, very long time, because I knew that they would not understand. But the isolation did not work. It made things even worse for me. I chased away all my friends. I quit my job and I hated you for what you did to me. Then my anger slowly turned into feeling sorry for myself, and I cried all day. I was hurt, lonely, and confused, mostly. I had no one I could turn to for comfort. . .no one around me to blame. When I finally gathered the courage to visit my parents, my father immediately made me feel responsible for everything that happened between us. He is an old man, you see, and his ideas about relationships are set in the traditions of the old country. To hear him speak, a man can do no wrong. And when my mother tried to help me by taking my side, I almost lost it. She knew all along, she said, that I was foolish to believe that you would marry me. I had wasted my life, she even told me. Can you believe that she said that?"

Eric could not help himself, and threw a smile at the last remarks. He remembered the many discussions they had in the early years of their courtship when they were madly in love. It was Laura who had insisted that marriage was never to be part of their relationship. *It would ruin everything*, she had said firmly, leaving no possibility for further discussion.

"I'm sorry I acted that way. You deserved better," he said, his voice carrying the heavy strain of regrets.

"Don't be sorry. I'm not sorry. It's probably the best thing that could have happened to me. I now realize that I needed a kick in the proverbial ass. I was just hanging on to an illusion. You were right to do what you did. I must thank you for that. One of us had to have the fortitude to put an end to this dysfunctional relationship. It would never have worked in the long run. Love alone is never enough."

She stopped for a second to sip on her drink. She looked genuinely glad to be able speak freely about all the things that had burdened her for so long. After a short pause, she pinched her lips and with a twinkle in her eyes, quickly added, "Besides, I met a wonderful man about a year after we broke up." She wore a triumphant smile on her face when she made her big announcement. But she was not bragging about how well her life had turned out to be after Eric. She was just thrilled that at long last she was certain that she had become the woman she always wanted to be.

Eric smiled thinly, still uncertain on how to take the news. "That explains it all, Mrs. Stephanopoulos."

"That's right, Eric. I'm now married to a Greek professor. He was doing some research for his PHD in ancient history at U of T, and I was killing time at the university taking one course after another when I bumped into him. He helped me a lot to overcome my fears, my need to point the finger at someone else to displace my own problems, and all the other hang-ups that have burdened me all of my life. I feel so good about myself now. I could not have done it without him, you know, Eric."

"You're a very lucky lady," Eric said with mixed feelings.

"I know, but enough talk about me. Tell me what happened to you in Morocco. Chantal gave me the highlights, but I would like to hear all the details. So Eric, please tell me everything. I have become a good listener, you know."

Eric nodded unhappily. At the mere mention of Morocco, memories of that episode in his life came flooding back in waves. So much had happened back then, and he would gladly have liked to be able to bury it all forever. But that was not possible. Not yet at least. Not until he had solved the trader's egnima.

"I'm sure that Chantal told you what a disaster my homecoming party in Morocco turned out to be. I went there with the hope that I would find all that had been missing in my entire life—all the pieces of the puzzle about me that I left behind when we moved to Canada. All the minute little details about my origins that always made me wonder where I really belong. You know the calling that all of us immigrants hear from our native land at some point in our life. The search for our roots, the urge to go back to our birthplace and find out for ourselves what it must have been like to live over there. All of the things in the back of our mind that always made us feel uncertain about our country of adoption. They became my obsession. And like all new settlers from a far away land, the call was far too powerful. It had to be answered. It was something I absolutely needed to do and so I went back, only to find a world that was totally foreign to me. It was not at all like I imagined it to be. Come to think of it, I did not really remember much. What I knew of that place was what my father had told me. I was far too young when we left Morocco to truly remember much about anything. And what was even worse about it, was that I did not feel like I belonged there. I was an alien in my homeland; sadly, that's how I felt."

Eric paused for an instant and seemed lost in his own thoughts. His struggle was apparent. What he had to tell was even more painful.

Laura was true to her words. She had indeed became a good listener and just observed the emotions streaming along on Eric's face—hope, disappointment, the desire to tell someone how he truly felt, sadness, and grief. She fought the urge to reach out and comfort him, sensing his need to liberate his soul of a heavy burden. So she remained silent, determined to let Eric pour out his soul.

After a long, thoughtful pause, Eric finally decided to resume his story, for better or worse

"The job offer from the investment bank boutique was a convenient excuse, and it turned out to be a huge mistake. I should have packed my bags and returned to Toronto right away after my first meeting with those bastards. When they mentioned the predictive algorithm, it should have raised enough red flags for me to want to decamp as far as possible from this place. But I was tone deaf. I was too full of myself to see it through, and what made it even more unbearable was that I was responsible for the death of so many people that trusted me."

"Don't be so hard on yourself. It was not your fault. There was no way you could have known."

"Yeah sure, tell that to Ivan; he put a bullet in his head rather than reveal the encryption that protected the algorithm. And what's even more horrible, to this day I don't even know what really happened to his wife and their little girl. I was so self-absorbed that I never saw it coming. No one offers you a ton of money unless they want something big in return. These monsters were after the algorithm from day one. That much should have been obvious to me from the get-go. But what did I do? I closed my eyes to everything that was going on around me, and they played me for the fool that I was."

"But the algorithm was of no use to them in the end. Right? Chantal told me they all perished on the ship off the coast of Gibraltar."

Eric's hands closed into a tight fist. Gone was the pleasure he felt when he held Laura tight in his arms moments earlier. He slowly exhaled through clenched teeth in some futile attempt to blow away the bitter taste that was rising in his mouth. "Yeah, that's how the story goes. But how do we know that's what really happened? They never found the bodies, you know." He winced at the thought.

Eric looked thoroughly disgusted with himself. Something about the way his eyes looked through her, told Laura to be careful if she was going to be of any help. Then she remembered Eric's strange question about some trader, and Chantal's mystifying answer when she asked about the purpose of Eric's visit to Istanbul. *He is chasing a ghost*, she had said. And suddenly it all became clear to her.

"Ah, now I understand why you asked me if I knew something about the trader. You're here because you think that somehow, someone—your speed trader for instance—has gotten their hands on the bank's predictive algorithm."

"You're so perceptive, Laura. You're the first one to get to the crux of what's been bothering me about this guy so quickly," Eric promptly replied, adding a smile that looked more like a twisted grin.

"So that's it. You are looking for this trader to get the algorithm back, and you think that once you find him you will stop him from doing whatever he is doing and everything will be back to normal with you, just like that. And you think that I'm here because I know who he is? Eric you are so...."

"So naive."

"No silly. I think that you're so desperate to undo what went wrong that you're grasping at straws. You see connections when none exist. You suspect everyone. You perceive threats and conspiracies everywhere."

"Like thinking that you might be my informant for instance?"

"Right. Do you see now what this obsession has done to you? You desperately want to believe that you can fix what went wrong back then. Even if you're right about this trader, it will not change anything. You see Eric, you cannot change the past. No one can. Not even the great Chinese emperors who tried to rewrite history because it did not fit their vision of things. For your own sake, please move on. Your life is passing you by, and it's time that you start thinking about yourself before it's too late. You just have to accept, once and for all, that what went terribly wrong in Morocco was beyond your control. . .You were not responsible, Eric!"

"You're so wrong about that. I have proof that the trader exists, and I have evidence that he is using the algorithm. I will find him and all his accomplices and they will pay for what they have done."

"Well, suit yourself, but no one at the bank seems to believe you. Chantal told me that the algorithm is most likely sitting at the bottom of the ocean, along with all the dead bodies."

"Chantal should not be listening to her husband. I don't understand Alain's motivations, but I can assure you that he has seen the evidence. They can't be simply dismissed as the fruits of my imagination."

Seeing the determination in Eric's eyes, Laura shrugged her shoulders as if to say, *this is hopeless*. Eric was going to do what he wanted to do. He always did and that was, in part, the cause of their many conflicts and the principal source of her frustrations when they lived together. Resigned to the fact that she would not be able to sway him away from his mad pursuit, she decided to take a more agreeable tack. That was something she had never done in the past, preferring instead to argue until Eric would walk away rather than giving up. She looked pleased with herself, having overcome another old bad habit.

"Well if you really believe that's the case, I hope that you're not doing this thing alone. It can be kind of dangerous, you know."

"I have help," Eric lied, knowing he had not told Interpol about the man who asked to meet him in Istanbul.

"Good, but be very careful would you? I don't want to lose you again, now that I found you. I'm hoping that we will renew our special friendship and get to see you often like the good old days."

Eric smiled and said nothing.

Laura gave Eric a full smile and slightly tilted her head sideways, a gesture he immediately recognized as a sign that something important was on her mind. As a woman who once loved him, as only a lover could, she wanted to help Eric find closure to what was troubling his soul. She now realized that she would have to accept that recovering the algorithm was his means of dealing with his demons. And while she desperately hoped that he was not chasing after an illusionary foe, she also knew that a deeper wound needed to be healed as well. Something that would only be cured by retracing the memory buried deep somewhere in the recesses of his heart. She was convinced that it was the only way that Eric would be able to let go of the guilt that plagued him ever since. *Chantal had been right all along,* she thought. *Fate had much to do with it. There is a good reason why our paths crossed in Istanbul after so many years apart.*

Eric's silence was perhaps the opening she was looking for, and she finally gathered the courage to broach the subject.

"Why don't you tell me about Valerie? What I have heard from Chantal is that she was an extraordinary woman," she asked, a slight edge to her voice now.

Eric felt like an electric shock had seized his whole body. It surged and reverberated in his head, stiffened his spine, freezing his throat and preventing him from breathing. He immediately recognized the reason for his intense reaction. A spirit from the past, one he thought he had crushed so hard that he would never have to deal with it ever again, had resurfaced. And now Laura had stabbed at the wound that would not heal.

He turned his head to look at the sun settling for the night over the Bosphorus, and swallowed hard on the lump in his throat that was threatening to choke him. He watched the large container ships sailing along the strait, leaving Asia for some distant destination. He observed the long line of passengers waiting patiently on the waterfront for the ferry that would soon take them across the large body of water that looked like a sea of enchanting gold. He let his mind float around like a meandering soul, and recalled his first visit to Istanbul, a city that had been conquered so many times, and endured so many miseries, yet never lost its will to flourish.

He remembered what a Turkish client had whispered in his ear a few years back, while they sipped Raki in the Summit Bar. "The Bosphorus Strait is the *soul* of Istanbul, my friend," his client had told him, his voice heavy with emotion. "This is where the city finds the answers to all its woes and pains."

Eric nodded to himself and looked wistfully into the distance. He felt the Bosphorus reaching out for him, slowly lifting off the veil of sadness that had descended over him. And then the metamorphosis took its hold.

Like magic, memories began to entangle in his head. One by one, vivid images began to invade his conscious mind. Nothing seemed too painful or too terrifying anymore. No secrets were kept from him. At last, he closed his eyes and his mind, slowly allowing his body to relax and his soul to roam around freely. When his gaze finally turned to Laura, the sharp pain he had felt all these years was still present, but at least now he was ready to talk about it.

"Valerie was a very special woman," he said with a lump in his throat. "She had more courage than most men I know. She was true to herself until the very end, and I wish I had listened to her more often. *Oh God*, do I wish that I had believed her when she begged me to have faith in her."

He spoke in a short, half-halting way, but seemed resolute to tell it all. "We were sitting at a cafe in Barcelona, just like you and I are sitting here today. She told me the whole truth about what really happened, about how her and her father had been manipulated, how they never knew what was really going on, and how they tried to stop the bastards when they found out what they were really up to. They both lost their lives while trying to put an end to that nightmare. Laura, you have got to trust me when I say that I so desperately wanted to believe her. I was so close and ready to accept her truth and put the whole bloody mess behind me. I tried so hard, you must believe me, but in the end, I simply could not overcome my goddamn fears and suspicions, and I'm now paying for it. She did not have to go back to Casablanca. All I had to do was to tell her that I trusted her and she would be with me now. The only thing left for me to do now is to stop these murderers from using the algorithm. If I succeed, I will at least have done something right in my life. It would not expunge me from my mistakes—that I know. But at least I could say that her death had not been vain."

"I believe you Eric, and I sincerely hope that you will find your peace sometime soon. But I don't think that you are going about it the right way."

"You still don't get it, Laura. There's no fucking way that I'm going to let these bastards get away with what they have done.... even if it means getting myself killed in the process."

"You don't really mean that?"

"You bet I do. If I get hold of the man who asked me to come here, I'll squeeze out of him everything he knows. And then they can try running away if they can. Trust me, there will be no happy ending for any one of them."

"I understand how you must feel, but don't be stupid. I beg you, Eric, you have to promise me one thing: do not waste your life chasing this trader and what you think he represents. Know how and when to cut your losses. Nothing you can do will bring Valerie back."

"I know what you mean. I may be stubborn, but I'm not crazy. I'm sure the fellow who called me holds the key to the whole thing. But if some reason his information does not pan out, or I find out that I was wrong about the trader, *I will close the file*—as they say in business."

"Good, but I hope that you're telling me the truth not just saying that to shut me up."

"You know that I can't fool you, Laura.... I never could."

"Now you are being cute. Really cute. Just come back to me alive. That's all I am asking."

Laura held his gaze for a moment, then something inside of her must have switched, as she suddenly changed the topic of their conversation." I must remember to thank Chantal for bringing us back together. But tell you what: I would really like you to meet Alexis. How about if I bring him over to meet you tomorrow morning? He can drop me off on his way to work at the university, and unless you have something really pressing to do, I could then show you around my new home town."

"Sure, that's sounds like a wonderful idea. But I must warn you, I'm expecting a very important phone call and I may have to drop you on a moment's notice."

"No problem. Why am I not surprised? I should be used to it by now with you. So alright, it's a date. I will pick you up tomorrow around 9:30 a.m.? Now, I better get going; Alexis is waiting for me at home, and he must be wondering what I'm doing. He is not the jealous type, but I have not tested him yet," she said, punctuating her last words with an infectious laugh.

It was now Eric's turn to smile first.

CHAPTER 14

A noisy crowd was gathered around the new tour buses that were parked in front of Hotel Conrad Istanbul. Hogir was plunked in the middle of the pack, surrounded by bus drivers and tour guides who were enjoying their free time. They had safely delivered their payload of passengers along with their heavy luggage, and they were now busy chatting, smoking, or just simply killing time. It was something they always did at every stop throughout their journey across Turkey. A close sense of camaraderie had developed among them during the tour and they all knew each other on a first name basis. To them, Hogir was someone they had not yet met, and thinking that he was a new guide on the circuit, they were eager to get acquainted with him.

Hogir had something else in mind. He had no bus to drive or passengers to take care of. His presence was required because his quarry was inside the hotel entertaining a woman. He was simply following orders to keep a close watch over Eric. He had always enjoyed that aspect of a mission. It was a simple thing for him to do that required only vigilance and stealth—skills that he particularly excelled in. The chat with the bus drivers and tour guides was a convenient cover, and he gladly took advantage of the opportunity.

Standing alone, not far from Hogir, Karzan extinguished his fourth cigarette. He looked more taciturn than usual. Hogir thought that maybe his comrade was tired of just standing around when nothing significant was happening. So he decided to invite him to join in the conversation. Karzan crushed the cigarette butt with more force than was necessary and looked away. Hogir thought better than to insist, and shrugged his shoulders at the man who had enquired earlier about Karzan.

Karzan was not bored. He was frustrated and felt they had wasted too much time with Eric. He could not understand why Abdullah did not agree with him. He saw Eric for what he was: a minor distraction that should be dealt with immediately. If it were up to him, a quick swipe of the sharp blade of his hunter's knife along Eric's throat would take permanent care of this nuisance. So why would they not let him handle it the way he took care of the American in Paris a couple of days ago? That way he would be free to focus all his energy on a much bigger problem, like finding out who had betrayed them for instance. Surely, everyone could see that the traitor represented a more lethal threat to the organization than Eric could ever be.

But Abdullah would not hear a word of it. He made it clear to Karzan. "Keep a close watch on Eric and he will deliver us the mole," he barked at him for daring to question his leader's command.

Although he kept to his assignment, Karzan could not put aside the thought that someone in their tight organization was a turncoat. He wanted to be the one that took care of that traitor as a lesson to all of those who might be tempted to follow his example. He watched Hogir as he distributed cigarettes to the small group that hovered around him. *He knows how to win confidence quickly*, he reflected, while admiring the ease with which Hogir was able to fit in seamlessly among strangers. But he quickly dismissed any suspicious thoughts about his comrade in arms. They had both suffered far too much and far too long to turn to the enemy now. In fact, he could not come to terms with the idea that any of his Kurdish comrades would do such a thing. It was simply unthinkable as far as he was concerned. And yet someone had betrayed them and brought Eric to Istanbul for a reason.

All along, a dark mistrust lurked in the back of Karzan's mind. No matter how hard he tried to convince himself otherwise, he had never been able to put his misgiving about the woman to rest. She was a foreigner after all, and no matter how much she had contributed to their cause, there would always be a mystery about her. Thanks to her, they were better armed and better organized than they had ever been. Iran and Syria were providing them with a steady supply of weapons and logistical assistance. The price for the armament was steep, but the foreign woman had given them a bottomless source of funds. No one knew where she came from and why she had joined their group. The software program she had brought along with her was an even bigger mystery. Her answers as to its origin were always evasive, and when pressed for details she would close the subject with a short but incontestable response, "What does it matter where I come from or how I acquired this algorithm? I have willingly given you a very valuable tool and I expect nothing in return but to be able to use it for your own benefit." Lacking a better counter argument, they finally agreed that she had a point and gradually dropped the matter altogether. Only Karzan remained skeptical. Her lack of clear answers could only mean that she had something to hide. He saw her only as a source of potential trouble down the road. He had his own reasons to suspect her and believed that the likelihood that she could be a double agent might not be too far-fetched after all.

Karzan was so deep in thought that he failed to see that Hogir was running in his direction, cell phone in hand.

"What's the matter with you, Karzan? Abdullah is on the line and he says that he has been ringing you for the past twenty minutes, and all he's been getting is your voice mail. Here, take my phone, he wants to speak with you immediately. He sounds very upset."

"Karzan, what the hell is going on?" Abdullah screamed on the phone.

"Sorry, my cell phone is not working; I think that the battery is dead. We're standing guard in front of the hotel where Eric is staying. He will not go anywhere without us. Is there something new? Any change of plan?"

"The next time this happens, borrow Hogir's phone for God's sake. Keep doing what you're doing and don't let him get away. Has he seen anyone since he arrived?'

"Yes, a woman. She's not from here. I was able to get her name from the front desk. She goes by the name Laura Stephanopoulos."

"What's wrong with you, Karzan? Don't you think this is an important piece of information?"

"Yes. But she is still inside with him and I will ask Hogir to tail her once she leaves the hotel."

"Karzan, this is an order. Listen to me very carefully; I will not tolerate any of your misguided initiatives anymore. You must keep me in the loop at all times. Is that clear?"

After a short pause, during which all Karzan could hear was the buzz of a muted line, Abdullah spoke again, "We will check her out. Make sure that Hogir tracks her down after she leaves the hotel. In the meantime, please do yourself a huge favor—get a new cell phone."

Slumped on the bed, remote in hand, Eric surfed the TV channels without paying much attention to what was on the screen. He was looking for a distraction to ease the tightness in his chest that had reached an excruciating peak since he landed in Istanbul. His mind was still reeling from the emotional roller coaster of his meeting with Laura that afternoon. He was glad that she had made the effort to find him, and he was truly grateful to her for what she had done for him in such a short time. Her openness had inspired him, and he appreciated the way she overcame his resistance to talk about Valerie and the nightmares that had been fueling his heart with guilt and remorse for the past three years. Relating these memories did not come easy, and the pain he felt, like an open wound that would not heal, had been almost unbearable. But in some way, the simple act of talking to someone about it gave him a renewed sense of purpose. Indeed, their reunion had been timely.

Tired of screening short snippets of mindless games and reality TV shows, Eric settled on CNN International, more out of habit than out of any real interest in the news. The evening broadcast was mostly about world politics, as no new major conflict had erupted that day.

"President Obama will be facing a tough road to re-election because of his support for gay rights," the announcer read from his teleprompter with all the certainty he could muster. "........Sarkozy lost his bid to get reelected. Hollande, a vouched Socialist, has beaten him by promising the French electorate that they can have all they want and so much more without new taxes and budget cuts....... Greece is in disarray. The election has produced a hopelessly fragmented parliament, and no political leader has been able to form a coalition government. The radical leftist Syriza Party, headed by a former communist, is the big winner in the election. They campaigned on the promise that if elected, they would scrap the massive E.U.-IMF bailout agreement, but offered no alternative, leading the Greek population to believe that they could go on living without paying taxes and doing away with austerity measures."

Eric listened to the news medley in amazement, wondering why TV producers kept on scratching their heads looking for new crazy ideas for their reality shows, when the real world was just full of fascinating stories.

He was thankful for the interruption when the high-pitched ring of the hotel phone filled the room. He pressed the mute button on the remote control and answered the phone right away. A woman was sobbing on the other end of the line. She sounded distressed and would not stop crying. This went on for awhile. He was about to hang up, thinking it was a crank call, when suddenly he thought he heard the woman calling him by his name. The voice sounded familiar but he could not be certain, so he remained quiet and waited for the woman to speak again.

"Eric, this is Judith," she said between sobs, and then coughed to clear her throat. "David has disappeared," she finally blurted out.

"What did you say?"

Judith sniveled. "David is gone and no one knows where he is."

"What do you mean he's gone?" When was the last time you saw him?"

"Two days ago. When he left for the office he told me that he would be having lunch with you, and no one has seen him since."

"Did you call the police?"

"Yes of course, for all the good it did me. They didn't seem to take his disappearance too seriously. All they were interested to know was if David and I were having marital problems. They even asked me if David had had an affair in the past. I tell you, only in France would the police act that way."

"They don't know David and they were just trying to test you in case you know more than you're telling."

"That's right, they don't know my David. He would never do such a thing. Anyway, I guess they got fed up with my calls so they finally agreed to talk to you since you were the last person to see him. Have they contacted you?"

"No. But that doesn't surprise me. I'm out of the country."

More sobs. A pause. Another throat-clearing cough. The discernible sound of Judith blowing her nose.

"Eric I'm worried to death. Something bad must have happened to my David. Please be honest with me. What is going on? Is David in trouble?" Judith pleaded, struggling with her voice

"Honestly Judith, I don't know. We are working on a file and all I asked him to do was to check certain facts for me through his regular contacts. He was in a great mood, and as far as I know, he headed straight back to the office after our lunch meeting. He did not seem worried or preoccupied about anything in particular. In fact, he seemed rather pleased to work on a project with me."

Eric stopped for a moment to think. He heard Judith's sniffles on the phone. She was clearly distraught, and he wanted to be helpful. An idea popped into his head. It was probably too obvious, but he decided nonetheless to give it a shot. "Come to think of it Judith," he said, "Do you know if the police have checked the hospitals to see if David was admitted?"

"I don't know. They didn't mention anything to me about what they were doing to find David. I will call them right away to find out. Thanks Eric," she said, and brusquely hung up.

Eric's eyes turned to the TV screen, and he instinctively pressed on the mute release button. A body was being pulled from the River Seine. The blue and red lights of an ambulance were flashing behind a reporter announcing the discovery of a man found floating in the river. According to the police officer being interviewed, the case was being treated as a murder investigation and the identity of the victim was being withheld pending notification to the next of kin. When the CNN reporter pressed the policeman for more information, he would only reveal that the man was an American.

Eric's eyes widened in absolute disbelief as the camera panned the scene behind the reporter. The body had been wrapped in a dark green blanket and was being wheeled away by two paramedics. But as they raised the stretcher to roll it inside the ambulance, the blanket caught the handle of the ambulance door and for a split second the dead man's face was left exposed.

Eric's heart froze. His jaw tightened in cold fury. In a primal scream that could likely be heard across town, he yelled out at the TV screen, "BASTARDS!"

CHAPTER 15

The room seemed like it had shrunk in the night. The shadows along the walls and across the floor had long vanished. Only massive furniture, better suited for giant Avatars than humans, remained standing. By sunrise most of the empty space in the room had been squeezed out, in a slow and inexorable clench. Seated at the edge of the bed and facing a large flat TV screen, Eric gasped at the confined space that felt more like a prison cell than a luxurious hotel room. He was alone and the walls of his angst were closing in on him.

He had not moved all night, transfixed by the news that spewed out on the television screen non-stop all night long. The scene of a body being pulled from the River Seine kept coming back at the top of the hour. He heard the same commentaries from the CNN reporter over and over again while waiting for the dead man's face to flash on the screen. A blink of an eye and the image was gone. Another hour before the image would return and Eric kept on waiting and praying that his eyes were fooling him.

At first David's death—or as he was now convinced, more likely, his murder—shook Eric's resolve

It is happening all over again. People who stand by me do not live long. As surely as the first call for prayer stirs the dormant city of Istanbul out of its torpor every morning, anyone who had the misfortune of being involved with him were doomed to face the same tragic end. It was an unavoidable byproduct—a kiss of death for anyone suspected of collaborating with him. And he now realized that not even his demise would end this cycle of deaths. Of that he was certain, for there would always be the lingering suspicion that someone in his entourage had gained access to the data.

So after much internal deliberation, he reached the only inescapable conclusion—there was only one way to end this madness, and Eric knew what had to be done. His pursuit had to put a stop once and for all to this vicious cycle of violence with the annihilation of the trader and all his accomplices.

Eric had a dizzy spell when he got up too quickly. He took a few tentative steps toward the bathroom and stopped for a second to steady himself. One look in the mirror told him the whole truth about his current state of mind. His body might have been weakened by his ordeal, and his eyes bloodshot from lack of sleep, but what he saw staring back at him was sheer determination. David's death and the murder of all the other innocent people who had shared his life in Casablanca had to be avenged. He had crossed the point of no return and was no longer afraid for his life. He leaned closer to the mirror, examined his face one more time, and brushed his day-old whiskers with his left palm. "It's time to get ready for my appointment," he informed his reflection in the mirror.

He hurried out of his hotel room, glancing at the time on his Armani watch. It was 10:40am in Paris, and after a quick adjustment for the difference in time zone, he calculated that he was only ten minutes late for his rendezvous. He had agreed to meet Laura and felt that he owed her that much after yesterday's afternoon chat.

Laura was waiting for him at the foot of the circular staircase in the main lobby. She greeted him with a gentle hug and a soft kiss on the left cheek. She seemed somewhat guarded and more formal than usual. Standing close to her was a man of average build with thick, curly black hair and strong Mediterranean features—bushy eyebrows, long eye lashes, and huge brown eyes set against a round and permanently suntanned face. He was smiling broadly while protectively resting his arm on Laura's shoulder.

"Good morning, Eric," Laura said in her enchanting voice. "Let me introduce you to my husband, Alexis."

Eric was slightly amused by the emphasis that she placed on the fact that Alexis was 'her husband'. It was not necessary, but he welcomed the taunt after his horrendous night of soul searching. He knew that if he was going to have any chance of getting even with the killers, he had to get a grip on himself quickly. This social call was as good an antidote as any. With a sense of relief, he finally turned his attention to Alexis, who had not lost his huge grin. His eyes sparkled with intelligence, and he looked younger than Eric, despite the thick lenses on his eyeglasses that gave him a serious and a tad severe appearance.

After a short, awkward silence, Eric shook Alexis's hand, cracked a big smile and said, "A pleasure to meet you, Alexis."

"The pleasure is all mine. I have heard so much about you. I'm so glad that we could meet at long last."

Eric faked a worried look and enquired, "I trust that you have been told just good things about me?"

Alexis did not miss a beat. "Absolutely. How could anyone have any bad thing to say about you?" he quickly replied.

The two men burst out laughing, and Eric took an instant liking to Alexis. Laura, who was standing on the sideline looking nervous and apprehensive, was visibly relieved at how well Eric and Alexis seemed to be getting along. She was determined to stay quiet and let the conversation between the two men take its natural course. She would enjoy the occasion as a vindication of what she had accomplished with her life. It was a moment she knew she would remember fondly and savor for a very long time. She gave Eric a quick look and then settled her gaze on Alexis, her face beaming with satisfaction and happiness.

"So what brings you to this part of the world?" Alexis asked.

Laura and Eric exchanged a knowing glance.

"Unfortunately, just business I'm afraid. Quite boring, really," Eric said, throwing an appreciative smile at Laura for keeping the real purpose of his visit to Istanbul a secret from her husband. He noticed the puzzled look on Alexis' face and quickly added, "But I'm also taking some time off this morning to do some sightseeing in your wonderful city. Laura has so graciously offered to show me around town."

"Yes, yes I know, she told me all about it last night. She is a wonderful guide. You're in excellent hands with her. She knows this city better than anyone. My only advice to you, though, is to skip the Grand Bazaar; otherwise, you will lose her for good. She's an addictive shopper. But I'm sure you already know that."

"Oh yes, I have not forgotten her wonderful qualities. I will try to keep her away from the shopping district, if that's at all possible."

"Good, my man. I don't think my credit card can take it anymore."

Throughout the exchange, Laura had a hard time keeping her emotions in check. Outwardly she remained stoic—Mona Lisa-like. But at any time she knew that she ran the risk of bursting out. She was overjoyed that the two most important men in her life were getting along so well. They were teasing her, but she preferred to take it as a good sign and not let her overly-sensitive nature get the better of her. *This has the potential to develop into a real friendship*, she thought, and hoped.

"Did I tell you that Alexis is a professor teaching at Istanbul University?" Laura suddenly interjected, wanting to stir the conversation away from her.

"No. You did not tell me that. What do you teach Alexis?"

"Ancient history. Would you believe it if someone told you that a Greek was a full-fledged professor at a Turkish university, teaching, of all things, history dating back to Troy?"

Eric nodded, appreciating Alexis' subtle message. The feud that festered between the Greeks and the Turks from ancient times was well known in the region. Not since Alexander the Great have these two neighboring countries been able to find a common ground for a peaceful and harmonious co-existence. It was a hostility, deeply-rooted many centuries ago, that continued to show its ugly face up to the present time. It culminated in a war between these two members of NATO, the outcome of which was a torn and divided Cyprus. More recently, the dispute flared up even more because of the stubborn resistance of Greece to the aspirations of Turkey to be part of the Euro zone. The irony of that latest spat did not escape Eric, knowing that in hindsight, Europe would rather have had Turkey's booming economy in its fold. Indeed, Greece was a source of grave aggravation for the folks in the EU headquarters in Brussels who were desperately looking for ways to salvage a sinking ship.

Eric empathized with Alexis' particular predicament. It had to be difficult for anyone to keep working and accept living in such an unfriendly and unwelcoming environment. He set his eyes on Alexis with new respect, but his curiosity got the better of him and so he asked, "How did you pull it off, Alexis? I would never have believedthat a Greek would have been invited to teach history at a Turkish university." "As far as they are concerned, I'm Canadian. Of course, being able to teach in English did not hurt either."

"He is too modest," Laura interjected. "Alexis is a renowned expert in his field and his reputation among his peers is absolutely stellar. He is a super star, and any university would be thrilled to have him on their staff."

"But darling, would that matter if they knew that I was Greek?"

"A naturalized Canadian of Greek descent, my love," Laura replied quickly.

Alexis tossed Laura a quick glance and nodded approvingly. He spoke softly while holding her hand. "Anyway, it does not matter anymore. I'm nearing the end of my term on my contract, and I'm not renewing it at the end of the semester."

Finishing his thought Laura proudly added, "That's right; Alexis wants to take time off from teaching to write a novel. So after Istanbul, we will be moving to Chania in Crete."

"A novel, that's wonderful, Alexis," Eric exclaimed. "What are you going to write about?"

"I'm afraid nothing really new. You know, the usual story about how difficult it is for anyone to start anew in another country, to learn how to live with cultural differences, and to even go as far as adopting and embracing them as if they were your own. I know it's a topic that has been explored by many authors and that many books have been written on the subject over the years. But in my case there is a personal twist. I really feel at home in Canada. It's my country of birth Greece that I have a hard time getting warm and fuzzy about. I often wonder if the reason for my choice is not simply a way for me to conceal a latent need to feel accepted by my adopted chosen country—a strong survival instinct and a deep and desperate sense of wanting to belong, if you will."

Eric eyed Alexis with renewed interest. There was so much in Alexis' life experience that he could identify with. He hoped that someday he would find the time to share with him his own thoughts on the subject. But for now, he chose to remain quiet.

An uncomfortable silence filled the air, and Laura immediately came to the rescue. "But you will find out the truth, my darling. Wait until you start writing; it'll all come to you."

"I know. At least, I hope you're right," Alexis said sullenly. "But for now, I must get going or I'm going to be late for class. Enjoy your day, you two—and Eric, please join us for dinner when you're free. Just give us a call; Laura and I would love to have you over."

"That's right. Eric, you're welcome anytime. I know that you're busy tonight, so just remember that you have an open dinner invitation from us that extends all the way to Chania." Then, turning to Alexis with arms opened wide, Laura added with a chuckle, "We too must get going my darling or there will not be enough time for Eric to go shopping."

"Where are you going?"

"To catch the elevators. Are we not going down to the underground parking to look for your car?"

"Silly you, if you want to tour my town you will have to do it my way. Let's walk down to the pier to catch the ferry, or *vapur* as they like to call it here. The best way to explore the historical Sultanahmet district is on foot."

Laura grabbed Eric's arm and led him along the road down a steep hill, heading for the waterfront of Istanbul. There was already a long line of people waiting for the ferry when they reached the docks at the end of the road. They were mostly locals on their way to work, as tourists generally preferred the comfort of taxi cabs and sometimes *Dolmuses* when travelling in a group large enough to entirely fill the cream-colored minibus. Laura used her electronic ticket to get them on board quickly. The commuter ferry was crowded, but no one was left behind waiting on the docks. Most commuters settled inside the large cabin so as to be shielded from the wind and the high waves that splashed the lower decks from time to time. A few passengers like Laura and Eric elected to remain standing outside, next to the cabin towering the Vapur where the captain kept a watchful eye.

The Bosphorus was calm that day, and they stood close to each other, their gaze directed at the sea, feeling the breeze gently brush their faces. They remained silent for most of the way across the long strait, fascinated by the *Yalis*—the grand residences of wealthy Turks of Ottoman Istanbul that bordered the shorelines of the Bosphorus. They gazed in awe at the grand and opulent *Dolmabahçe* Palace. At a distance, they could see the mouth of the Golden Horn emerging in the horizon, glistening under the famous *Galata Bridge*.

When they finally reached their destination at the *Eminönü Piers*, Eric's mind had been totally purified of all the dark and gloomy thoughts that had kept him awake all night. The Bosphorus had worked its magic again, opening his soul to all the wonders for him to see and appreciate. They walked holding hands along the ancient Hippodrome where Roman chariots once raced. Then they visited Hagia Sophia, a cathedral turned into a mosque on the order of Sultan Mehmed II following the conquest of Istanbul by the Turks, and now a magnificent museum.

It was not until they reached the famous Blue Mosque that his uneasiness returned. He was sure that someone was following them. He felt a presence lurking behind the massive pillars. He could sense eyes watching him, hidden in the shadows of the gigantic mosque. It was another one of his gut feelings—something he had learned not to ignore at his own expense. But all he saw were gigantic domes decorated with beautiful blue calligraphy and walls adorned with pieces of blue, green and white tiles from Iznik. A couple of men down on their knees and hands facing east caught his attention for an instant. But there was nothing to worry about there, just bare footed Turks going about their business finishing their morning prayers.

Laura felt Eric's grip tightening in her hand and noticed the way he kept looking back at every opportunity. Something seemed to worry him all of a sudden, and she wondered what might be the cause. "Are you alright?" she asked.

"Yes of course. This place is absolutely incredible. It's breathtaking. Thank you so much for bringing me here."

Laura looked incredulous. Eric's response sounded forced and unnatural to her. She looked straight into his eyes, trying to figure out for herself what was bothering him. She hit a wall and could only sense his anxiety.

"So why are you constantly looking behind you?" she asked skeptically.

"Oh that. It's a terrible paranoid habit of mine that I unfortunately acquired over the years. I can't get rid of it; it's a residual from the past that simply won't go away. You know, once bitten always fearful—constantly on the lookout," Eric shrugged.

"I see." It was now Laura's turn to shrug her shoulders. "Are you ready for the grand finale then?"

"Sure. What could that be, I wonder?"

"The fabulous Topkapi Palace; it's only a few minutes away. We could start with the Imperial Treasury where some of the world's biggest emeralds and diamonds are on display, or we could begin, instead, with the Harem quarters where the Sultans spent most of their time."

"The Treasury of course. I want to see what I would never be able to afford."

"You're such a liar," Laura quipped breaking into a giggle.

This was not the first lie that Eric had told Laura that day. His somber expression masked a deep uneasiness. The murder of David Luchatel weighed heavy on his mind despite his attempts at putting a brave front for Laura's benefit. The anger had returned in full force, and he felt a strong pang in his heart. He let go of Laura's hand and glanced over his shoulder, sensing a presence behind him. He caught a glimpse of a man for a fraction of a second, before the suspected stalker had time to hustle behind a large tree. His face was obscured in the shadows on the side of the stone pathway. But there was no mistake this time. He had seen this man before.

CHAPTER 16

Their eyes locked. Instant recognition turned into unbridled rage. Their first encounter in the south of France had been brief, but it left them with deep scars permanently etched on their souls. Circumstances had made them adversaries; their actions transformed them into mortal enemies. They stood a few feet apart, sizing one another up, appraising their relative positions, envisioning their next move. Neither man dared take the initiative, not wanting to miss out on a better opportunity. It was a dance timed by the rhythmic beat of two hearts as the two enemies eyed each other, ready to pounce.

Karzan shook his head from side to side to get rid of a sudden tightness in his neck. He was angry at himself. He had let his guard down for a split second, no more than a solitary heartbeat, but that was all the time Eric had needed to catch a glimpse of him. This was not supposed to happen. Not to him at least, with all his field experience and his instincts well-honed after so many years at war. It was a good thing that he was alone stalking his prey, for he could not bear the fact that he had made a mistake. "No one must know and no more mistakes," he swore under his breath. The bloodied face of his dead comrade killed in Antibes suddenly burst into his mind. A vivid reminder of an earlier error in judgment. The image lasted just long enough to flood his heart with even more bitterness. Sensing the danger, he rapidly set aside the mounting fury and slowly relaxed his body to let his brain do its work. He had to think fast, knowing that a confrontation in such a crowded place could only produce greater problems, and would only attract the undesirable attention of the *Polis* who frequently patrolled the Palace grounds.

Eric turned to Laura to let her know what was going on, but the words never came out of his mouth. No explanation was needed after all. Laura had sensed the urgency and sadly nodded her acquiescence.

Without warning, Eric tore after Karzan. *Be careful*, Laura mouthed to his retreating back; *please come back to me alive.*

But Karzan had anticipated Eric's action and was already running frantically, his feet and hands beating the pavement and air in unison. The Imperial Gate was a short distance away, and he made good use of the mass of approaching visitors to lengthen the distance between them.

Eric had lost a few precious seconds, not expecting Karzan to run away from him. He had hoped, instead, for a fight to the death from the man who had threatened his life. He rubbed the scar under his left eye as if he needed an incentive, and willed himself to run even faster, ignoring the pain in his chest and the fire in his leg and thigh muscles. There was a swarm of tourists roaming around the Palace courtyards. He just cut right through, pushing and shoving his way through the crowd, mumbling apologies that most people did not or could not understand. For an instant, he thought he had lost his quarry in the throngs of people that had gathered in front of the main gate. Then he spotted him at a distance, dashing out of the Palace walls and sprinting towards the *Cağaloğlu Bath*. He redoubled his efforts to catch up with Karzan, not wanting to lose sight of him in the tortuous streets that snaked in every direction throughout the peninsula shaped like a giant rhinoceros horn.

Karzan glanced over his shoulder and saw Eric hot in pursuit. He wished he could stop running away like a coward and deal with this vermin once and for all. "A quick swipe of his knife would put an end to this foolishness," he cursed loudly. But Abdullah was on his case and he could hardly afford to screw up. Catching the traitor who was feeding information to Eric was the primary objective of the mission. Abdullah would not have it any other way. Eric had to remain alive in order to lead them to the traitor in their midst. Failure would not be tolerated. Abdullah was very clear about that.

Karzan was barely feeling the strain of the chase; his regular regimen of mountain climbing and long jogs in the countryside had prepared him well for this sort of thing. But being hounded like a thief was not his idea of fun. He thought about ways to turn this pursuit to his advantage, and brusquely cut left, heading for the Grand Bazaar.

Once Eric cleared the Imperial Gate, he was able to keep pace with Karzan. But he had not gained any ground on him, and the sudden change of direction made him lose a few more precious seconds.

"This is not going well," Eric cursed under his breath. When he realized what Karzan was up to, he was even more enraged by the man's cunning.

The Grand Bazaar of Istanbul loomed ahead. It was renowned for its vast maze of narrow and circuitous alleys lined with thousands of shops, cafes, and tea houses that were scarcely illuminated under an intricately painted vaulted roof. The market place was a completely covered gigantic labyrinth of shopping madness visited by over 300,000 tourists daily. In short, Eric knew the Grand Bazaar would be the ideal place for someone who wanted to break loose.

When Eric reached the *Nuruosmaniye Gate*, he was breathing hard but nowhere close to catching the man he was chasing. Karzan had simply vanished into thin air under the canopy of thousands of booth-like shops and an even greater number of shoppers. He paused for a second to allow time for his eyes to adjust to the artificial lights. When it all became clear, what he saw was even more disconcerting. The Grand Bazaar was more chaotic, hectic, and wilder than he could have ever imagined it to be. The narrow lanes were cramped with a sea of onlookers. Shopkeepers in all corners were hustling every tourist that happened to walk by, and shoppers everywhere were haggling for better deals. Shops were bursting at the seams with merchandize sprawled out on makeshift wooden countertops, piled up on the carpeted floors, or simply stacked on top of large and tall cardboard boxes. T-shirts, souvenirs, fabrics, bags, and leather belts of all colors, styles, and brands were hanging three and four layers deep along thin wires encircling the tiny booths. The Grand Bazaar of Istanbul was a treasure trove of secret hideouts.

It would be easier to find a needle in a haystack then to find Karzan in this maze, but Eric was not about to give up.

He took a few steps past the gate and hesitated for a moment to scrutinize the vicinity, looking for a sign, a hint, or anything that might reveal the presence of Karzan. He had nothing to hang on to but luck, and he knew that he was not blessed with good fortune of late. The whole pursuit looked rather pointless; his stubbornness alone made sure that he continued to forge ahead.

Eric kept a steady pace as he slalomed around the horde of visitors looking for souvenirs to take back home. He made sure to stop and carefully examine every dark vaulted alley that crisscrossed his path on either side. He must have spent the better half of an hour searching for Kazan in this web-like network of dark and crowded lanes, without success. Time was wasting, and he knew that the odds of finding Karzan were lessened at every tick of the needle.

He reached another blind alley and stood still for a minute, wondering what to do. "Where is he?" he growled in frustration. After a short pause, he took a deep breath and then began to retrace his steps, looking for another passage. He was feeling equally discouraged, angry, and desperate when he happened to glance over his right shoulder. A sudden jolt shook his entire body, and his head snapped sharply in the direction of a small group of Asian women.

He had spotted Karzan.

He could not believe his eyes and his good luck. At the end of a side lane, a mere thirty feet away, the Kurdish terrorist was hustling a bunch of Asian tourists like a seasoned shopkeeper. Their faces half hidden by sun visors, the women were gathered all around him, giggling like little girls while covering their mouths with their white gloved hands. Karzan seemed to be enjoying the attention he was getting and did not appear to notice Eric bolting his way. Within seconds, Eric had reached the small group, elbowed his way to the middle of the gathering, and charged with his hands aiming straight at Karzan's throat.

But Karzan was ready for him.

It was a carefully planned trap. In one swift movement, Karzan sidestepped Eric, raised one knee below waist level, crushing his groin, and followed with a well-placed elbow under his nose.

Eric staggered away, fighting to get his breath back. For a moment, he looked like he was going to crash, but somehow managed to remain on his feet. He lunged at Kazan, fists flailing, hoping to hit something—anything.

But Karzan was too quick. He shrugged his shoulders, sneered, and swiftly punched Eric in the solar plexus, knocking the wind out of him. Eric's body hung in the air for a second, and then landed on the cement floor with a thud.

No one in the shop had moved, too petrified to run, let alone scream. Glares were exchanged, but nothing more. It suited Karzan just fine. He had no longer been able to bear the thought that an amateur had caused him so much trouble. Eric had to pay for making him look bad. Abdullah would no doubt press him for explanations, and none would be good enough in his leader's mind. But that didn't matter. His honor was at stake. Karzan took one last look at Eric as he lay sprawled on the floor, moaning in pain, gasping for air. He gave him a kick and a smirk, and then hustled out of sight before anyone had the bright idea to call for help.

Satisfied that Eric would not give him any more trouble for some time, Karzan pulled his cell phone from his pocket and gave a few quick instructions to Hogir, who was waiting outside the bazaar. When he emerged from the side lane, he deliberately slowed down his pace. In an attempt to look more like a tourist than a terrorist on the run, he stopped a few times, pretending to admire beautiful hand-woven carpets and a couple of displays of gold watches along the way. It was all for show of course, but it was a necessary precaution in case the incident with Eric had been reported to the local police. Every so often he would discreetly glance at the reflection in a mirror or pretend to tie a shoe lace to take a quick peek around. It would take him a little longer to reach the east gate of the Grand Bazaar, but he knew that in his line of business one could never be too careful.

Meanwhile, Eric had slowly recovered his senses and gladly accepted the helping hand of the shopkeeper to get back on his feet. He inhaled a few deep breaths to fully regain his composure, and wiped the blood away from his nose with the tissue that was handed to him. The Asian women had taken a few steps back and seemed to hesitate about what to do next, but Eric had no time for explanations, expressions of gratitude, or any more apologies. He turned his attention to the shopkeeper who had witnessed the whole incident. The man immediately understood the silent inquiry and with a barely noticeable tilt of the head, indicated which way Karzan had gone.

The merchant stood at the doorway unfazed by what had just happened in his shop, as if this sort of thing was a common occurrence in the bazaar. He watched Eric run for a short while and then glanced back at the women who were by now fidgeting nervously in the far corner of his store. With a wide smile he picked up the beach towel from the floor that Karzan had been peddling and wasted no more time in getting back to business.

Karzan stared in shock at the man tearing his way through the crowd and storming in his direction like a maniac. "I don't believe it. The man doesn't know when to quit," he cursed out loud.

And then he realized there was an even greater danger looming.

A small crowd had gathered at the entrance of the jewelry store where he'd stopped to admire a gold watch under a locked glass display. All eyes were staring at him menacingly. The whole mall could hear Eric yell," *Imdat, Imdat,* help, help, stop him; he is a thief."

This whole thing was spinning out of control. Karzan took a mere millisecond to assess the situation and devise the best exit strategy. "Move!" he barked at the salesman blocking his way. He bolted out of the store before anyone had time to react. This was the second time he had underestimated Eric, and it could never happen again—not to him—not to a seasoned fighter who had outfoxed the blood-thirsty hordes of Saddam Hussein's army in northern Iraq.

But there was no time for self- recrimination. Eric was rapidly gaining on him, yelling for help and causing a commotion along the way. There were shouts of alarm in all directions. Shopkeepers pulled out their cell phones, distraught bystanders stared at each other, and tour guides gathered their brood protectively. But by some miracle, the wall of people parted in front of him like the Red Sea, offering a free and unencumbered passage to the nearest exit gate. Fear had replaced the initial bravado of the crowd. No one wanted to take a chance with a thief who might be carrying a weapon. *Let the Polis take care of the thief*, was now on everyone's mind. Karzan took full advantage of the opportunity and fled out of the bazaar before Eric could ever gain on him.

Eric reached the east gate in time to see Karzan hop on the back of a motorcycle and take off in a cloud of smoke. He started to run after the motorbike, but stopped after a few steps, quickly realizing the futility of his action. Gasping for air, he focused his mind on the street ahead of him. He surveyed the surroundings, scrutinized the people, watched the traffic, looked for an opportunity that might present itself, and mostly prayed for another lucky break. The motorcycle had already veered to the left at the first intersection. He stomped the pavement in frustration, and his lucky break made its appearance in the shape of an old, beat-up Toyota delivery van. The driver was napping inside the cabin, passing time in between two delivery jobs. With its engine idling and the wheels on the passenger side parked over the sidewalk, the white van offered an easy target.

Eric leapt across the street, yanked open the door of the vehicle, pulled the startled driver out onto the side of the road, and gunned the engine out of its parking spot. He left behind him a bearded old man, cursing and shouting every imaginable insult at the stranger who had stolen his van and its precious cargo of olive oil. There was not a second to spare. As far as Eric was concerned, nothing else mattered at this point but to catch his man.

He swerved the van, made heavy by its liquid cargo, in and out of the traffic without regard to his safety or the other vehicles that happened to be in his way. When faced with a bottleneck, he would not hesitate to pull the battered Toyota over the sidewalk, bullying the innocent pedestrians out of the way and leaving a trail of incensed screams and angry shouts behind him. He finally reached the intersection and swerved the van sharply to the left, cutting off the oncoming traffic. On the opposite side of the road, brakes screeched and cars honked loudly. He ignored the stream of infuriated drivers and their middle fingers pointing angrily at him, and floored the gas pedal, hoping that the old van had a little more juice left under the hood. To his surprise, the engine responded well, and with tires burning the asphalt underneath, the Toyota roared forward and started to close in on the motorcycle.

The race was on, and nothing could stop Eric from catching his man.

Ahead on the road, Hogir glanced in his side mirror. A white van had jumped into view, blasting its way towards them. One quick glance at the driver was all the time he needed to recognize Eric. He nudged Karzan with his elbow to alert him. Karzan stared down the street incredulously. A peek at Eric at the wheel of the oncoming van made him realize that he had made his third mistake of the day. Eric had given him no respite and he began to resent his leader's orders even more.

"This can't go on; I must put an end to this whole madness once and for all!" Karzan spat out in disgust.

The motorcycle veered off the main road and turned into a very narrow lane lined with street vendors on both sides. The lane had been transformed into a long and cramped fruit and vegetable market for the day. The motorbike zigzagged its way through the crowd and the vendors' stands, barely slowing down to avoid the obstacles in its path. Hogir was an experienced driver who seemed to relish the challenge. He maneuvered the powerful motorbike with control and agility, never hesitating or second-guessing himself. They made it to the end of the busy lane without incident and in excellent time—but Karzan was not happy.

Eric had kept pace. He too had not been fazed by what had been thrown his way. With horn blaring and engine roaring, he used the old Toyota like a bulldozer to slice open a passage through the mass of people and the vendors' carts blocking his way. He ploughed through more stands, carts, and crates than he cared to remember. There was no stopping him. His prey was within his grasp and he could smell blood.

Karzan pointed Hogir in the direction of *Kennedy Cadessi*, a wide avenue that circled the Golden Horn along the edge of the water. This was the spot that Karzan had chosen for the final act—a wide open laneway with light traffic and few people, far from indiscreet eyes and within reach of an escape route—the Galata Bridge. With the palm of his hand facing down, Karzan signaled Hogir to slow down. He pulled his gun from under his belt on his back, turned his body sideways, aimed, and pressed the trigger twice in quick succession.

Eric was driving like a man possessed. His eyes focused on his target. He held his hands tightly on the steering wheel, getting ready to ram the motorcycle at any time. In a split second, all hell broke loose: a loud explosion, the bang of metal crashing against metal, followed instantly by the hissing noise of a pierced air bag. Eric had lost control of the van, and the chase was abruptly over.

Eric was in shock. He could hear the tinkling of falling glass, the plaintive sound of the punctured radiator, and smelled the rancid stench of olive oil mixed in with the explosive odor of gasoline. But the dreadful realization that blood was pouring down his face kept him paralyzed in his seat. The lamppost made a last squeaking noise like the broken branch of an old oak tree in the wind, and the Toyota jerked back down on its wheels with a loud bang. His head hit the steering wheel, and he closed his eyes in pain.

Then came an eerie silence.

It lasted a few seconds before mayhem erupted. Cars screeched to a halt, horns blared, and people screamed. A few brave souls tried to pry open the doors of the van but gave up after a few unsuccessful attempts. And then the banging began—first on the windows, then on the doors, and finally on what was left of the windshield. The wailing of an ambulance in the distance put a temporary end to the frantic activity. Women pulled their husbands back as they tried to inch forward to get a clear view of Eric inside the wreck. Men stared at each other with worried looks. The crowd stood still, hesitating, deliberating, and feeding off of its nervous energy.

"We have to hurry to get him out of the truck," a man yelled, "it is going to catch fire at any time!"

Another moment of indecision, enough time for the meaning to filter through the crowd, and then pandemonium started all over again. Everyone sprang into action at once, in a mad rush to haul Eric out of the rubble. Ambulance or not, in danger or not, no matter what—the crowd was convinced that Eric needed to be rescued immediately.

Slouched behind the wheel, his head resting on the steering wheel, Eric thanked his good luck one more time before passing out.

CHAPTER 17

Hogir and Karzan stood at the edge of a large group of men and women who were gathered around to catch a glimpse of the van crushed against a bent lamppost that threatened to fall over at any minute. They had safely hidden their motorbike behind a large bush half a kilometer away, and were cautiously scrutinizing the surrounding area for any sign of trouble. Satisfied that no one was paying any attention to them, they approached the site of the accident, making sure to blend into the crowd as if they were just two curious bystanders. They were there to find out what happened to Eric and to tie up any loose ends in the event anything had gone wrong.

Karzan briefly observed the policeman who was directing traffic, making ample use of his whistle to strongly discourage anyone who tried to stop for a quick look at the mangled van on the side of the road. The news of the terrible crash had spread like wildfire, and the overworked policeman glanced several times in the direction of his two companions who were busy canvassing the crowd, notepad in hands. They were interviewing witnesses to collect statements for their report to headquarters. Karzan watched them going about their business, and finally focused his attention on the younger of the two policemen, who was eagerly taking copious notes.

Standing at his side, Hogir looked weary and worried. He had barely slept in over twenty-four hours. A day earlier, he had followed the woman with a Greek name to her apartment building in the European quarter. Stationed next to a small tea and coffee shop, he had kept a close watch over the entrance of the building all night long. He had not eaten for an entire day, and to keep his mind sharp and alert, he drank seven cups of strong Turkish coffee and smoked two packs of cigarettes. He had kept a constant vigil, not ever letting his guard down for a second. When the woman, accompanied by a man (whom he assumed to be either her lover or her husband), emerged from the apartment building in the early morning hours, he was ready for them. He crushed his last cigarette butt on the pavement and hopped on his motorbike, ready to tag along behind their tiny Fiat. He kept them in sight from a safe distance, but never allowed more than two motor vehicles between them. For some reason, he was not surprised when he realized that the little car was leading him back to the Conrad Istanbul Hotel. *I must have acquired Karzan's gift of premonition,* he reflected, poking fun at himself.

Later on that morning, Hogir found Karzan chatting with a man who he assumed to be the driver of the large bus parked along the ramp that led up to the main entrance of the hotel. The two partners exchanged brief eye contact, and shortly afterwards, Karzan excused himself to join Hogir. They did not speak to one another, knowing full well the reason for their presence in front of the hotel. They waited for a good hour, scrutinizing every face that walked in and out of the lobby.

When Laura finally emerged with Eric, they both looked away to conceal their faces. They watched them as they walked down the hill and waited until they were a fair distance away before they started to follow. Karzan took the lead, shadowing the couple, and after a few short steps he appeared to change his mind. He stopped Hogir in his tracks and told him to stay put. "I will take care of the tail alone," he told him. Hogir started to protest but the look Karzan gave him quickly silenced any thoughts he might have had about raising any strong objections.

To Hogir's dismay, their entire mission began to unravel from that point on. Karzan had started to act irrationally. *It was so unlike him,* he thought. He could sense that something was troubling his partner, but could not figure out what it could possibly be. He had caught Karzan studying him a couple of times, when Karzan thought he was not paying attention. And he also noted the harshness in Karzan's voice when he gave him instructions to wait for him. He knew that Karzan had taken an unnecessary risk when he decided to follow Laura and Eric alone. *That was highly unusual, especially when two targets were involved. He must have known that, so why did he insist on doing it alone?* Hogir mulled it over, somewhat mystified by his comrade's strange behavior.

Hogir looked intently at Karzan, trying once again to decipher what was on his partner's mind. He was clearly perturbed by how the situation had evolved, but tried not to show it for fear of his partner's wrath. Besides, there was something else that was troubling him even more.

"Abdullah is not going to be happy," Hogir said.

"Eric did not give me a choice. It had to be done."

Hogir looked skeptical. "I don't understand. What happened in the bazaar?"

"The traitor must have warned him about us. Eric set up a trap and was ready for me," Karzan lied.

Hogir looked away and drew a deep breath. *This damn business is getting messier and messier.* He took a moment to mull over what Karzan had just said, and then gathered enough courage to dare challenge his partner's explanation.

"But you did not have to shoot him. What good is he to us if he is dead?"

Karzan growled, "Who do you think I am? A crazy lunatic or some dimwit?"

"No, no, of course not. But what are you going to tell Abdullah?"

"The truth, of course. Relax, will you? I shot the two front tires. That's why he lost control of the van and hit the lamppost. Don't stare at me that way. I'm sure everything will be fine. Just stay put; I will find out what happened to him."

Hogir started to say something and then decided to let it go. *Better let Karzan handle it,* he reflected, fearing what Abdullah might do when he found out that Karzan had disobeyed him.

Karzan smiled as he walked resolutely toward the young policeman. He kept his gaze focused on the policeman's eyes to make sure that he was conveying the impression that he had something important to tell him. It did not work, but at least he caught the young police officer's attention.

"Stop there. No one is allowed beyond this point," the police officer barked, pointing at the yellow tape demarcating the scene of the accident.

"It's alright officer. I'm not here to interfere with your investigation. I just want to know if the poor driver of the vehicle was badly hurt."

The policeman studied Karzan suspiciously. No one had shown any interest or seemed to care much about the driver's well being. What most people wanted to know was how did the crash happen. So at first the young policeman was somewhat taken back, and did not know what to make of Karzan's enquiry. He glanced over at his superior and then thought better of it. The fellow seemed genuinely concerned, he thought, and thus decided to handle the matter himself.

"He was conscious when they carried him over to the ambulance. The medics said that he should be alright. They made him move his legs and arms and he appeared to be coherent," the policeman replied.

"Allah is great." Karzan said, as he looked up to the sky in a sign of prayer. After a dutiful pause, he kissed his index finger then rested the palm of his hand on his chest at heart level, then recited a verse from the Koran. The policeman was impressed by the kindness of the man.

Karzan gave an empathetic smile. "Would you know, by any chance, where they have taken him?"

"Yes, of course. The American Hospital."

He thanked the young policeman and informed him that he would check at the hospital to make sure that the poor man was alright. He started to walk away when, like an afterthought, he stopped in his tracks and turned to ask another question.

"Do we know how this accident happened?" He asked.

"That's what's really puzzling about the whole damn thing," the policeman replied. "I have witnesses who told me that he was driving like a maniac and must have been on drugs. Yet others thought he was chasing after another car and lost control of his vehicle. Some people even told me that he had stolen the van and was running away from the police. Go figure it out. The bottom line, I guess, is that we will never know what really happened unless, of course, the driver decides to be communicative."

"Oh I'm sure he will be. It's in his interest to co-operate with the police. In any event, I'm sure that you will be able to piece together the events leading up to the accident. I must run now to the hospital to offer him my assistance. Thank you so much for your co-operation."

Karzan was relieved. The news was good. There was no mention of a motorbike or gunshots. Above all, Eric was well and alive. There remained only one issue that had to be dealt with swiftly. He must find the informant before anyone else gets hold of him, for he knew that Abdullah would see through his weak fib about Eric having been tipped off.

Hogir watched the interaction with the policeman from across the road. The tautness in Karzan's face was gone. He did not break stride when he reached Hogir.

"Let's go," Karzan said.

"Where to?"

"The American Hospital."

"The hospital. What did you find out?"

"I will tell you on the way. Go get the bike."

CHAPTER 18

SYLVERSTONE AND PARTNERS LLP, MONTREAL, QUEBEC

Paul severed the connection for the fifth time. He gazed over his desk in disgust. Legal files were stacked a foot high, his morning correspondence was left unopened on the corner of his large mahogany desk, his coffee was cold, and his gold cufflinks were hidden somewhere under the mass of paper. He felt the urge to light a cigarette, something he had not done in over a year, ever since his break up with his wife.

The new blond bombshell girlfriend had turned out to be a big flop, but that was not what was preoccupying him at the moment. He picked up the five page report from the top of the pile of documents in front him and read it for the third time. It was written in a forthright, almost telegraphic style, like a police report. Most importantly, however, it contained information that he knew would be very helpful to Eric. The report hinted strongly at the possibility of a breakthrough in the case. But there was just one problem—he could not get hold of his brother. He tried calling his cell phone, but all he got was his voice mail. He had no better luck trying to reach him in his apartment or his office—just the annoying beep, and then the taped monotone voice of Eric instructing the caller to 'please leave me a short message and I will call you back promptly'.

So much for promptness, he fumed. He had made his first call over five hours ago.

Paul eased back in his leather armchair and pulled a small, white index card from the Rolodex next to his computer. Then he picked up the telephone one more time, dialed the long distance number inscribed on the card, and waited for an answer.

"*Bonjour, Monsieur Lepetit. C'est Paul Martin sur la ligne. Comment allez-vous?*"

"I'm fine, and you?"

"Well, things could be better. But I guess I should not be complaining too much. It's no longer snowing and the temperature in Montreal is a balmy 10 degrees below zero."

Alain Lepetit laughed."Good. At last, someone with a positive attitude."

Paul cleared his throat and waited for Alain Lepetit's laugh to subside. There was no reason to feel nervous about calling his brother's boss, but the findings of the report and Eric's silence had rattled him.

"The reason for my call is.....well I'm sorry to bother you with this small matter, but in fact I'm looking for Eric. I called his office earlier, but all I'm getting is his voice mail."

Alain Lepetit growled. "It's unbelievable. They were supposed to take care of this days ago."

"I'm sorry, I don't understand, but what was supposed to get done days ago?"

"Change the message on his voice mail, for God's sake. Your brother is no longer employed at the bank. Has he not told you?"

"He quit the bank?"

"Yes, that's what I said. It's a habit of his. This is the second time he has done this to me."

"I was not aware. He keeps things pretty close to his chest, you know."

"Tell me about it. But you can also add stubborn, obstinate, and pig-headed to his list of wonderful personal qualities."

"I prefer to think of him as being persistent. It's a family trait, you should know."

Alain Lepetit chortled on the phone. Paul took the opportunity to grab his notepad, and scribbled a few words to remind him to tell his brother that he knew of an excellent lawyer in Paris that could help him negotiate a good severance package.

"I suppose that you would like to know where your brother is," Alain Lepetit said.

"Yes, Of course. Do you have any idea where I can find him? I have some important information for him."

"Not really. The last time I heard from him was in an email informing me that he was resigning from the bank He gave me no explanations, no reasons, nothing at all that might at least give me a hint as to why he was calling it quits, except of course that he wanted to take care of some unfinished business.

Goddamn it. He didn't even have the courtesy to let me know about his intentions face to face, like a man," Alain Lepetit shouted. His frustration with Eric had been brewing inside of him for a long time. He knew that he had little influence over Eric, but that was not an excuse. And it certainly did not appease any remorse he might have had trying to manipulate Eric for his own selfish needs. He was convinced that if something were ever to happen to Eric, it would come back to haunt him in some shape or form for the rest of his life. He was being blackmailed by people who would take pleasure reminding him of how he screwed up big time. He could not lie his way out this mess this time out.

At the very least, his outburst made him feel better for a short while. He took a deep breath and managed to stifle, somewhat, his fit of temper—but not his anger. On the other end of the line, Paul had been quiet. Like a good lawyer, he understood the power of silence. A witness was almost always more communicative if left alone to wrestle with his own angst. He had successfully tested that simple truth in court several times. Now, Alain Lepetit was going through the motions, and Paul knew that it would be a matter of time before his brother's former boss would start talking.

"I'm sorry, I'm venting. That's not very helpful," Alain Lepetit said after a long pause.

"It's quite alright. You would not believe the number of times I have wanted to twist my brother's neck. I love him dearly, but I know how infuriating he can be at times."

"Well I suppose there's something else I should tell you. It's not much, but it might be helpful. His assistant booked him on a flight to Istanbul before he left the office. I have no clue what this trip is all about, but who knows, it might point you in the right direction. I don't understand your brother at all, you know. I offered him an incredible promotion in Australia, and all he could do to thank me was to cause me aggravation with my superiors."

At the mention of Istanbul, Paul glanced at the section of the confidential report where Istanbul was mentioned as the probable epicenter of the numbered companies' ownership. *That would certainly explain Eric's presence in Turkey,* he quickly surmised.

"I'm sorry to hear that my brother would do such a thing, but I'm sure he must have had his own good reasons."

"Yeah sure, but as far I'm concerned, he better not come back to me looking for another job ever again."

Paul ignored the last remark, attributing it more to frustration than sour grapes. "Did you say he's gone to Istanbul?"

"As I said, he asked to be booked on a flight to Istanbul the day he left the bank. I have no clue about his current whereabouts."

"Well at least I have a lead to work on. I will contact the Canadian Embassy in Ankara. Maybe they can help locate him for me. Thank you very much for your assistance. "

"My pleasure," Alain Lepetit replied, and then quickly added, "I have an important message for your brother. I would greatly appreciate it if you would give it to him when you find him. You see, despite all his mischief, I don't hold a grudge against him. I don't know why, after all he has done to me, but I still want to help him anyway I can. Please tell him that the police found David Luchatel at the bottom of the Seine River with his throat slashed from ear to ear."

Paul swallowed hard at the news. This last piece of information confirmed his worst fears about Eric's reason for requesting a special investigative report.

"I will certainly convey that message to him. But for my own benefit, what's David Luchatel's connection to my brother?"

"David was doing some private digging for information on the side for Eric. I don't know what they were looking for or working on, but by the looks of things, somebody did not appreciate that David was poking his nose into their affairs."

"I see. I hope that this has nothing to do with Eric's disappearance. Thank you again for being honest with me."

After hanging up, Paul mulled over the entire conversation. His many years' experience as a trial lawyer had triggered some serious doubt about the sincerity of Eric's former boss. Alain Lepetit was holding back something. There was no doubt in his mind. While Eric was capable of acting out on impulse if he felt down deep in his guts that it was the right thing to do, he knew his brother would act responsibly when it came to his job. Alain Lepetit's statement that he did not know why Eric had quit the bank just did not ring true. The whole account seemed contrived, and the way Alain Lepetit volunteered the information bit by bit was a sure telling sign that he had not been entirely forthright with him. *What else did Alain Lepetit know about Eric's sudden departure that he would not share with me? Why put on such an act?*

Paul felt a sharp pain in his neck when he buzzed his assistant to get him the attaché at the Canadian Consulate in Ankara on the phone. While he waited for the connection, he took a look at the two charts on the last page of the report. The first one was a sketch depicting the ownership structure of the various numbered companies that Eric's high-speed trader had used to make his transactions. The chart was crisscrossed with various dotted and solid lines of various thickness and color, linking the companies to one another in an ever-increasing number of layers. The organization did not look like any of the pyramidal configurations he had seen before. A half dozen or so elliptical boxes were highlighted in red with arrows pointing to a larger rectangular box under which was inscribed 'Istanbul' in bold red font. The ownership connection looked tenuous in Paul's eyes. The report ascribed a better-than fifty percent probability that the company set up in Istanbul was at the heart of the whole organization.

The second chart looked even more convoluted. Under the heading: 'Transaction Flows,' lines crisscrossed the page in all directions with no apparent logical patterns. The author of the report was careful to note that the chart illustrated only the electronic transfers of substantial transactions. It also pointed out that it did not necessarily show the destinations of where the funds were ultimately deposited. In fact, according to the report, the circuitous routes where funds traveled electronically were more likely designed to confuse and hide the origin and recipients of the funds. More often than not, the author reiterated, foreign IP addresses were used to hide the true identity of the trades. A series of nodes marked the locations of the custodian banks that were employed, and the size of the nodes indicated the relative proportion of funds that flowed through them. The larger the nodes the more significant the amount of fund flows that passed through that point. Istanbul was again highlighted in red, as well as a couple of other major banking centers such as Frankfurt, Dubai and the Cayman Islands. One node in particular caught Paul's attention. The node was relatively small by comparison, but its significance, as far as he was concerned, was nerve-racking. A single transaction representing a substantial sum of money had been wired to Casablanca, and that was the tipping point that convinced him that Eric was onto something serious and dangerous.

When he finally got his telephone connection with the Canadian attaché, he wasted no time explaining to him that finding his brother Eric was a matter of life or death.

PART THREE

"Daylight follows a dark night."
MAASAI PROVERB

CHAPTER 19

AMERICAN HOSPITAL, ISTANBUL

The nurse pinched his left cheek gently and whispered something in his ear. Eric stirred in his bed and moaned a few unintelligible words. Encouraged by the reaction of her patient, she took his hand in her hand and squeezed it lightly. She held his hand sqeeezing if ever so gently several times, and then waited patiently for Eric to come to his senses.

Eric lay in a semi-conscious state on a bed that was a tad too short for his aching body. He could feel the presence of the nurse at his bedside and hear her pleas imploring him to open his eyes. At first, he tried to comply with the nurse's request and will himself to pry one eye open, then the other for a mere millisecond. The bright light in the small hospital room quickly put an end to his effort. The throbbing pain he felt in his head grew in excruciating intensity, and he winced as he tightly closed his eyes once again.

The nurse nodded at the doctor who walked into the room. She placed a cold compress on Eric's head and then stepped aside.

"Mr. Martin, I'm Doctor Yilmaz. Please listen to me. I need you to open your eyes so that I can finish examining you. It will not take long if you co-operate. Trust me; the procedure will not cause you any pain."

At first Eric seemed unaware of the doctor standing over him. Nothing in the room seemed real or made any sense. Every object spun around him, caught in a vortex of light and diffused shadows. His mind and body had ceased to be connected, and he was sure that he was undergoing an out-of-body experience. He was light-headed, nauseous, and on the verge of passing out again. The voice of the doctor reverberated in his head, bouncing around in his skull in deafening echoes.

Gradually, the medicine they had given him started to kick in. He could sense at first—and then slowly feel—the warm touch of the doctor's hand on his face, holding his eyelids wide open. He no longer resisted the strobe light pointed at his eyes, and he started to breathe normally. The room slowly began to take shape around him. He could now see clearly the nurse holding his hand while the doctor hovered over him.

"Please keep your eyes open for one more minute," the doctor said, as he moved his laser like strobe light around Eric's pupil. "Good. I'm finished now. How are you feeling Mr. Martin?"

"Like shit. How do you think you would be feeling if you had hit a totem pole at one hundred kilometers an hour?"

The doctor laughed. "Well, I see that at least you have not lost your sense of humour. That's a good sign."

"I'm glad you think so," Eric replied. He then shut his eyes tight and pressed on his forehead with the tips of his fingers, trying to squeeze out the pain thumping inside of his skull. "Can you give me something to take care of this damn headache?"

"I have already given you two extra strength Tylenol 3s. I'd rather not prescribe you any more pills for now, just in case. You have had a mild concussion, and while I do not think it's serious, we should wait awhile to make sure that there are no unwarranted side-effects. Better to be prudent, would you not agree?"

Eric frowned. "Yes of course. But how long is this excruciating headache going to last?"

"For a day or two, I'm afraid. But the good news is that you escaped from this horrendous accident without a single broken limb. You have a few bruises and cuts here and there and a gash on your forehead. The abrasions on your arms and face were most probably caused by the windshield that exploded on impact. Other than that, you're in good health. Your organs are fine, no injury there. I found no trace of any internal bleeding, and the lab results came back with a clean bill of health. I don't see any reason for keeping you in the hospital any longer. You may leave as soon as you feel up to it. You're a very lucky man, Mr. Martin."

"I have been told that before," Eric quipped. He looked at the doctor and quickly regretted his curt response. "Thank you, Doctor. I don't mean to sound ungrateful. I do appreciate all the care you have given me, but this stupid headache is driving me nuts."

"No problem at all." The doctor smiled and then shook his head in disbelief. "You don't know how lucky you are, Mr. Martin. The van is a total wreck. It's a miracle that you got out of it alive, with just a headache to complain about."

"Someone is watching over me," Eric replied in a tired voice.

The doctor took the clipboard from the nurse's hands and scribbled a short note on the medical form. He shot a glance at Eric before accepting the outstretched hand. "Please make sure to stop at the front desk before leaving the hospital. You must sign a few forms and, of course, pay your bill. I trust you have good travel insurance, but if you don't, we accept all the major credit cards."

"I'm fine. I will take care of the bill."

"Well in that case, here is my business card. Please call me if you need any medical attention. Oh by the way, before I forget, there are three policemen waiting outside who want to see you as soon as you're ready. I told them that it might take a while, but they insisted on seeing you as soon as possible. Should I tell them to come in now?"

Eric nodded. "I might as well deal with what the police want from me right away."

The doctor and the nurse were just about to leave when the three policemen stormed into the room with a short burly man leading the charge. He stood rooted in front of Eric's bed, scrutinizing him without speaking. He wore a dark blue uniform with two stripes on his right sleeve, and his upper lip seemed to quiver under a thick moustache. He stared at Eric with menacing dark brown eyes, and under the neon ceiling lights his clean shaven head gave him an even more eerie appearance. The second policeman, also in a blue uniform but without stripes on his sleeve, parked his body on the right side of Eric's bed while the remaining officer, in a perfectly fitted charcoal grey suit and a red tie, went straight for the window at the far end of the room.

Eric briefly wondered who was in charge of this police enquiry. The man in the grey suit paid little attention to him. He stood tall. His face was even-featured, and his full head of black hair made him look like a matinée movie star. He kept fussing around his jacket looking for an invisible piece of lint, and once, Eric caught the distinguished brand mark of a Cartier watch on his wrist. He seemed unconcerned, somewhat removed, and most definitely bored. Meanwhile, the other police officer standing at his bedside with a small notebook in hand looked the part of the perfect second in command. He too wore a stern face, the mandatory mustache, and the same dark piercing eyes.

The booming voice of the stocky man, staring him down at the top of the bed, left no doubt as to whom he would have to answer to.

"My name is Captain Sevim," he barked loud enough to make sure that everyone in the room was paying attention to him. "The hospital records show that you registered under the name of Martin. Is this your real name?"

"Yes. My name is Eric Martin."

"Why did you come to Turkey, Mr. Martin?"

"Why do people come to visit Turkey, I wonder?"

"Mr. Martin, if I were you, I would do away with the sarcasm. In case no one told you, you are in deep trouble with the law. I would co-operate and answer my questions if I were you."

"As I said, I came here as a tourist. I heard so much about your wonderful city and I decided to see it with my own eyes at the first opportunity."

"Mr. Martin, I don't like your attitude. I don't even like you. But that's beside the point. With what I have against you, I can put you away for at least twenty years. So just answer my questions and we can get this over quickly."

"Really? What do you have on me?"

"Alright, if this is the way you want it, let me tell you about some of the charges I'm going to file against you. How about possession of stolen property, reckless endangerment of public safety, speeding, drive-by shooting, damage to public property, and damage—no, even better—total destruction of stolen property, to name just a few. Mr. Martin you stole and totally wrecked a vehicle from a poor man who depends entirely on his delivery van for his livelihood. Do you realize what you've done to this poor man?"

"Give me the bill; I will pay for all the damages."

The captain looked like he was about to explode. His face turned a dark shade of red and his bulging eyes threatened to pop out of their sockets at any time. He had heard enough. He shoved aside the officer who stood in his way and stepped right next to the bed, his overhanging belly pressed against the metal frame. Standing above Eric's face with fists clenched, he shouted, spit coming out of his mouth, "Where do you think you are? In some underdeveloped country or somewhere in the Wild West? You think this is Texas where all you have got to do is flash your money around? You Americans are all the same. You think you can bully your way around with your mighty dollar."

"Alberta."

"What?"

"Where I come from, we consider Alberta to be our Wild West. That's where we keep our oil rigs. I'm Canadian not American."

"Canadian, American, you're all the same. I have heard enough." The captain turned to face the other police officer and howled, "Book him!"

At that very moment the mobile telephone of the man in the grey suit purred softly. He had watched the heated exchange between the two men with a dour, almost blasé expression on his face. He waved off the other two policemen and stepped outside to answer the call. Less than a minute later he popped his head in the door and gestured for the two officers to join him in the hallway for a private talk.

Eric welcomed the interruption. It gave him time to ponder his options. He was in trouble with the law and knew that his attitude had only served to further exacerbate the situation. He debated whether or not he should tell the Turkish police the whole truth. *What do I've to lose if I tell them what I'm really doing in Istanbul? Will they try to stop me or help me out?*

His mind was still reeling, when the officer in the grey suit walked into the room alone. The fact that he had dismissed the other two policemen did not surprise him. He immediately thought of the good cop/bad cop routine. The officer wore the same humorless expression on his face as he glanced around the room like it was the first time he had seen it. With his lips twirled, he pulled a silver case from his pocket and studied its content of unfiltered black Turkish tobacco cigarettes. He tapped the metal case twice and rolled a cigarette with his index finger, hesitated for a moment, and then thought better of it. He quickly snapped the cigarette case shut and put it back inside the side pocket of his perfectly tailored suit jacket. He then leveled his gaze at Eric.

Eric observed the entire act in silence. He had still not decided how he would handle the second part of the police investigation. He assessed the impeccably dressed officer for a second time, considered what he might be willing to reveal to him, and finally nodded to himself indicating that he was now ready to talk. He had decided that the best way to handle his predicament would be to let the truth run its own course, for better or worse.

"I'm Captain Aslan, from Turkey's Counter Terrorism Unit. I must apologize for my colleague's behavior earlier."

Oh great, another police captain. He let an uncomfortable pregnant pause pass, and then broke into a faint grin.

"It's quite alright officer. The man was just doing his job, I suppose," Eric said in a flat voice.

"Well if you want my opinion, I think he went too far with the insults."

"He was provoked," Eric replied taking on a more conciliatory tone.

"You know the strange thing about it, is that in all honesty, he is a gentle soul. I guess that's why his parent named him Sevim. Believe it or not, but his name in English roughly means 'lovable'.

Eric instantly burst out laughing and took an instant liking for the officer's quirky sense of humor. "Let me be straight with you and tell you what really happened out there," he said.

"No need to," Aslan quickly interjected. "I am releasing you. You're a free man, Mr. Martin."

"Really, just like that?"

"Well, not just like that. I received a call from Interpol a moment ago. They are taking you under their care. In fact, Mr. Bartolli personally vouched for you. I don't have a clue what you did for him, but I know Bartolli well. He would never stick his neck out for anyone unless he wanted or needed something really bad. But that does not concern you anymore. One of his agents is on the way to pick you up as we speak."

Eric was mystified, relieved, and pleased in that order. He wanted to know more about the circumstances for his release, but instinctively knew that it would be a big waste of time to try getting any information out of Aslan. He had to accept, for now at least, that for some reason the Turkish police had agreed not to press charges against him.

"I don't know who I must thank the most for my discharge, you or Bartolli, but I want you to know that I will never forget what you did for me today."

"Don't get me wrong, Mr. Martin. I did not do anything special for you. In fact, I placed a very important stipulation in our agreement with Interpol. You have twenty-four hours to leave Turkey or I will personally put you in jail and throw away the keys."

Eric nodded dolefully.

"Got it."

"Good. Have a safe trip home."

Aslan reached into his jacket pocket, and for a moment Eric thought that the anti-terrorism officer had finally given in to his urge for a smoke. Instead, he saw him pull out what looked like a small pendant, and was totally taken by surprise when Aslan handed it to him.

"Before I forget, please take this. The medics found it on the front seat of the van. I don't know who it belongs to, you or the owner of the vehicle, but I figure you will need it more than him. Here, keep it. Consider it a gift, a souvenir if you will of your short visit in Istanbul."

Eric rolled the blue and white bead in his hand. He recognized the amulet by its Turkish name, and remembered seeing it dangling everywhere in the Middle East where good luck was always needed.

Mavi boncuk, the amulet that protects the wearer from the evil eye.

CHAPTER 20

The call to prayer from the mosque nearby echoed in the small hospital room. At that very moment, a ray of sunshine broke through the window and nested its warm shaft of light on Eric's face. He was still in bed, entranced by the melodious chant of the Imam. It rekindled in him memories of a time where everything seemed so easy and simple—of time spent around the kitchen table in Montreal listening to his father recount his incredible adventures back to the good old days in Morocco. In the sunroom of the family summer home in Antibes where, around a simple meal of cheese and wine, the activities for the day ahead were discussed and sometimes argued with gusto. And later on in his office in Toronto, when the main preoccupations at the time were where his next deal would come from or what it would take for his client to buy into his latest high yield debt proposal.

Those days were long gone.

Somehow Eric had lost his joy for life when he decided to take on the job in Casablanca. His stay in Paris had made matters even more taxing. He now realized that Laura had been right all along. He must confront his obsession head on in order to free himself of its entanglements. His salvation was his informant. The problem was that he had lost contact with the only man who could help him find the truth about the trader. Istanbul had turned out to be a nightmare, even greater than he could have ever imagined, and all his efforts now seemed doomed to failure.

Eric was holding in his hand the blue and white amulet in the shape of an eye, when Stephanie barged into the room unannounced. She dropped a heavy shopping bag on the bed and sniffed the air a couple of times before heading straight for the window.

"I hate the smell of tobacco," she bellowed.

"Then you picked the wrong country, and by the way, how about a hello and a how are you?"

"You don't deserve it. You don't know how much shit you caused me back at the office when they found out that you had taken off without warning. Bartolli, my boss and your protector, in case you have forgotten, was beside himself. You, Mr. Martin, made me look like an idiot at the agency. I don't appreciate it one bit. What lousy excuses have you got for yourself?"

"None. I got a phone call from someone who seemed to know a lot about what was going on, and I jumped on the first plane to Istanbul."

"But you could at least have given me the courtesy of letting me know what you were up to. Besides, we had a deal. You were supposed to go back to your normal routine at the bank and let us take care of this matter. Right!!"

"If it's any consolation, you look beautiful when you're mad."

Stephanie threw him a glare that could kill.

"Bartolli was right about you. You're nothing but trouble. You don't even have a clue as to what you're up against. Did you not think in that little brain of yours that this whole thing might have been a trap? That they wanted you here in Istanbul to take care of you once and for all?"

"As a matter of fact, the thought had crossed my mind. But all things considered, I came to the conclusion that it did not really matter. There is no other way to put an end to what these guys are doing; and for that matter, I don't think Interpol has any clue of what's going on either. You told me that much when we met in Antibes."

"You're a bloody banker, for God's sake. The last time I checked, banking was not a contact sport!"

Stephanie stared angrily. A vein in her neck started throbbing. Eric had a way to get under her skin and she knew that she could not allow herself to fall for his taunts again. She swallowed hard to let her heartbeat settle down and clear her mind. *Eric is frustrating, but right about certain things,* she finally admitted to herself. That was the problem with him—maddeningly blind and careless when it came to his own safety, yet extremely perceptive and logical when dissecting thorny issues.

"Let me tell you something that we do know. What you did was utterly stupid. You could have gotten yourself killed. We're here to help you. We're on your side. The enemy is out there. So unless you agree to let us do our job, I will leave you behind here in the care of Sevim and his colleagues. I'm not bluffing Eric."

"If you put it that way, I'd rather be in your care."

"You're a royal pain in the ass, you know. What are you waiting for? Get dressed. I bought you some new clothes; they're in the bag. The ones you were wearing are covered with blood and torn to pieces."

Eric grinned. "Wow, you really meant it. You do want to take care of me." Eric pulled a light blue shirt, khaki cotton trousers, a blazer, and a pair of brown loafers out of the bag. Everything in the bag spelled cool comfort and easy elegance. "And you even picked the right size. I'm impressed."

"Stop with the childish behavior. Get dressed quickly; we must leave this place before Aslan changes his mind. Let's get going. I don't have all day."

"Are you not going to—you know— give me something called privacy?"

Stephanie burst out laughing and almost choked in between a spat of gasping coughs.

"At least I know one other thing about you. You're not only slow to take a hint and totally dense as far as taking instructions goes, but you're also a prude. Stop wasting my time and get dressed. We must get out of here."

"Where are you taking me?"

"To your hotel to get some rest. You have an early flight tomorrow. For your sake, make sure that you're ready at seven o'clock sharp. I will personally drive you to the airport. There, are you happy now?"

Eric nodded without great enthusiasm. He fixed his eyes on Stephanie, signaling a wish to change the tone of the conversation.

"Tell me something, will you? I can't figure it out and this is really bothering me. If they brought me here to get rid of me permanently, as you said, why have they not killed me yet?"

Stephanie wrestled for a moment with how much information she should share with Eric. Aslan had told her about a number of PKK cells that operated out of Istanbul and Ankara. They had not been able to penetrate any of them, but one in particular was rumored to be flushed with cash. According to an informant, this cell had established their center of operations in Istanbul about three years ago. Aslan could not vouch for the veracity of his spy's information, but he suspected that if this terrorist group was sitting on a large stash of money it was most probably derived from some illicit businesses like drug trafficking or even prostitution. He would not be surprised if they had not already laundered some of their money by investing it into legitimate enterprises. While they were not able to make a connection with Eric's trader, the timing of the emergence of a cash rich terrorist cell three years ago and the probability that they would want to recycle their money could not be discounted as a simple coincidence. Like Aslan, Stephanie had her reasons to suspect that something was afoot. And there was also the matter of the man that she shot and killed in Fort Carré. Aslan was able to trace the fingerprints of the dead operative on their massive database of known terrorists. "The man was definitely PKK," he wrote in his email. "But he seemed to be a 'floater' with no strong affiliation or allegiance to any one group in particular. That he belonged to the Istanbul gang at the time of his death was a reasonable assumption, if not a likely possibility," he reported in his email to Interpol.

Stephanie mulled over all the facts they had uncovered during their investigation. But one look at Eric's facial expression convinced her that it was best, at least for the time being, to keep him in the dark. Despite her misgivings, she felt the need to protect Eric by taking him as far away as possible from Istanbul. *Better get him out of here as fast as possible,* she thought, *even if it meant that the case might never be solved as a result.*

"If they have not already killed you, it's because they want or need something from you. Let's suppose for a moment that I believe that your spy is for real. Then in that case, it would make sense for them to follow you closely so that you could lead them to him. In any event, you have blown their cover and now your source will never get close to you if he values his life." Stephanie spoke in a flat monotone voice, preferring to let the plain logic do the convincing.

Eric nodded enigmatically. He had no answer for what he considered having made a huge mistake. His mind was reeling with an odd combination of self-blame and anger. *When will I learn that I'm way over my head and accept help when it's offered to me?*

Stephanie tossed him a glance. She had given Eric only one option. Her patience was being tested as she waited for Eric to come to terms with it.

Eric did not disappoint her.

"Time to pack up and leave this city," he said, his tone somber and tired.

She simply nodded her approval by way of response.

They both kept to their thoughts in the taxi that took them to the hotel. Stephanie was already planning her day ahead. She had to draft a call report for her superiors, send a thank you note to Aslan that reiterated Interpol's strong desire of co-operating closely with the Turkish Anti-Terrorism Unit, and last but not least, as proof of her total devotion to her job— babysit Eric back to Paris. She liked to keep busy. Normally, it gave her a sense of purpose and accomplishment, but this time what she was really doing was trying to avoid thinking about Eric.

Eric was more mystery than puzzle to her, and Stephanie did not like leaving challenges unresolved

Sitting next to Stephanie in the back seat of the white taxicab, Eric kept his eyes shut for most of the ride, heavy with fatigue. He was struggling with the murder of David Luchatel. *How am I going to explain to Judith that her husband died because of what I asked him to do?* He bemoaned.

Stephanie left Eric at the door of his hotel room with instructions to get some rest and a reminder that they had an early flight to Paris in the morning. She stood in the hallway until she heard Eric lock the door with the deadbolt. Satisfied that he had settled in his room for the night, she checked her watch and rushed to her suite at the end of the hallway. She had an important call to make to the office.

Eric removed his sports jacket and slipped silently into his room. His migraine had subsided significantly, but by some strange quirk of the brain, he felt worse because of it. He was painfully aware that a clear head did not necessarily mean a conscience free of remorse. He was alone in his hotel room, but he could sense a presence lurking in the dark.

He sat on the bed, feeling weary and worn-out. His neck and shoulders were sore from the after effect of the violent collision that was, by now, taking its toll on his entire body. But he knew that despite it all, sleep would not come easy that night. He was about to lie down in bed when the vibration of the BlackBerry in his pocket nudged him out of his dark thoughts. He pulled the phone out of its leather pouch and stared at the screen without great interest, his eyes moving up and down at the endless list of emails streaming along. He kept scrolling on and on to bring more and more unread emails into view, all along cursing himself for not having purchased an iPhone with a larger screen.

The vast majority of the emails were from well-wishers who had found out about his sudden resignation from the bank. Most were shocked and saddened by the news, and their good wishes seemed sincere. Others were simply more concerned with their own job security, fearing that a restructuring was in the works, and pointedly asked if he had jumped ship or was pushed out of his job.

He smiled broadly when he clicked on an email from Laura. She wanted to know if he was alright and begged him to give her a call as soon as he had a minute to spare. She had signed off her note with a postscript, "We're worried, please let us know what we can do to help." He made a mental note to contact her as soon as he was settled back in his apartment in Paris. Paul had also sent an email. His message was short, to the point, and with his initials by way of sign off and salutations. It simply read, "I've got news, Istanbul is the key. Call me asap. PM"

When he was done reading, Eric began furiously working the delete button. The procedure had a therapeutic effect on him, as he derived an immense pleasure and great satisfaction from the quick and repetitive process. At the touch of a button, he felt as if his entire troubled past had been instantly erased, just like that, by magic. The whole task took him less than a minute to complete. He then turned his attention to the contact directory and briefly deliberated whether he should wipe it clean as well while he was at it. He stopped what he was doing when his eyes caught the small icons at the top of the screen telling him that he had three voice mails and two unread text messages. All five messages were from his brother and revealed an increasing level of frustration over the course of the recordings. He started dialing Paul's office in Montreal, then thought better of it. "What does it matter what he uncovered in Istanbul. It's of no use to me now," he said aloud before hanging up.

But the Blackberry refused to give him any respite. It purred again as soon as he put it down on the night table. He tried to ignore it, fearing that his brother was trying to reach him again. But the phone just kept on vibrating, relentlessly demanding his attention. He finally gave up and picked up the pestering communication device, wanting to destroy the damn thing.

"I'm very, very upset with you, Monsieur Martin."

Eric recognized the voice instantly—the same accent, the same curt manner, and the same absence of caller identification. His heartbeat increased tenfold and his headache came back with a vengeance.

"I gave you very specific instructions to wait for my call. And what did you do?" the caller hissed.

"I waited for you, but your call never came," Eric replied.

"Two days, Monsieur Martin. Wait two days for my call—that's all you had to do. But no, that was too difficult for you. You had to give them chase on your own."

"I did not go after them. They were the ones who were following me. I recognized one of them as the man who tried to kill me in Antibes. So I took my chances to get even with the bastard."

"I don't care how you feel about this guy. I don't even care if you get killed, Monsieur Martin. But when you decided 'to take your chances' as you so aptly put it, did you not think for a moment what that meant for me? Did you not realize that you were putting my life at risk?"

"How so?"

"This was a big mistake. I should never have contacted you in the first place. If you can't see how you were endangering my life by doing what you did, it's hopeless. This whole stupid thing has been a great waste of my time. Good-bye, Monsieur Martin."

"Wait. Wait. Listen to me. You got it all wrong. You have to understand that they must have known that I was in Istanbul. They were waiting for me and must have been following me from the moment I landed. Somehow, they must have figured out that someone was helping me out. The good news in all of that is that they did not kill me when they had the opportunity. And the reasons are obvious. Think about it. They must not know who you are, and they don't know how much you told me about them. They must also be thinking that maybe others are also in the know. They are looking for you mister."

The phone went suddenly silent. Time kept ticking away and still no sound came from the other end of the line. A minute passed, then two. At the count of three the voice came back, preceded by a nervous cough.

"You're the only one who could lead them to me. I think it's best that we part ways right now."

"Wait. I can make this worthwhile for you. Just name your price."

The caller's voice took an angry tone.

"All you can think about is money. You really believe that I'm doing this for money? I've got news for you. There are lots of easier ways to make a living. No sir, money has nothing to do with it, but you would not understand."

"Try me, I might surprise you."

The caller appeared to hesitate for a moment. His well-honed instincts as a seasoned terrorist screamed to put an immediate end to the conversation. But he knew that he had gone too far. Eric had touched a sensitive chord by questioning his integrity, and this was something he felt very strongly about. He would never allow anyone to question his lifelong commitment to his people's aspiration for an independent Kurdish homeland.

"The root cause of all our problems is money—too much money, as a matter of fact. All the troubles started with that evil foreign woman and her damn computer program. My leaders seemed to lose their will to fight the moment she joined our group. They are more interested in getting rich than fighting for the freedom of the Kurdish people."

Eric's senses were alight with anticipation. A real opportunity was presenting itself out of the blue. The man was still talking. If he played his cards right, he might be able to convince him to tell him more and find out, once and for all, whether his suspicions were well-founded.

"What woman? What program? What happened?" he asked in quick succession, sounding more eager than he intended to.

"Never mind, forget what I said. This will not get us anywhere except to draw trouble to myself."

"But I can help you get rid of that woman and her computer program. You have to understand, this is also very personal for me. Let me you tell a story about my experience in Casablanca."

For the next twenty minutes Eric did all the talking. He spoke about how he had been lured to work for a boutique investment firm in Morocco, how they used him to get what they wanted, and what happened as soon as they got hold of the man that had developed the sophisticated predictive algorithm. He ended his story by revealing his suspicions about the fate of the algorithm and how it was being employed by a high-speed trader.

The caller on the other end of the line listened carefully to Eric's story. He did not interrupt or seek further clarification, to the point that Eric wondered whether he had done the right thing by confiding so much to a total stranger. When he was finished relating his story, there was another long, silent pause. The response the caller finally gave him was more than he could have bargained for.

"We can't discuss this anymore over the phone. It's not safe. Take the first flight to Nevsehir tonight. We can meet there—and who knows, I might change my mind and reciprocate with the information you seek. But if I find out that you have not been careful and allowed someone to follow you, the meeting is off and you will never hear from me again."

"I will be very careful, trust me," Eric said.

CHAPTER 21

Fidgeting at the back of the taxicab, Stephanie gave a dirty look to the driver who was ogling her in his rear view mirror. She had no patience for this sort of thing. And now was certainly not the right time. It was dawn, the sun was barely breaking above the Bosphorus, and she was in a hurry. She rolled down the window, filling her lungs with fresh air that was heavy with the scent of the sea. All was peaceful and quiet as the taxi sped through the sleeping city. A cool breeze caressed her face and gently loosened her hair. Across the strait, the gentle waves were the color of ripe tangerines. In another time and in another place, she would have taken the opportunity to work out the tension straining her neck and shoulders and suck in a few more deep breaths to clear her mind of all negative thoughts. But on this day, she was incapable of letting go. She flipped her hair away from her face and crossed her arms across her chest. Istanbul was going through its daily renaissance ritual, but Stephanie was having none of it.

The taxicab's tires screeched to a sudden halt at an intersection.

"Careful. Will you!" A startled Stephanie yelled at the driver.

"Sorry madam, I thought I had enough time to beat the red light."

Stephanie thinned her lips. "I know I told you I was in a hurry to get to the airport, but I would like to make it in one piece, if you don't mind."

The driver grumbled something under his breath and gunned his vehicle as soon as the light turned to green. The streets of Istanbul were empty at this very early hour of the day. This was when the bearded taxi driver liked his job and the city the best. No traffic, no sign of the police anywhere, and two quick fares to-and-from Ataturk airport and his daily quota would be a thing of the past. He could afford to spend the rest of day with his wife, or better still, join his friends for a game of backgammon at the local drinking hole. Yet he had another reason to be happy. The pretty passenger seated just behind him had agreed to pay for the return fare—and to top it off, with a generous tip if he made it to the airport in half an hour or less. He could not believe his good luck. All he had to do was pick up another passenger wanting to go to the city, and he could take the next morning off as well.

The sign pointing in the direction of Atatürk airport whizzed by the passenger window, and Stephanie finally accepted the inescapable reality of her predicament—in a foreign country, and in a city where she barely knew her way around, it would be virtually impossible to find Eric without any help. She could sense her frustration turning into anger. Twice she had been entrusted with a simple task, and twice she had failed. But her incompetence, if that's what it was, was not a valid excuse. Despite all her misgivings, her duty was to let Bartolli know as soon as possible what was going on in Istanbul.

"What! You lost him again?" Bartolli screamed over the phone.

Stephanie stifled her annoyance and let her silence smother her tone. After a short pause, she managed to clear her mind, and in a level voice gave a detailed account of what happened. "He looked pretty beat up when I picked him up from the hospital yesterday. I immediately took him back to his hotel room and made sure that he was settled in for the night. But when I went back to check on him, he was no longer there. I looked everywhere for him in the hotel, thinking that perhaps he went to grab something to eat. But I could not find him, and no one had seen him."

Stephanie paused for a moment and swallowed hard, attempting to gather the courage to deliver the final piece of information to her superior. "I'm afraid he's taken off after the trader on his own again."

"This is becoming a bad habit, Stephanie. How can he do that to you twice in a row, just like that? Are you getting soft or something?"

Stephanie's temper flared up immediately. "You want to take me off the case?"

"No, don't be silly. It's just that it's so unlike you to make the same mistake twice. You're so obsessively thorough."

"Anal. Just say it, that's what you think I am. But it won't happen again, trust me on this. This guy pissed me off so much that if I catch him right now I will cut off his manhood."

"Easy there tiger, let's think through this rationally. Where are you now?"

"I'm on my way to the airport."

"You think he's flying out of the country."

"I don't know, but I really hope so for his own sake. How he survived the crash virtually unscathed is unbelievable." Stephanie said, feeling suddenly uncomfortable.

She was clearly puzzled by what caused her to express any concern for Eric. She should still be raving mad for what he had done to her. Feeling sorry for him seemed so out of character—such a strange thing for her to do.

But for now, Bartolli's silence was telling. She could hear him sighing on the phone and knew by experience that this was a sure sign that his patience was just about to run out. She had to regroup and get back on track and finish her story quickly or else more trouble would be coming her way.

"When I could not find him in the hotel, I stepped outside to talk to the drivers of the taxis parked across the street. One of them told me that he saw a man fitting the description of Eric jump in the cab just ahead of him, and later on heard on the radio the driver give the dispatcher the airport as destination of his fare." She paused for a beat, waiting for Bartolli's reaction, hoping for the best.

"Good. Very good. You may have a chance to catch up with him."

"Not a chance in a million years, I'm afraid. He's got a three hour head start on me. My only hope is to get permission to take a peek at the flight manifests and find out where he's headed—assuming, of course, that he booked the flight under his real name."

"Did you contact Aslan to get you access to the manifests?"

"Yes, but he won't help me unless you speak to him first. Why he would not trust me is beyond me. It must be a male thing."

Bartolli ignored the last remark. "I will call him right away. Consider it done. Let's hope that Eric has decided to go home on his own. And, by the way, is he fitted?"

"Yes, but I'm not getting anything."

"Let's hope we have better luck with the manifests."

Bartolli breathed heavily and ended up coughing a couple of times."I need you to do something for me while you're in Istanbul," he added cautiously. "Now listen carefully and don't scream at me when I tell you what I want you to do. This is a direct order from your superior."

Stephanie pressed the phone on her ear, fearing the worse. She had heard that nervous cough and formal tone in his voice before. This was the way he delivered all his bad news to her.

Bartolli cleared his throat a few more times and then added. "You're going to take what I have to tell you like a pro. Are you cool with that?"

"Stop with the drama already, and give it to me straight. I'm not a flower child for God's sake. What's on your mind boss," Stephanie said.

"Well, it's like exchanging one favor for another. I would like you to pick up Jules at the airport and take him to Aslan."

"What!!!" It was Stephanie's turn to scream. "Another babysitting job? Is that why you sent me here? Is that what you think of me—a bloody babysitter? You must be joking!"

"Calm down Stephanie. Listen to me, please. Jules has done an excellent job of figuring out what Eric's trader did to hide his handy work. It was so clever and so complex and convoluted, it boggled my mind. I still don't understand it all despite having spent countless hours with Jules, who tried his best to simplify it for me. The trader is a genius, but thank God we also have a genius on our staff. There is still a lot of work to be done, but Jules may have found a good lead. And now we need the help of the Turkish Special IT unit to fill in some of the blanks. Aslan is very excited about Jules' findings, and he wants him here to work with his people."

"But what do you need me for? I'm not a chauffeur, for God's sake."

"I talked to him before he left. He is fully briefed about his mission. He is not there to cramp your style. I just want to make sure that he has a field agent on the spot to go to and help him if necessary. That's all."

"That's all?"

"That's it. Now get busy finding Eric. We need to catch up with him before he gets into more trouble."

Two hours later, Stephanie had still not found any trace of Eric. She had spent most of her time scouring the entire length of the departure concourse, mingling along the way with the passengers waiting in line. She stopped at the boarding stations of every foreign airline, Eric's picture in hand on her smart phone, to enquire if, by any chance, anyone had seen him. She then climbed up the stairs that led to the footbridge overlooking the departure lounge and spent a long time scrutinizing the face of every man that bore the slightest resemblance to Eric. She even used her badge a couple of times, bluffing her way to order patrolling customs officers to keep an eye open for Eric and to report to her immediately when they spotted him, knowing full well that she had no authority in Turkey. "It's a matter of national security," she told them to make her request sound official.

In spite of everything, she came up empty-handed. All her efforts to find Eric wound up heightening her level of frustration by more than she cared to handle. And that was when she started to doubt herself. *What if this is all just a decoy—a way for Eric to throw me off course while he remains in town to give chase to the men who shot at him? What if his spy had told him where to find them?* Her mind was reeling from one possibility to another, from one devious scenario to a string of even more cunning tricks played on her by Eric—a man who, in her opinion, was possessed with a very unhealthy fixation. *Eric is really starting to annoy me in a big way.* She cringed at the mere thought of his tricks.

There was only one thing left for her to do at that point. She snatched her phone from its leather case attached to her belt and dialed a long distance number. The phone rang once.

"Mr. Paul Martin, I'm Stephanie Brulé, how are you sir?"

"Fine. What is it you are selling?" Paul replied grouchily.

"Nothing sir. I'm sorry I did not introduce myself properly. I'm special agent Brulé, Interpol. The reason for my call is that I'm looking for your brother Eric. Have you heard from him recently?"

"No."

"I see. Do you have any idea where I may find him?"

Paul gave the same monosyllable answer. "No."

Stephanie realized that talking with Paul was going to be a waste of time. So she tried to end the conversation.

"Well if he should contact you, could you please call this number and ask for me or Mr. Bartolli. It is very important that we speak to him. We have uncovered new data that will interest him greatly."

To her surprise Paul Martin's voice suddenly came alive.

"You work with Bartolli?" He asked, his voice now sounding more crisp and clear.

"Yes, he is my boss."

"The Bartolli who helped my brother in Morocco?"

"Yes, the one and only one in the organization."

"In that case, let me fill you in with what I know. It's not much, but who knows, it might help you. Eric asked me to look into certain documents and data for him. He wanted to know their origins. I may have found something, and I have been looking for him since yesterday to let him know. Quite frankly, I'm very concerned that he might be in some sort of trouble. I tried calling him at his office and on his cell, and left several voice and text messages, but nothing so far. All I've been getting for the past two days is total radio silence and his voice mail box. I even called the Canadian Embassy in Ankara for assistance. They told me to contact the local police. So much for our tax dollars in action, wouldn't you say?"

Stephanie hesitated, and then said, "Mr. Martin, does the information you have uncovered have anything to do with Istanbul?"

"Yes, how did you guess?" Paul quickly replied.

"This is the reason why I'm in Istanbul right now. We too think that Istanbul is the key, and we want to help him."

"I see, all roads lead to Istanbul. It's hardly surprising; the city was also built on top of seven hills. Sorry for the cliché, Stephanie, but it increasingly looks like history is repeating itself."

"So it seems," Stephanie said. "It's critically important that we find Eric as soon as possible. Please call me as soon as you get wind of his whereabouts. And yes, you're absolutely right to worry about him. I'm afraid that he could be in serious trouble if he insists on doing it alone."

Stephanie shoved her cell back in its leather case, thinking that the phone call had not been a total waste of her time after all. Her conversation with Paul had helped her gain some insight into Eric's motivation. The truth was that Eric did not entirely trust Interpol with the data he had uncovered. He had used his brother as a backup Plan B. Eric's lack of confidence in the agency did not shock or even surprise her—he was known to like doing things his own way, and more to the point, his past experiences with Interpol had not been exemplary. But the implications of his sudden disappearance were more profound and personal this time out. She too had to face the fact that Eric harbored certain doubts about her as well. That realization hurt even more than she cared to admit to herself. She made a mental note of this new revelation for her next encounter with Eric, and made up her mind about what to do next.

"I have wasted enough time looking for him this morning," she muttered while glancing at her watch. She was a good half an hour late for her next assignment. She threw a quick glance around and immediately spotted the elevators leading down to the arrival lounge.

This time she got lucky.

Jules Betton was a good foot taller than most people, and his bushy red hair made him an easy target to spot. What she did not expect, however, was the way that he was dressed. *The man is from another planet,* she immediately thought at the sight of the tall, lanky man who had both hands gesticulating in the air to catch her attention. She suppressed a laugh, and remained riveted on the spot while watching him make his way toward her through the crowd. He had on a safari shirt, a pair of khaki Bermuda shorts, long brown socks rolled up to knee level, heavy tracking boots on his feet, a knapsack over his shoulder, and a large money belt around his waist. *My God, all he needs now is a Tilley hat and a butterfly net and he would fit the part perfectly,* she chuckled under her breath.

Jules Betton rushed to greet her with outstretched arms.

"Don't," she said, "a simple hello will do."

Jules Betton was taken aback and tried to hide his disappointment, not very successfully as it turned out.

"I told you we would end up together in some exotic place," he said with a wide grin pasted on his face.

But his attempt at humor fell flat on Stephanie's ears.

"Let's get a couple of things straight. As long as you're in Istanbul I'm your boss and you will do what I tell you to do. Got that?"

"Yes ma'am," he replied, his grin now long gone.

"Secondly you're going to stop calling me ma'am. I'm not your mother, and I have a name. Sarcasm does not suit you."

"OK, Stephanie."

"Thirdly, you're going to go to the bathroom over there and change out of this ridiculous outfit. And lastly, while you're working in Turkey you will keep your mouth shut and your ears and your eyes wide open. If you hear or find out anything about the case we are working on, you will call me immediately and speak to no one else about it until I give you my permission. Is that clear?"

She stared him down as he opened his mouth, about to protest.

"Good. Now go get changed while I get a cab to take us to Aslan."

Jules nodded in agreement, and then blurted out in a single long breath, "No need for a cab. Aslan is here. He was looking for you and left a few minutes ago to take care of some urgent business. Anyway, he told me that he would be waiting for us in the security office on the second floor."

Moments later, Stephanie and Jules Betton were standing in the cramped airport security quarters, surrounded by three police officers in navy-blue uniforms, and Aslan. All four men had the same blank, humorless expressions on their faces. No one greeted them when they walked into the office. They just kept staring at her, looking rather uncomfortable. *It must be the female factor again*, she mused. So she took the initiative and spoke first.

"Hi boys," she said, her gaze held on Aslan, who held a silver cigarette case in his hand. "You already met Jules Betton. I guess there is no need to introduce him to you?"

"That's right; I met him downstairs after he cleared customs. We chatted briefly while waiting for you, and I complimented him on his work," Aslan replied.

"That's for sure. He has done a great job, and I hope that with your co-operation we will be able to get to the bottom of this case quickly. At least, that's what I'm hoping for. But for now, I need a little favor."

Aslan pulled out a piece of paper from the breast pocket of his perfectly tailored jacket, tapped the document with his fingers a couple of times, and then said, "Your little friend has decided to challenge me, it seems."

"How so?"

"Well, either he thinks I did not mean what I said or he wants to play the tourist while he is in Turkey."

"Aslan you're not making any sense. What's going on? What is it you are holding in your hands?"

Aslan glanced around the room and exchanged rapid glances with the other three police officers. They seemed to be enjoying the way he was putting the foreign woman back in her place.

Aslan cracked a barely visible smile under his moustache and then said, "Here is the flight manifest you want. Eric was on a Turkish airline flight that landed in Cappadocia over an hour ago."

CHAPTER 22

Yilmaz was the happiest man on the planet the day his young, beautiful bride held his hand and made her vows of eternal love, devotion, and fidelity. Being married to the favorite daughter of a wealthy merchant from Iznik was indeed a dream come true for the boyish looking newlywed. On that afternoon, he could finally look forward to a happy life, reassured by the thought that a bright and very comfortable future was ahead of him.

The wedding was a grandiose affair. The wealthiest and most powerful families in all of Turkey had attended the service and paid their homage to the bride's father. The large vaulted reception hall where the exchange of vows took place was full to capacity. More than a thousand guests had crammed the interior of the palatial chamber with walls carved in white marble. Some had traveled from as far as Van in Eastern Anatolia and Kastamonu near the Black Sea to honor the bride and the groom on their special day.

"You deserve this blessing, my son, for you've worked so hard," his mother had whispered in his ear moments before the wedding ceremony. And Yilmaz had walked tall and proud, his head full of a sense of entitlement, as he greeted the guests with his pretty bride at his side.

Yilmaz was the first born son of a bookkeeper who had worked all of his life for the father of the bride. While it was in her father's office that the two young lovers had met for the first time, it was in the football field that their romance flourished. For Yilmaz was the star in a semi-professional football league. He was very well-liked by his coaches, envied by his teammates, and admired by his fans. He had the knack of being always at the right place at the right time, ready for a breakaway from one end to the other end of the football field. He could dribble the ball at breathtaking speed through the slightest opening in the defence line, and score goals in a 'banana kick' like fashion from angles that everyone would have thought impossible. It was said that he was born with a football at his feet, and scouts from the Turkish Super League such as *Besiktaş J.K.* of Istanbul and *Trabzonspor* of Trabzon who followed every one of his games closely, certainly agreed with that assessment.

Yilmaz reveled in his success, confident that a lucrative contract in the major league would be waiting for him at the end of the season. Life was indeed full of great promise for the young Yilmaz, if it were not for the fact that fate soon struck twice.

Shortly after their magical wedding, his mother-in-law succumbed to a mysterious illness, and less than six months later her widowed husband took a much younger woman as a wife. A new, favorite girl was born soon after from that union, and Yilmaz's wife stopped receiving her father's generous allowance that helped the young couple maintain their opulent lifestyle.

At about the same time, in a strange coincidence that could only be explained by bad karma, the football career of Yilmaz took a turn for the worse. One day, his team was protecting a one-goal lead with less than five minutes on the clock, and the coach had left Yilmaz on the field to showcase his defensive skills to the scouts in attendance. The stakes were high; the winner of the match would have earned a spot in the season end championship game. Yilmaz responded in kind, and took matters in his own hands, playing like a one-man team. He seemed to be everywhere at once, constantly frustrating the offensive drive of the other team. The crowd loved it, cheering loudly every time he took possession of the ball. And the reaction of the fans energized him even more.

That's when disaster struck for the second time.

He never saw it coming, his mind and heart caught in his own frenetic display of football prowess. A short, stocky defensive mid-fielder had tackled him from behind, feet and cleats crushing and twisting his knees to the ground. Agonizing in pain, he lay sprawled on the grassy ground for a long time. The crowd gave him a standing ovation when he was carried off the playing field on a stretcher. The team went on to win the qualifying game and prevailed in the championship match without him. He was never cheered by an adoring crowd or played another game of football again. The fabulous football career never materialized.

Fifteen years later, Yilmaz had lost more than his youthful exuberance and athletic build—slightly overweight and somewhat paunchy at the waistline, he was now in the habit of dragging his feet as he made the rounds along the long corridor of Atatürk airport. He felt that life had not been kind to him, even though his wife remained loyal at his side after the accident. She gave him three beautiful daughters and kept her silence when he declined her father's job offer. But that was where she drew the line. She was her father's daughter, after all. Maintaining appearances was paramount. She would not have it any other way, even if Yilmaz had a hard time keeping up with her insatiable demands for expensive designer clothes and fine jewelry. And, as it turned out, his three daughters had not only inherited their mother's good looks, but also shared her passion for the finer things in life.

Yilmaz was always the first one to volunteer for overtime work to supplement his modest wages as a police lieutenant, and because this was never enough for his wife and daughters' ever increasing needs, he also took a second job as a night security guard. So when a stranger approached him one day with an envelope full of cash and a request to *not look too closely* at a package about to clear customs, he took it gladly. He asked no questions again, the next time he was asked to help expedite the clearance of an airline passenger. He just took the envelope, never bothering to count the money inside, and gave it to his wife.

After dropping his lunch bag in the airport security office on the second floor, at the break of dawn that morning he was approached by a man who gave him a very thin envelope. There was no cash in it this time—just a photograph of a foreign-looking man and a slip of paper with a handwritten phone number.

"If you see this man, call the number in the envelope and you will be generously rewarded," the man said, his eyes constantly sweeping the hallway.

Yilmaz did not like the way the request had been made. Money was always paid up front. *This change in procedure shows a certain lack of trust,* he thought, and he briefly contemplated declining the proposition altogether. However upon further reflection, he thought it would be best to look for the man in the photograph. The reward could be substantial after all.

Despite the early hour of the day, the airport was already bursting with energy. Turkey was a popular tourist destination, and a steady flow of visitors kept the understaffed airport personnel hectically busy all the time. Yilmaz walked the entire length of the airport in short, measured strides, while paying special attention to every man that crossed his line of sight. Once in a while he would stop to take another look at the photograph, and once satisfied that it did not match the face of the man who just walked by him, he would resume his search as if he were on regular police patrol. The airport was a vast complex of long interconnecting corridors, and after forty minutes of non-stop walking, his knees started to hurt. He stopped in front of the Turkish airline ticket booth and leaned against the counter to rest his legs. About a dozen or so travelers were waiting in line, but he paid little attention to them while he rubbed his sore knees. A young, smiling couple—obviously in love—suddenly appeared in front of him to ask for directions. Yilmaz looked up, slightly startled, and immediately straightened his back when he noticed the beautiful young woman staring at him. He watched the couple walk away holding hands, with more than a resentful stare.

Someone asking for a return ticket in English snapped his attention away from the young couple. When the man turned sideways to pick up his passport and airline tickets, he immediately recognized Eric. Despite all the cuts and dark bruises somewhat altering his facial features, there was no doubt in his mind that the man standing at the ticket counter was the same person in the photograph.

For Yilmaz this was also a moment of decision.

A phone call would fulfil my end of the bargain, but will the reward be forthcoming? He held his gaze on Eric for a moment, his mind wrestling with the few options available to him. Again, the appeal of a hefty reward overcame any resistance he might have had. He followed Eric at a safe distance and watched him as he cleared the security scanner. Then he waited until he saw Eric board the airplane. At that point, he pulled the phone from his pocket and dialed the number written on the piece of paper. *That way,* he thought, *I've done what I was asked to do.* But by letting Eric board the plane, he had hedged his bet. "Just in case the man decides to renege on the reward," he chuckled, as he listened to the phone ringing.

The man on the phone was pleased with the news. He made him repeat the destination and the flight number twice, and thanked him with the promise that a very thick envelope would be waiting for him in his car. He was never questioned about the veracity of his claim. *A sure sign that I have not lost my handlers' confidence,* he thought with more relief than satisfaction.

He was about to leave the departure lounge, pleased with himself, when he felt a tap on his right shoulder. He turned to see his superior eyeing him strangely. His immediate reaction was one of fright of being caught. He feared that somehow his superior might have overheard his conversation. His stomach tightened into a knot and he started to cough loudly.

"What's wrong with you, Yilmaz?" Are you sick or something?"

"No, I'm alright; it's just my wife's cooking. You know how lousy a cook she is." Yilmaz made up the quick excuse, hoping that it would ring true.

"Oh, I understand, my poor Yilmaz. I hope you feel better soon because I need you. I have a top priority job for you. Counter-terrorism called a moment ago. They want us to immediately gather the passenger manifests of all the inbound and outbound flights. Someone by the name of Aslan is on his way as we speak to collect them."

"Do we know what they are looking for?" Yilmaz asked, feeling somewhat relieved.

"A foreigner I think. But that's all I could pull out of them. These guys at HQ are not the chatty type, if you know what I mean."

"I will get on with it right away. We don't want this Aslan poking his nose around here too long." The two men laughed as they headed in opposite directions.

Later on, as Yilmaz observed the Interpol agent standing in the airport security office, he wondered why her male colleague with the messy red hair was not in charge of the investigation. She looked fearless when she burst into the office, alone among four men. Not once did she pay any attention to him. He disliked her tone and the cavalier way she addressed the counter-terrorism officer. But he gained respect for Aslan as he stood his ground, taking his time to give her the information she so disrespectfully demanded. Then another more interesting thought crossed his mind. *Perhaps his handlers might also want to know that Interpol was after their man. Eric Martin is the target of an international man hunt. Who knows what that piece of information could be worth?* Yilmaz speculated with glee.

CHAPTER 23

Nevsehir, Central Anatolia (Cappadocia)

Eric was greeted in Cappadocia by a bright, blinding sun and a gust of dry desert heat. He closed his eyes for a moment and filled his nostrils with the scent of the arid land which morphed into a sapphire sky in the distant horizon. He loved the feeling of burning heat on his face and the acrid taste in his dry mouth. It felt like home, where he was born—a modest dwelling on a small triangular piece of land in the northern tip of Africa, where he discovered his passion for the desert. As mariners love to sail the sea, with nothing and no one in sight but the ebb and flow of undulating waves, so he loved to roam the parched wilderness with the sun and the solitude as his only companions. There was never any doubt in his mind that he would one day return to this barren expanse of sand and shifting dunes on the edge of the Sahara. It was in that bleak land that his soul belonged. After all, he had often heard the wind whisper in his ear that the nomad always found his way back to his tribe. It was not just a matter of survival, more a way of life, where authenticity and faithfulness meant everything.

The road to Nevsehir—or Nyssa, as the picturesque town was called in antiquity—snaked down a valley in the middle of a wide area of fairly flat, sun-baked land. There was not an ounce of shade anywhere in this stark lunar landscape, and the temperature inside the rental car kept rising a degree or two at every turn of the road. He drove with his window wide open and his arm rested on the sill. To him, air conditioning was an unnatural invention of modern times—definitely not something he would ever contemplate using. Once in a while he would stick his neck out the window in a show of defiance against the elements, and then he would shake his head from side to side, letting the hot wind brush his hair back. This was something he had often done as a child to cool himself off while his father drove his brother and him to town in the deep south of Morocco.

After a couple of miles, he swerved off the main road and turned onto a gravel trail that led to a plateau populated by a remarkable array of conical pillars, mushroom- and pedestal-shaped rock formations. He glanced at his watch and gave himself a fifteen minute break. *Just enough time to get a quick desert fix*, he reflected. At one point, the winding trail became more uneven and challenging as it steepened sharply around a jagged ridge. The rental car swerved and bounced around widely under a cloud of dust while he navigated his way through a cluster of massive rock cones. On at least three separate occasions, he almost lost control of the vehicle in the fine sand that blanketed the twisting incline. But he kept on driving, drawn by the air of mystery that pervaded Cappadocia with its natural rock statues and huge expanses of silence.

The dirt path was narrower than a mule trail when Eric finally acknowledged the impasse. He slammed on the brakes and parked the vehicle under a phallic looking rock structure that stretched at least one hundred feet into the sky. He climbed out of the car and took a few tentative steps towards the edge of the ridge. A deep layer of sand, warm to the feet, covered the grounds, and he firmly planted his feet in it every step of the way as he carefully descended the steep slope. By the time he reached the bottom the sun was fast approaching its zenith, and he wished he had thought of bringing a bottle of mineral water with him. It had taken him almost half an hour to reach the flat terrain spiked with magnificent cone shaped pillars. He wiped the sweat off his forehead and gazed around at the incredible sight of sensuous rock formations that stretched as far as the eye could see. Before him was an astonishing landscape of elongated, golden-beige obelisks capped with large bulbs, majestic honeycomb cliffs, and towering pedestal rock columns topped by basalt stone that defied the law of gravity. The remarkable open-air sculpture museum, chiseled by Mother Nature herself, took his breath away.

"Amazing, isn't it?"

The sound of the voice startled Eric. He whipped his head around to see a short, bearded man standing a few feet behind him. He was smiling at him while keeping an eye on a small group of hikers who were precariously making their way down the steep cliff. By the look of things, Eric judged the man to be one of the many tourist guides that abound in the region. One by one the rest of the group reached the bottom of the escarpment, and the guide handed them some water bottles, which they immediately gulped down under the shelter of a giant mushroom-shaped rock.

"Beautiful, don't you think?" the guide asked again.

Eric slowly exhaled, letting the tension in his body dissipate. He cracked a thin smile and gave the guide a guarded one-word answer.

"Breathtaking," he simply said.

The guide made no attempt to move closer, sensing Eric's unease.

"The elongated, capped-cone structures you were staring at were called 'fairy chimneys' by the early inhabitants of this region because they believed that they were the chimneys of fairies who lived underground."

The guide gave Eric a reassuring smile, and without waiting for his response, turned his attention to the group of hikers who had not yet fully recovered from their descent.

"Folks, this is nature's gift to the world. Look at it. Admire its sense of harmony. Absorb its positive energy. Touch its spirit. This is what real art ought to be. This is the work of nature at its finest. You will never see anything more beautiful anywhere on the planet."

He stopped to sip some water from a bottle, wiped his mouth with the back of his hand, and smiled broadly. "Now, please look at the snow-capped mountain looming in the horizon on your right. In fact, it is not a mountain in the strictest term of the word, but a gigantic volcano called *Erciyes*. This is where everything you see before your eyes today was created some thirty million years ago when erupting volcanoes, including that one, blanketed Cappadocia with ash some forty to fifty meters thick. Over time the ash solidified into a soft, easily eroded, volcanic stone called 'tuff', superimposed in places with layers of much harder lava rocks. And then nature began its wondrous work. It took her thousands of years with the help of rain, wind, and flowing rivers to carve out valleys, canyons, and of course those amazing statues. It may have taken her a very long time to get it done, you might say, but what a masterpiece she created in the end. Would you not agree with me?"

The guide took a deep breath, nodding his head up and down. He may have told the same tale a thousand times in five different languages, yet his enthusiasm for Cappadocia was as fresh and fervent as the first time. He paused briefly to catch his breath and then went on, more passionate than ever, telling his incredible story.

"Erosion shaped the incredible moon-like landscape of Cappadocia, but man also had a hand in this wondrous work. If you take a closer look at the cone-shaped formations over there, you will see that they are honeycombed with caves that were carved out of the rock by the first settlers in the region during prehistoric times. Tomorrow we will drive to *Derinkuyu,* about thirty kilometers south of Nevsehir, where we will visit the underground cities excavated by the Hittites and later on expanded by the early Christians who sought temporary shelter from the persecution of Roman soldiers. Just imagine subterranean cities extending seven and eight levels into the earth, carved from the soft volcanic tuff. Entire cities hidden underground with a network of caves, tunnels, living quarters, storehouses, wine presses, stables, kitchens, and even churches, dug into the soft stone so that the inhabitants could hide away for months at a time from the Roman soldiers who were persecuting them. Folks, another fascinating adventure awaits you tomorrow, but first let's take a closer look at the amazing site surrounding you."

The mention of Nevsehir electrified Eric, jolting his mind to what brought him to this part of the world in the first place. He saluted the guide with a brief gesture of the hand and rushed back to his vehicle. The side trip to the plateau had taken him a lot longer than he expected. What he initially took as a minor distraction was, in fact, not something he could have resisted. The inner urge to set foot on the stark expanse of land full of majestic rock sculptures was simply too strong. It reminded him of the gut-wrenching calling he had once felt at the sight of an oasis near Marrakech.

It was the same instinctive reasoning that made him sneak away from Istanbul without telling Stephanie. He appreciated her help and trusted her, but deep down he felt it was something he had to do alone. Besides, Eric was sure that his contact would never reveal himself if he found out that he had involved Interpol. "Stephanie will simply have to wait," he muttered under his breath, shrugging off any guilt he might have felt at the moment.

As he turned the ignition key, a man ambled up by the passenger side of the vehicle and tapped on the window. Eric's heart missed a beat. He was at the wheel, engine running, and for an instant thought of gunning the car. He thought better of it and remained frozen in his seat, his hands firmly holding onto the steering wheel. The man tapped on the window for a second time. The knocks were more insistent and reverberated loudly inside the car. He took a deep breath and furtively glanced at the intruder from the corner of one eye. It took him a second to realize his mistake and smiled broadly when he reached out across the passenger seat to lower the window.

"Are you alright? You left in such a hurry that I thought you must not be feeling well," the guide said grinning warmly. "One ought to be very careful with the sun at this time of the day, you know. I brought you a bottle of mineral water just in case."

"Thank you. That was very kind of you, but you didn't have to do that. I'm fine, really. I 'm just late for an appointment," Eric replied, feeling more at ease.

The guide gazed at Eric, unconvinced by his explanation. He pulled the cold water bottle from his back pack and handed it over to Eric.

"Here take it anyway, you might need it."

Eric thanked the guide and drove away in a cloud of dust. The guide waved at him and waited until Eric's car disappeared around a bend in the road to pull his cell phone from his knapsack.

Eric glanced a couple of times in his rear view mirror as he gunned the rental car along the dirt road. *What a nice guy*, he thought, as he manoeuvred the car along the winding path. When he reached the main road, he pulled over at the intersection and switched the engine off. He spent several minutes staring at the vast, barren wasteland inhabited by majestic stone structures that seemed to reach for the sky under the glaring sun. But mostly, he listened to the sound of the wind and watched the flow of vehicles that whizzed by him.

Reassured that no one had followed him, he kick-started the engine and pressed hard on the gas pedal. He was heading for Nevsehir, guided by the GPS attached to the dashboard. He encountered heavier traffic as he neared the town. The landscape seemed less desolate with its rich fields of sunflowers and sugar beets. He was back on track and getting closer to his destination. In a short while he would meet his informant; and this time, he was determined to find out once and for all the name and location of the trader. He had pushed the man as hard as he could to get him to agree to a face-to-face meeting. But that was only half the battle. More than ever, he now had to find a way to get him to talk.

By most accounts, Eric should have been satisfied with the way his escape from Istanbul to Cappadocia had unfolded. Yet, behind the wheel he could not put away that nagging feeling that all was not well. He could not put his finger on the reason for his misgivings. To reassure himself, he went over all the precautions he had taken so far. He had been extremely careful and alert leaving Istanbul. He had exited the hotel at dawn, using the rear entrance so as not to be seen by the staff. Once in the taxi cab, he made sure they were safely out of earshot before telling the driver that he wanted to go to the airport. He had briefly considered leaving a note for Stephanie, to apologize for taking off on her for a second time without warning—and then thought better of it, fearing that she might find the note before he had a chance to catch his flight out of Istanbul.

At the airport he had been even more vigilant, constantly scanning his surroundings to make sure that no one was following him. He treated every glance in his direction suspiciously until he was satisfied that it was only an innocuous fleeting gaze by an innocent traveler. The only time he felt somewhat apprehensive was when a policeman stared at him while he waited in line to purchase his airline ticket. Later on, he noticed the way that policeman studied his face while standing in the secured waiting area. And then again, he felt the policeman's stare behind his back when he handed over his ticket to the attendant before boarding the twin engine plane. But then when the woman passenger seated next to him enquired about what had happened to his face, it all became clear to him. He surmised that the policeman had simply been intrigued by the cuts and bruises on his face, just like that charming lady seated at his side on the plane.

All was going as planned and yet he could not get rid of that nervous feeling that was growing inside of him. It was not an emotive reaction that he could explain rationally, nor one that could be rejected outright. Were his guts sensing danger lurking ahead? Was he feeling that way because he was about to find out the whole, unfiltered truth that had eluded him for all these years? Or was it because he was afraid of the consequences the revelation might bring out, that unnerved him? Was he about to repeat the same mistakes of the past, yet again? Eric could not be certain of anything. He had learned a long time ago to trust his instincts, and right now they were blaring that something was wrong. At that point, Eric felt he had only two choices—first, to call Stephanie for help and run the risk of scaring away his contact for good, or secondly, to pursue his quest alone and let things unfold as they should. The more he thought about his dilemma, the more he felt there was only one way to go. He stowed his concerns aside and chose the second option, not realizing at the time how prescient his decision would turn out to be.

Eric had little difficulty finding a room in a decent hotel in Nevsehir. Over the years the capital of Cappadocia had grown as a good starting base for touring the region. The surrounding tuff formations and troglodyte cities were the main attractions, and throughout the year thousands of tourists from every corner of the world stopped in Nevsehir for a night or two on their way to the underground cities. Fortunately, the town was well-equipped with ample accommodations to suit the most discerning tastes and budgets.

The lobby of the hotel was crammed with tourists, eagerly waiting for their tour guide to hand them over the keys to their room. They were standing in large circles, blocking anyone from passing through who did not belong to the group. Luckily for Eric, the front desk was clear of visitors, and with elbows leading the charge he managed to thread his way through the crowd, heading for the first available receptionist. She welcomed him with a well-practiced smile and set his passport aside, requesting instead his credit card. With the same smile that seemed to be permanently glued on her face, she enquired about the length of his stay before handing him the key to his room, but not his passport. "It's for security," she explained, still smiling.

At least the service in this place is efficient, Eric mused as he unlocked his door with the electronic key. The room was cool and dark. He paused at the door for a second, giving enough time to let his eyes adjust to the darkness. He pawed his way along the wall looking for the light switch and only managed to stumble on a chair. Totally frustrated, he decided that a change of course was in order and headed straight for the window. In one swift arching motion, he pulled the heavy drapes, meant to shelter the room from the blazing sun, wide open. An abrupt brightness engulfed the room and momentarily blinded him. He slowly opened his eyes and stared at the spectacular landscape of jagged peaks and grey and beige pointed mounts honeycombed with cavities.

He stood by the window with the palms of his hands pressed on the warm glass, transfixed by the sheer beauty of the scenery. At a distance, multicolor hot-air balloons drifted by like giant Christmas balls suspended in mid-air by invisible strings. The hot-air balloons floating about aimlessly reminded him of what was really troubling him—a sense of powerlessness, of being pulled, pushed, and played with like a puppet. After all, he was no further ahead now than when he first landed in Turkey. In fact, the whole affair had definitely taken a turn for the worse. He had received threats on his life, been ridiculed by his boss, shot at, and almost got himself killed in a car crash. And then there was David, the only banker that agreed to help him—and in return for that help, had been murdered. All Eric had to show for his efforts was a vague promise to find out the identity of the mysterious high-speed trader. For that, he was first told to fly to Istanbul, then asked to travel all the way to the middle of Turkey in Central Anatolia, and then ordered to wait for a phone call.

But the phone call never came. Instead, someone slipped a note under the door while he was busy gazing out the window. The note was not signed, but its contents left no doubt as to the identity of the author. Nonetheless, Eric had not expected a handwritten message, and he read it with great interest.

Meet me in Göreme at 2pm. The museum is not far. Ask for directions at the front desk. The museum should be buzzing with visitors at this time of the day. A perfect place for a private chat.

I'll find you.

I trust you remember our little arrangement. But to be absolutely clear, make sure no one is trailing you—otherwise, forget about our meeting.

He felt tightness in his chest as he read the note for a second time, and will himself to ignore the pain. Now was not the time to back down.

It took him less than half an hour to find the Göreme Open-Air Museum. He parked the car in between two enormous tour buses at the very end of a dusty lot. There must have been more than a hundred cars and at least two dozen large buses crammed into the two parking lots reserved for the patrons of the museum. At the gate, visitors were lined up in pairs from as far back as the parking lots, some five hundred meters away. At any time, the line threatened to block the access to the lots, and frustrated drivers were constantly hammering on their horns. Eric took his place in the line and waited for his turn to enter the museum, barely able to contain his apprehension.

Under different circumstances, the wait would have been worthwhile. The site held an incredible array of extensive dwellings, churches, and monasteries carved out of the soft volcanic tuff by medieval orthodox Christian monks, dating back to the 9th century. He had more than one hour ahead of him and used the time to act like a tourist. He wandered around, stopping by here and there, listening briefly to the tour guides reciting their well-practiced discourse about the origins of the rock-cut chapels and the people who lived in them. He stopped for a minute to watch a few people, mesmerized by the Byzantine frescoes decorating the walls and ceilings of many of the churches built by the early keepers of the faith. All along, he kept his mind focused on his surroundings, blending with large groups of visitors whenever he felt the need to vanish from sight, and changing direction often to confuse and lose anyone following him. But mostly, he chewed away time, anxiously waiting for his contact to show himself.

"Where the hell are you?" he muttered under his breath, realizing that the author of the note was by now more than two hours late. Impatience quickly turned to frustration, and then gradually evolved to apprehension before finally settling on despair. He wondered if he could live without ever knowing the truth. But the mere thought of another let-down angered him even more.

Eric shoved his hands in his pockets, hiding away his clinched fists as he surveyed the grounds for a last time. The oddly shaped rock structures with their gapping caves suddenly took an ominous appearance. The magic was gone. It no longer felt like a welcoming holy site. He must have cursed out loud without being aware of it, when he noticed people staring at him.

"Time to leave this place," he finally decided as he walked briskly toward the exit.

When he reached the parking lot, he noticed two men waiting at the entrance. Both men were short, muscular, and coiffed with identical crew cuts, military style. They did not attempt to hide the fact they were staring at him. One of them grinned as they marched in his direction, fully aware that Eric had spotted him.

Eric observed the two men carefully, his mind reeling, his senses on full alert. Friends or foes, he wavered for a second or two, and then turned around.

Behind him another pair of even more menacing-looking bullies blocked his retreat. He stopped dead in his tracks, gave the immediate area a rapid scan, and quickly reassessed his options. There were none. The trap was set, and the four men were closing in on him. He turned his back to make a dash across the road. It was too late. A van squealed to an abrupt halt on the roadside, cutting off his last and only chance for an escape. Before he could mutter a single word, arms grabbed him from behind and shoved him into the back seat of the van.

CHAPTER 24

The van sped away, leaving behind a bunch of onlookers wondering what had just happened—a police raid, someone being kidnapped, a prank? No one knew; no one could decide. Eric had been whisked away in broad daylight and truth be told, no one really cared. Vacationers on a trip of a lifetime, the few witnesses who remained at the scene, gathered around at the entrance of the parking lot and quickly agreed that what they had seen was none of their business. Something best left alone.

Inside the van, the tension was palpable. The whole abduction had barely taken a few minutes. It had been carried out with military precision and efficiency. From the moment Eric had been spotted up to the time he was hurled into the van, not a word had been spoken. None was necessary. When the vehicle reached the top of the hill overlooking the open air museum, the driver gently released his foot off the gas pedal. He had driven on this road many times and knew that the *Jandarma* were always patrolling the area. He cruised at the speed limit for a little while and kept glancing in the rear view mirror. As soon as he was satisfied that he was out of reach of the police's radar, he roared the engine back into high-speed. His accomplices remained quiet all along.

In the back of the van, Eric was still shell-shocked. Squeezed between his abductors with his hands tied behind his back, he sat transfixed, not able to move. He felt the cold steel barrel of a gun held firmly against his rib cage. It was more for assurance than absolute necessity. He was barely recognizable under the white fedora on his head and a long scarf wrapped around his face. He was also blind as a bat under the opaque sunglasses hanging over his nose. His captors had been thorough and very professional.

The crackling of the shortwave radio broke the silence. Eric felt movement on his right side as the man shifted in his seat. There were more sharp sputters on the radio, the roar of the engine, but still no voice transmission. Beyond the snap of a cigarette lighter and then the long drawn exhale of a man smoking to relax himself, Eric strained his ears for familiar sounds. This was his only connection with reality, and somehow it helped him regain his emotional balance.

"Who are you? What do you want from me?" he asked, his voice muffled by the scarf.

"Shut up," his captor yelled, driving the barrel of his gun deeper into his rib cage.

Eric remained undeterred.

"People know where I am. You won't get away with it." It was a lie of course, but he knew he had to try something, anything to get him out of this mess before it was too late.

"I told you to shut up." The man punched Eric in the stomach and pressed his gun against his head. "The next time you open your mouth, I will blow your head off."

A voice broke through the shortwave radio, putting an immediate end to the confrontation. The man released Eric from his grip and glanced at his comrade. A nod from the other man confirmed his suspicion. The voice was clear and commanding. A few words spoken in Turkish followed by an equally brief response from the front passenger, and the two-way radio went dead again. Silence ripped the air inside the cabin.

Moments later, the van swerved off the main road and screamed to a full stop on the graveled pavement. Eric's body tensed, expecting a fatal shot at anytime now. He closed his eyes, not that it mattered much. He was like a blind man under the thick glasses. But like a silent prayer, the gesture had a fleeting effect on him. The gunshot never came. In fact, nothing happened for some time. No hustling or sudden movement. Not a sound either. Nothing to indicate what was going on or what his captors were going to do with him. They simply remained rooted in their seat with Eric sandwiched between them. *They are keeping me in the dark for a reason,* he dreaded. Not knowing their intensions drove him crazy. Panic settled in slowly, and fear entangled his throat. His lungs screamed for air, and he gasped in pain. Feeling totally powerless was even more excruciating. Yet, he was still alive, and as long as he able to breathe, there would always be hope.

Tolling in the silence time ticked away, and Eric knew that he was running out of options. He was about to burst out with another plea for his life when the distant howl of an engine caught his attention. His abductors heard it too. The effect of the incoming vehicle was electrical. He could hear the men fussing around in their seats. Snappy orders were given, guns were cocked, the four doors swung wide open, and all four men leapt out of the van at the same time. Someone grabbed Eric by the collar and hauled him out of the vehicle. The man kept prodding him on the back with the barrel of his gun, pressing him to walk faster. After few hesitant steps, his foot caught a rock and he tumbled to the ground head first. He groaned in pain and lay sprawled on the dirt with blood gushing out of the old wound on his forehead. The man snarled and kicked him hard in the groin. Eric screamed, his legs shaking in the dirt to ease the pain. The man did not allow him any respite. He kneeled down and hissed in his ear, "Get up right now or you will never be able to walk again."

His first attempt to get back on his feet was unsuccessful. Feeling disoriented and dizzy from the blows to the head and groin, he fell back on the ground, his face smashing the ancient lava rocks. The taste of dirt and blood nearly gagged him. His hands were tied behind his back, and he could not wipe his mouth clean. So he just spit the blood out of his mouth as hard as he could. The man poked him again with his gun. This time it hurt even more, and Eric responded more out of spite than from pain. The throbbing ache in his head doubled in intensity, but somehow he found the strength to get up. He crushed the sunglasses covered with his own blood and kicked the hat in the dirt. Satisfied with this small act of defiance, he leveled his gaze at his captors.

"You have made a big mistake. You have the wrong man. I'm just a Canadian tourist," he said before spitting more blood out his mouth.

His abductors just looked at him and then burst out laughing. They were an odd bunch—crew cuts and thick moustaches were the norm. Even their dress code was similar. They all seemed to belong to some sort of army unit, only not one ever seen in a military parade. When the laughter subsided, the man who appeared to be the leader stepped in ahead of the small group to confront Eric. He measured Eric with his eyes, carrying a look of disdain on his face.

He growled, "I don't think so. You're definitely our man. Get in the car, NOW!"

On cue, two men grabbed Eric from behind and dragged him into the SUV. Moments later the two vehicles screeched away in a cloud of dust, heading in opposite directions. The occupants of the van had apparently completed their mission. Inside the SUV, Eric was pretty much left alone to his own thoughts. His hands were still tied behind his back, but no one had bothered about the hat or the opaque sunglasses that had kept him from seeing where they were taking him.

This time the ride was rough and bumpy. The suspension of the all-terrain, four-wheel drive vehicle was hard pressed to keep up with the many potholes and deep crevasses littering the dirt road. He almost fell off his seat several times, and once, his head even hit the roof top of the SUV. They traveled at high speed through particularly challenging canyons and frightening precipices, but never once did the driver lift his foot off the gas pedal.

Eric tried to clear his mind. Through the window he caught sight of the van vanishing rapidly behind them. A tiny dot on the horizon was all that was left of the four men who had abducted him. Now, two well armed men were driving him at high speed towards a distant mountain range. God only knew what fate would be waiting for him once they reached their destination. An escape seemed totally unrealistic at this stage. What then? He pondered for a moment, and then retraced in his mind how he got to this point, trying to figure out what went wrong. He remembered the phone call he had received a day earlier. Initially, the man on the phone had seemed hesitant. That in itself should have given him ample warning. But then the caller had agreed to meet him at Göreme after he heard what happened in Casablanca. But then again, the caller never showed up at their rendezvous. What would be worse—that he had been totally naive about the whole thing, or that he fell into a carefully laid out trap? In either case Eric knew that if he wanted to get out of this predicament alive he had to come up quickly with a credible reason to explain his presence in Cappadocia.

The dirt road ended at a farmhouse nestled against the side of a mountain that dwarfed the valley below. A small, whitewashed structure made out of mud bricks, the farmhouse looked like an oddity in this isolated patch of land. A wooden rooftop spiked with a weird looking assortment of antennas, a massive studded oak door, and steel bars on the windows added to the notion of incongruity. Two oversized Hummers were parked on either side of the small structure like guarding lampposts. Close by, large storage bins and tall metal containers were lined up alongside a large moving van. Other than a small, cultivated lot nearby, the place looked more like a military camp than a farmhouse.

No one came to greet them.

The driver bypassed the farmhouse and cut off the engine at the far end of a graveled path. Three dogs rushed out of the adjacent barn, barking loudly at the occupants of the SUV. Nearby, a flock of sheep wandered around freely under the watchful eye of a young boy standing on a mound, a walking stick in his hand. Someone whistled from inside the barn and the dogs retreated back to their quarters. The driver climbed out of the vehicle, holding his Uzi at his side. He signaled for Eric to get out and to follow him. Eric looked up at the young shepherd. They exchanged stares but not thoughts.

Dusk was quickly settling in, and the whole valley went eerily quiet.

They shoved him inside the farmhouse to a windowless room that had been carved out of the flank of the mountain. The room was dark and damp. Small bags of grain were piled up in one corner. The rancid smell of old olive oil pervaded the air. A stool had been placed in the middle of the room across from a small wooden table and a chair. An ancient brass oil lamp flickered on the table, projecting ghastly shadows on the walls.

The driver pointed at the stool. "Sit," he shouted, and then left the room, locking the door behind him.

Eric shivered. His abductors were obviously not in a great hurry. He used his time to try to devise a way out of his predicament—payment of a generous ransom, a promise to co-operate, a pledge never to reveal his abductors' identity—anything, whatever it took.

Loud footsteps coming his way and dogs barking outside mercifully put a quick stop to his anguish.

"So this is the famous Eric Martin," Abdullah's voice echoed in the room. "You don't know how much grief you have caused us, but I'm sure you would be glad to put an end to it. Wouldn't you agree, Mr. Martin?"

"Listen, I don't know who you are, and quite frankly, I don't care. Let me go and I will forget about the whole thing. If it's money you're after, I'm sure we can come to a satisfactory settlement."

Abdullah burst out laughing. His whole body convulsed like a bad cough. He was still wheezing and panting when he finally replied. "Really, Mr. Martin? You will let us continue our business without interference? You will stop your enquiries? You will instruct Interpol to end their investigation? Just like that!"

"I don't know what you're talking about. As I said to your friends earlier, I'm vacationing in Turkey. A well-deserved vacation, I might add. That's all."

"I see. You chased Karzan in the Bazaar because you like jogging. You tried to run him over in Istanbul for the sheer fun of it. And you traveled all the way to Cappadocia for a holiday. And we should just believe you? You know something—I wonder what Alain Lepetit would say about this fantasy tale of yours?"

"What do you know about Alain Lepetit?" Eric asked, clearly intrigued.

"Oh, but I know a lot about your old boss. He is not very fond of you, you know. I would not trust him if I were you. But that's not important. We have found a way to make him an honest man. That is, as far as our little business is concerned, of course. And he has told me lots of interesting things about you, like you do not know when to give up."

Eric sighed. "Alright, let's cut the bullshit. You would not have kept me alive if you did not need me for something. So tell me what it is you want to know and let's end this charade."

"Good, that's better. Start by telling me about Çelik."

"Çelik? Who is he? I don't know anyone by that name."

Abdullah clenched his fist, "I thought you said that you were ready to cooperate? Tell me how, when, and where you met Çelik."

"Honestly, I don't know this man."

The door suddenly burst open and before Abdullah could stop him, Karzan lunged for Eric's throat, his fingers tightening around it like a deathly vise while punching him in the face with the other hand. Abdullah stepped back to watch Karzan going at it with full force and furry. He knew that there was no love lost between the two men, but he did not realize how deeply Karzan resented Eric. The beating went on for a long while. Eric was on the verge of losing consciousness before Abdullah finally stepped in and waved off Karzan.

Eric's face was a bloody mess. His right eye had swollen to the size of a small orange and his head hung low on his neck. Abdullah told Karzan to untie Eric's hands and ordered him to get a wet towel. He then waited for Eric to regain his composure.

Eric's ears were still buzzing when he finished wiping the blood off his face. He took his time—his final act of defiance, now that there was no longer any doubt in his mind he would never leave this place alive. Information is what these men wanted. The flimsy piece of intelligence he had been able to uncover so far was the sole reason they had not shot him already. That thought hardened his spirit even more. And he made up his mind—he would not give his abductors any satisfaction.

Abdullah grabbed the chair and set it in front of Eric. He sat barely a breath away and lifted Eric's head to meet his eyes. He leaned closer, meeting Eric's forehead with his own. His voice was soft and quiet as a whisper when he spoke.

"Çelik is a traitor. We know that he brought you here to talk—to fill you in about us. The greedy bastard wanted it all to himself. Unfortunately, he shot himself before we had a chance to get to him. Now, you're going to tell us what he told you and who else knows about it. Otherwise, my friend here will cut you up in pieces, one finger, one eyelid, one toenail at a time, and when he is done, I guarantee that you will beg us to listen to you."

Karzan grinned from ear to ear as he pulled the long blade out from its leather sheathe. He waved the knife in front of Eric's face, barely missing his left eye with the tip of the blade.

Eric did not flinch.

"I told you. I did not know his name. He was very suspicious and guarded. He has not told me anything. We spoke on the phone, and I convinced him to meet me for a chat. That's when he asked me to wait for him at the Göreme museum. That's all I know. I'm sure Alain Lepetit already filled you in on what I found out at the bank. The rest is old news. Your men picked me up and brought me here."

"What about the woman agent from Interpol? What does she know?"

"Nothing at all. After the car crash in Istanbul she came over to check on me at the request of an old friend. I did not tell her that I was coming here. She is probably still waiting for me at the hotel."

"Liar!" Abdullah slapped him hard across the face. "Stop lying to me. Don't take me for a fool. We know that she followed you to the airport. What was she doing there? What's that weird looking man who is accompanying her doing here?"

"Don't you understand? I don't know anything more than what I already told you. And even if I knew, I would not be telling you; I'm through talking."

"Enough," Abdullah bellowed. "You're going to tell me what I want to know right now."

Abdullah got up suddenly and kicked the chair away from underneath his feet. It was not an act. Even Karzan was surprised by the sudden outburst. Abdullah looked out of sorts and motioned Karzan, who was standing at his side with knife in hand, to take over the interrogation.

"Stop!" yelled the woman who had just entered the room. "Abdullah, order him to stop immediately!" she howled.

CHAPTER 25

Karzan stopped the blade in mid-air, mere millimeters from Eric's throat. With his teeth clenched, he stared at Abdullah, eyes pleading him not to listen to the command of the foreign woman. For an instant, no one dared move. Everyone remained frozen in place like statues. Only the heavy breathing of Karzan could be heard. Abdullah finally shook his head and Karzan cursed under his breath.

The woman sighed in relief. She ignored Karzan and addressed Abdullah as if the two of them were the only ones in the room.

"There is no longer any need for this. The entire system is being reprogrammed with new codes. New IP addresses are being assigned as we speak. No one would be able to trace the trades back to us. And if by some miracle someone were lucky enough to break into our system, they would never be able to decipher the data without the keys."

"Are you absolutely certain?" Abdullah shouted back.

"When have I ever disappointed you, Abdullah? You can take what I said to the bank. We are closing shop here."

Something about the woman's voice sounded oddly familiar to Eric. The intonations, the quick firebrand delivery, the way she mispronounced certain words. All added up to a voice from the past.

"My poor Eric; look at what they have done to you."

Eric was momentarily taken aback. His ears were still buzzing from the beating and he could barely see from his good eye. Yet, he detected something familiar about the woman's voice. He raked his memory banks for answers. Scattered impressions flashed through his mind, some more vivid than others, some more recent than others. A series of images flickered in his mind in quick sequence, only to vanish even more rapidly into his subconscious. Voices, faces, places, events, and feelings came and went in rapid succession. He could sense through the fog of his buried memories the shadow of a face slowly emerging. And then a name from the past popped out from the deep recess of his psyche like a flash of lightning. He had found a match. The neurons in his brain leapt to merge with one another, completing the final connections in his conscious mind.

"Tania? Tania? Is that really you?"

"Yes Eric. Your eyes are not playing tricks on you. It's really me."

Eric rubbed off the blood dripping into his eyes. Several thoughts raced through his mind in quick succession—doubt, disbelief, mistrust, anger— in that order. He drew his breath to quell the bitter taste rising in his mouth. He fought the natural impulse demanding immediate retribution. The thin smile Tania gave him made it even more difficult for him to control his thirst for vengeance.

"But how did you manage to come out alive? The ship was totally obliterated. No one could have survived that inferno."

"My poor Eric; don't look at me with such disbelief in your eyes."

"It's incredible. I just want to know what happened. The U.S. Navy told me that there were no survivors!"

"Well, as you can see I did survive the massacre, and yes I'm alive and well. But unlike you, no one came to my rescue. I was simply not onboard. After all, someone had to take care of Yvan Berdyek's wife and their precious little girl. And now, after all these years, we meet again. I'm sorry for the circumstances, but are you not happy to see me?"

"Don't push it, Tania. You did not bring me here to reminisce about the past. I already told the thugs that always seem to be hanging around you everything I know. The well is dry. I've nothing more to tell you."

Karzan shuffled impatiently on his feet. He could barely tolerate the presence of the foreign woman in their midst, and now her babbling was driving him mad; a big waste of time as far as he was concerned. He held in his hand a more direct and effective extraction tool. But for some unfathomable reason, Abdullah, his leader would not give him the go-ahead. He stretched his neck to relieve the lump in his throat that threatened to suffocate him, bit his tongue hard in frustration, and drew blood in his mouth.

Karzan's restlessness did not escape Tania. She threw a furtive glance at Abdullah and registered the silent nod.

"Eric, before we continue with this very interesting conversation, let me take care of my friends here," she said, her voice carrying a slight strain.

"It's ok boys. You may leave me with him alone. He is harmless; besides, we're in the middle of nowhere, where can he go?"

After a brief hesitation, Abdullah led the way out the door. Karzan followed reluctantly but not before slamming the door behind him.

Tania rolled her eyes.

"You see what I have to put with? They are all a bunch of ungrateful and selfish bastards. I brought them fortune, a means to achieve their long standing dream of independence, and this is how they treat me. I guess I should not expect more as a woman."

Eric snickered.

"I never considered you a weak link. Quite the opposite. You are a natural born survivor. If there's anything about you that can't be disputed is that you know how to take care of yourself. And you sure know how to use your assets to manipulate the opposite sex. How am I doing? I could describe you in less flattering terms if you'd prefer."

Tania burst out laughing, a raw combination of high-pitched chuckle and joyful snorting. "Eric, this is not fair; flattery will not get you anywhere. But let me show you something that might help you change your mind about me. And who knows, it might even convince you to join me in this new venture."

"You tried that once. It did not work. Remember!"

"Now, now, don't be negative. Come with me; I will show you something that will blow your mind away."

Tania waved off the man standing guard at the door and led Eric through a poorly lit hallway. The farmhouse was more spacious than its outward appearance had initially led him to believe. The small dwelling was just a front. Behind its facade, a long and narrow tunnel-like passage with connecting rooms had been excavated inside the abutting mountain. The walls in the rooms were at least a meter thick. The place was built like a fortress on the inside. Eric counted six rooms along the way and a dozen or so well-armed men. For the most part, the guards were either cleaning their guns, smoking water pipes, or just lounging and killing time. But Eric was not fooled by their apparent laisser-faire manners. They were trained soldiers who would immediately snap to attention and kill him if he made any threatening move.

Tania glanced over her shoulder and noticed Eric's gazing at the tunnel.

"Amazing, isn't it? We didn't build it though. Legend has it that it was a gold mine in the old days. We just restored it," she said without slowing down for Eric who was trailing behind.

At the end of the hallway, a narrow staircase snaked around a stone column leading to a vast chamber at the bottom. The room was brightly illuminated by a row of hanging neon light fixtures. A large generator was humming in the corner, and tall white metal cabinets connected to each other by an array of multicolor electrical wires filled the entire space in the middle. The walls were covered with super large computer screens spewing out at lightning speed, row upon row of data and flow charts superimposed on shifting maps of the world. Three young men with keyboards resting on their laps were busy typing faster than most people can think, while at the same time watching their output on the giant screens. They paid no attention to Tania and Eric as they entered the room.

"Now Eric, this is what Jeff Offenbach and Marcel Loeb could only dream about," Tania exclaimed with delight.

Eric shrugged. "Jeff and Marcel are long dead. Good riddance," he shot back.

"You can't tell me that you're not impressed Eric?"

"Impressed with what—a bunch of computers on steroids and a couple of geeks playing computer games?"

Tania feigned being hurt. "Are you serious? You have not yet figured it out? I guess I overestimated you. I'm really disappointed in you, Eric."

"Don't you worry Tania; I know exactly what's going on. You stole Yvan Berdyek's algorithm and somehow managed to break the codes to enter into the system. But you are not that smart. You must have had help to figure out how to do it. So tell me now, who helped you?"

"No bad, not bad," Tania replied, breaking into a silly laugh.

"Are you going to tell me how you did it?"

"Do what Eric?"

"Decipher the codes without the keys?"

"Oh, that's what you really want to know. It was so easy, you'd not believe it. You see, I knew that Yvan had one weakness. He could not keep any secrets from his wife. And to make a long story short, they had a very beautiful daughter. She adored that child. So you can see that it did not take me long to persuade her to show me where Yvan had stashed away his program notes. She led me straight to the basement of Yvan's parents' home in Prague. *Et voilà*, the codes, along with all the keys, were mine, and I immediately started my new venture. I was looking for protection in exchange for my new toy. The PKK looked like a good match."

"And now you're busy playing the stock markets with the financial model that you have stolen." Eric spited out in disgust..

Tania giggled.

"You're the high-speed trader that has been plundering the bank's investors," Eric shouted.

"One of the high-speed traders. These geeks, as you called them, have taken Yvan's model to another level. We're on the verge of going global with more opportunities available to us than ever before. That's right. We will no longer be limited to bank stock trades. It's going to be a brand new ball game from now on. Yvan was an absolute genius, don't get me wrong. He set the groundwork to make it all possible. We could not have done it without him. But now thanks to my little team of whiz kids, unlimited trading possibilities in all the major industrial sectors will soon be opened to us. I'm so excited at our new prospects. My God, it almost gives me an orgasm to think about it."

Eric feel his anger mounting. As far as he was concerned, Tania and her team of programmers were just a bunch of scavengers feeding off someone else's clever work. But what they had done could have catastrophic consequences—the integrity of global financial markets were at risk. As he realized the enormity of what Tania had accomplished, he could only castigate himself for not having been more farsighted. *If only if I had left a note to Stephanie.*

Tania observed Eric intensely, trying to read his mind, looking for a hint in his body language that would guide her in her attempts to win him over. She had used all her tricks, but as always her efforts had failed so far. Eric had always remained a total mystery to her. Her charm, her wit, her sex appeal had no effect on him. He seemed weak and gullible, but that was a front, merely a mask for a determination bordering on obsession. He intrigued her beyond belief, and that was what made him even more attractive. Her attempt to save his life in Casablanca and her seductive offer to become lovers were more heartfelt than she would ever care to admit to anyone, let alone to herself.

She raked her eyes over the full length of his body. She needed to test herself one more time. Unsure of herself, she struggled with her feelings, swallowed hard, hesitated again and stared square into Eric's eyes. In the end, despite all her efforts, her willpower wilted away, shattered beyond recognition. She felt totally vulnerable for the first time in her life. And then she whispered in his ear something she thought she would never say to anyone.

"You know Eric; I was sincere when I asked you to join me in Casablanca. It was not just a ploy to get you working for us. I really meant it. I like you very, very much. It's not too late to change your mind, you know. Look what I have accomplished. I have already amassed a small fortune. Millions are stashed away in secret accounts and much more will come our way once the new software program is launched. This could be all yours as well. With your knowledge of bank security systems, together we will always be ahead of the game. Stay with me; let me save your life."

Eric said nothing, knowing that silence was his best and only weapon. He raised his chin and shook his head by way of an answer.

"They are going to kill you. You know that. This time no one will come to your aid. Please accept my very generous offer. Life will be good together. Don't waste it over some silly scruples."

"My conscience is clean. Yes, I blame myself for what happened to Yvan and all the people who died because of the algorithm. Don't think for one minute that I don't have any regrets, that I don't wish that I had done things differently. But do I have a bad conscience? Not at all. Why should I? The guilty ones are you and all your accomplices who murdered innocent people out of greed, fanaticism, and who knows what else that might have corrupted their filthy minds. Your offer is not so generous. It's a sure one-way ticket straight to hell where you belong."

Tania's face distorted into an expression he had never seen before. Her eyes tightened to a feral slit and her lips pursed into the thinnest of lines. In an instant, her whole outward appearance metamorphosed into a cobra about to strike.

"If that's the way you feel about it, then suit yourself. You have just signed your death warrant," she howled in cold fury.

Alarmed by the commotion, Karzan and two guards bounded into the room with their guns fully drawn. They immediately formed a defensive line in front of Tania. Eric ignored them and spoke to Tania right through the three men menacing him with their drawn weapons.

"Now that we understand how we feel about each other, can you at least do the compassionate thing and tell me what have you done with Yvan's wife and their daughter?"

"It's none of your business," Tania hissed. "Take him. Do whatever you want with him. I'm through wasting my time with this idiot."

Karzan scratched his moustache with the tip of the blade of his knife as Tania looked on.

CHAPTER 26

Eric looked up at the dark sky and an infinite abyss of nothingness stared back at him. He breathed in deeply, filling his lungs with all that was no more and welcomed the void that stripped away all his senses. No more worries or fears, they had been sucked out of him. He was omnipotent, reborn free of afflictions.

But his time of blissful quietude was short lived. A loud roar on the horizon followed by a thunderous rumbling over the mountaintop broke the stillness of the night like an angry god. Dampness quickly replaced the arid air of the desert. A gust of wind swirled the grey dust over the barren land. A second roar shook the earth, and high above, a streak of lightning tore the sky in half. The thunderstorm brewing in the valley hidden by the jagged peaks had announced its arrival like a stampede of wild prairie horses. Cappadocia—the 'land of the beautiful horses'—was making a comeback, and the world below trembled at its sight.

A cold shiver ran down Eric's spine. He raised the collar of his stained cotton shirt and wrapped his arms tightly across his chest. The guard gave him a silent stare and then inhaled the smoke from his cigarette, seeking warmth that would not come. The vehicles that had brought them to this desolate patch of land were no match for the frigid draft that battered their faces and shivering bodies like sand needles.

His captors had left him behind with a single sentry, while they were busy clearing boulders with crow bars and hands at the foot of a cone-shaped mound. They had badly hurt him. The beating had been severe, but his throat had not been sliced open and left to bleed to death. There would be time later on for the slaughter. There was no doubt in his mind of what fate awaited him. More than a hindrance after what he had done, seen, and heard, he knew that he represented a huge danger to his captors if kept alive for long. As time was ticking away, the men who were holding him captive seemed too busy at work over a hole in the ground to bother with him.

They had taken him across the valley at the foot of a dormant volcano, without even a hint of how or when they would dispose of him. Surveying the sparse surroundings, he wondered if that was the site they had chosen for his last resting place. He briefly pondered on how they would kill him and whether they would choose to let him die a slow and painful death. He once again looked up at sky above and saw a streak of lightning slice open the night. A drop of rain rolled down on his forehead like a calling card. He took it as a good omen.

Abdullah shifted his weight from one foot to the other. His solemn expression could not hide a deep unease. He turned his head to scrutinize Tania's face. They had been watching the progress of the men excavating the entrance of the tunnel. It was hard work, and his men did not look happy. He knew that they resented what they had been asked to do. And it made matters worse when the men found out that the order had been made at the request of the foreign woman. He finally broke silence when Karzan angrily tossed a bent crow bar on the ground.

"There's an easier way to deal with him," Abdullah said sullenly.

Tania ignored him and continued gazing into the darkness. Standing erect and tall in the blustery weather, she was lost in her own thoughts. She did not flinch when the frosty gust blew her headscarf away.

Abdullah hesitated for a moment, unsure whether she had heard him or was simply not paying attention to him. He waited a while longer and then spoke again, his tone firmer this time out.

"Karzan is furious, you know. He vowed to kill Eric with his own hands after what happened in Antibes. One swipe of the knife and it will be over quickly. Why waste so much time when we have so much to do to clear up camp?"

"I know, but this is how I want it done."

Tania brushed away a strand of hair from her face and locked her gaze on Abdullah. There was fierce determination in her eyes. The look of someone accustomed to having her way when it really mattered.

"You can't refuse me this wish, after all I have done for you and your men," she said with finality in her voice.

Abdullah brooded over Tania's reply. He had never met a woman like her before—a rare combination of cunning intelligence and reckless energy. And there was so much more about her that appealed to him. She was sensuous and contemptuous, perceptive and decisive, dogmatic about the way she fought for what she believed in. But above all, he knew that she was also capable of extreme cruelty, without the slightest trace of remorse—and that was what fascinated him the most about her.

He held his gaze on Tania for a short while longer, and then reached the only conclusion that was possible for him. "Karzan feels responsible for the death of his comrade. He wants retribution. It's a matter of honor as far as he is concerned." The last words were spoken with conviction bordering on anger.

"Eric did not kill his accomplice. The Interpol agent shot him and your man fell to his death," Tania snapped back.

"It does not matter how he died. In Karzan's mind, Eric was responsible for his partner's death. That's all that matters to him. Besides, you want the same thing. I don't understand you. Why delay the inevitable?"

"Because I want Eric to know that he's not the only one who lost someone dear in the icy waters. I want him to feel the pain I felt. I want him to understand that he also made me a victim. Let him stew in that hell hole until he dies. That's what I want."

Tania went quiet suddenly. Her outburst had shaken her. She felt her throat tightening as she expressed her true feelings. Gasping for air, she needed time to recover. But a deeper fear was also at play. She was terrified that somehow she might have let her guard down. It almost choked her to death to think that she might have revealed a speck of weakness, a chink in her armor, a vulnerability deeply buried behind an iron will. The expression on Abdullah's face was a sure telltale sign that she had been in real danger of crossing that line. There was no place for personal vendettas in their world. Respect was earned through bravery and single mindedness in the pursuit of a goal when a greater purpose was at stake. She saw the revelation of her inner angst roll down on Abdullah's eyes like a bad scene in a B-movie and sought to quickly mask her mistake by appealing to Abdullah's ego.

"We are a good team, you and I. I've provided you with more money that you could ever dream of, and you in turn made sure that your men remained focused on our objectives. But now we're ready for much bigger things, you and me. I'm about to make it possible for you to increase your power and effectiveness at least tenfold with the changes I'm about to make in the predictive financial model. Believe me, Abdullah, your place in history in the free Kurd nation will be what legends are made of. You will be revered as a hero for generations to come."

A hint of pride brushed Abdullah's face. He nodded with a faint smile and a look on his face more friendly and caring than she had ever seen before. Gone was the strain and anger in his voice, and his penetrating eyes carried more than a trace of concern when he spoke in a hushed whisper.

"I'm going to grant you your wish because I'm not ungrateful. I'm very appreciative of what you have done for me and for our cause. Your contribution will not be forgotten either. But you must understand one thing Tania; your usefulness is nearing its end. I'm worried about what's going to happen to you now that the struggle is almost over. I received word last night that the Kurdistan Workers Party is about to sign a peace agreement with Ankara. It's only a matter of weeks, days perhaps, before we're asked to withdraw to the safe havens in northern Iraq. Less fortunate freedom fighters might even be told to lay down their arms. Others might be asked to join the political wing of the PKK to ensure that our rights are enshrined in a new constitution. The three-decades-old insurgency will be over shortly. You must understand that, Tania. That's the reality we must all face, and in this new world order, your magical algorithm will no longer be needed."

Tania's neck stiffened and she gave Abdullah a defiant look.

"Then I will move on," she said, her voice struggling to find the right tone. "It's not as if there's a lack of freedom struggles in the world. Who knows, I might end up in Chechnya or in Pakistan helping the Taliban. Don't worry so much about me. I will be fine."

Tania bit her lower lip, suddenly realizing that there was more to Abdullah's interest than a partnership of convenience. She saw the hurt in his eyes, and not knowing what else to do, she forced a smile on her face and touched his arm lightly. "Thank you for the forewarning," she said softly. "I know you did not have to do it, and I will forever be grateful to you."

She paused for a moment, allowing her words to sink in. Hogir's heavy footsteps making his way toward them caught her by surprise. She immediately removed her hand from Abdullah's arm and gave Hogir a fierce look, wishing him far away if she could.

"What is it, Hogir?" Abdullah bellowed.

"We have finished clearing the entrance of the tunnel."

"Good. Go get Eric. We must hurry; we have much to do." He then turned his gaze back to Tania. "Let's go and get this over with quickly, before the storm breaks out," he said.

Tania smiled, satisfied with herself, and waited until Hogir was out of earshot before moving closer to Abdullah.

"Thank you for granting me my wish," she murmured, her lips brushing his ear.

Eric could not stop shivering as Hogir led him to the hole in the ground. His soggy shirt and pants clung to his body, and the cold that greeted him as he walked hunched over down the narrow passage was like another blow to the face. With his fists tied in front of him, he could barely maneuver his large frame through the low- ceilinged tunnels and sharp angular passageways. Every squat under each new bend resulted in an agonizing tear or deep cut to the top of his head, hands, elbows or shoulders. The place was not built for the modern man. It was tight, infuriatingly narrow, and the bare walls of hardened ash were like sandpaper against his bare skin. He felt as if tiny glass fragments were ripping his flesh to the bone.

The tunnel led to a cave-like chamber that had been carved out of the greying ash. It was surrounded by smaller rooms with vaulted ceilings and arched entrances. The rooms must have been built to serve different functions. They were of different shapes and sizes and had a large number of niches, cavities, and alcoves dug into the walls and flat grounds. Long, narrow passageways linked each room to one another that in turn, were connected to a network of tunnels that led farther down into the hollowed out underground. At the access points of these tunnels were huge stone wheels that, once rolled in place, were virtually immovable.

Hogir pointed his flashlight at a steep flight of narrow steps ahead of him. He was leading the small group through another claustrophobic tunnel slopping dangerously further and deeper below ground. Each new tunnel led to more cavernous chambers; every chamber had its adjacent rooms, some no larger than stone cells, and in turn every room was connected to a seemingly endless number of tunnels and blind passageways. By now, Eric had totally lost his sense of direction. He could never have imagined that the famous underground cities of Cappadocia would have been so vast and intricate. He estimated that at least two to three hundred persons could easily have lived in these subterranean dwellings.

The early keepers of the faith were no fools, he thought. The underground settlements were impregnable. Built like honeycombs, they were dug deep within the earth for defence. The labyrinth of long and tight tunnels was a sure killing zone for anyone who dared enter the underground city without permission. No matter the size of the attacking force or how well armed they might have been, invaders would have to advance single file with little more than their short centurion swords to protect themselves against the armor piercing arrows and large boulders catapulted in their direction by the warrior defenders. Their retreats would have been cut off by heavy millstone trapdoors that could be easily rolled down in place by removing small wooden wedges that held them back in place. Caught hundreds of feet below the earth, the invading force would have been decimated one man at a time, without mercy.

Eric was breathing hard as they reached yet another communal chamber. He guessed that they were at least four levels below ground, and wondered how many more there were before they would reach bottom. The room appeared larger than most he had seen earlier. It could have easily accommodated three to four times the size of the party accompanying him. He also noted that more care seemed to have been given to the finishing of the walls and ground. There were no sharp edges anywhere, corners had been rounded, and walls had been sanded and smoothed. A tall rectangular stone had been erected like an altar at the far end, underneath a small oval-shaped alcove that had been carved into the wall. Blackened vessels hanging over either side of the alcove suggested their use as probably primitive oil lamps. Faint remnants of once colorful frescoes and biblical images plastered the vaulted ceiling. At the center of the room, two rows of long stone slabs, edges rounded and polished by years of use, served as reminders of the purpose of this sacred sanctuary where the keepers of the faith gathered in prayer a long time ago.

"An amazing place, isn't it?" Tania said as she entered the ancient church."To think that the Hittites, and the early Christians after them, using primitive tools were able to tunnel entire towns into the rock itself with as many as eight stories hundreds of feet below the ground. It's mind-boggling, don't you think, Eric? And did you know that over two hundred cities like this one have been discovered in the region? My God, weren't they industrious people back then. They were like little ants, I'm telling you."

"You did not bring me here to give me a history lesson or to impress me with human ingenuity and its capacity for hard work. Why don't you end this charade and ask your men to do their dirty deed right now."

"Not so fast, Eric. If I were you I would take a good look around. This is the last time you are going to be able to see this rocky wonderland. Take your time and explore the rooms around you. It's quite fascinating. You see, the early settlers built this place with the idea that they would have to hide underground for months at a time. They did not only build living quarters, they also dug into the stone: storehouses, stables, livestock pens, kitchens, elaborate churches, and even wine presses so that they could live for weeks or months until it was safe for them to go back to the surface and return to their villages."

"This is all very interesting, but why are you telling me this?" Eric asked, looking more annoyed than puzzled.

"Because this is where you are going to spend the rest of your miserable existence. You will have plenty of time to enjoy the amenities. Except of course, you will find the shelves bare of food and water. But, on the other hand, you will have lots of time to yourself. Yes, that's right, plenty of time for you to ponder what you have given up when you declined my offer. Is that not wonderful, Eric?"

"I'm thrilled," Eric quickly replied, and then added as a dare, "Don't you worry about me, I was not planning to go anywhere, not yet at least, unless of course you would like to let me go right away to save me the trouble."

Tania burst out laughing. She was the only one in the room laughing, but that did not seem to bother her. Hogir was quick to note the reaction of his comrades and immediately stepped forward, placing his body between Eric and Karzan. Standing beside Tania, Abdullah was not amused either, and was struggling against the urge to let Karzan have his way with Eric. He took a deep breath and then exhaled slowly. He repeated the heavy breathing exercise twice. Once certain that his temper was in check, he stared Tania down in silence, ordering her with his eyes to end the nonsense immediately.

Tania pursed her lips, her face breaking into something that looked more like a grimace than a smile. She glanced around the room, taking stock of the charged atmosphere. The dour look Abdullah's men gave her left no doubt that she had better stop her tirade, even if she did not like taking orders.

"Fine. I'm glad that you chose to co-operate," she said with her lips curling up into a snarl. "Hogir, untie our friend before we leave him. He is going to behave now."

Abdullah's patience had run out by now, and he immediately signaled his men to head back for the tunnel. Tania followed closely behind. She stopped at the entrance of the narrow passageway, appearing to hesitate for a moment. A lopsided smile painted her face as she turned pointing the beam of her flashlight at Eric.

Eric had not moved. He looked calm, almost serene.

"Don't look so sad, my poor Eric. I did not leave you here to die alone. In the small room that served as antechamber for the priests you will find good company—except they were not as fortunate as you. You see, Martina and her little girl were never given your privilege. They never saw the place of their burial ground before they died."

The grinding sound of a one-ton circular keystone sealing the entrance of the ancient church buried her laughter and Eric's curse echoing behind her.

At first, Eric remained impassive. No panic. No fear. No thought raced through his mind. He felt nothing at all, as if all his senses had all been taken away from him. The cave-like church vanished from his sight. Darkness erased the outer walls and ceiling above him. Silence filled the space with its deathly presence. He closed one eye, then the other, searching for an image in his head of what he had seen moments earlier. None emerged, for his brain was frozen like a computer with too much data being processed all at once.

They had left him in the dark, and the darkness was total, darker than dark—absolute, primordial darkness. He remained in a Buddha-like state, rooted in the same spot for a long time. He could imagine what was ahead of him in the following days or as long as a week perhaps, if he was strong enough. Death would come slowly, but he did not fear it. But as much as he accepted death as an inevitable outcome of life, he was mortified by the realization that two innocent victims were buried in a cave barely a few feet away from him. Riddled with guilt and gut-wrenching remorse, his brain had shut down, no longer able to deal with the emotional overload.

And for all this time, the byzantine church hidden deep within the heart of the earth had kept her vows of silence.

As time passed, he slowly became aware of his breathing—a faint, barely audible murmur. He trained his ears to pay more attention to the first sign of life from deep within him. He placed his hand in front of his mouth and felt the warm breeze flowing out of his nostrils onto his fingertips. He raised his hand to his face and was surprised by the way his skin felt to the touch. Soon, he could hear the drumbeat of his heart echoing in the empty chamber that once served as a place of worship.

And then his survival instincts kicked in—nothing drastic, no brusque reaction or need to scream for help. He just felt a slow growing desire to move and explore his surroundings. He took one tentative step forward, unsure of where he was heading, then thought better of it and moved to his right, looking for a wall to guide him. He chose his steps carefully, remembering the stone benches in the middle of the room. Holding his hands outstretched in front of him like a blind man for protection and guidance, he finally managed to reach the large and smooth surface of a wall. It felt cold and damp, but it reassured him nonetheless. He had found his guiding light that would help him navigate in this subterranean mausoleum. Now all he needed to do was to find the way out.

He racked his brain to pull the last image of the man-made cave out of the small recess where he stored the things he had seen or done. The picture of Tania standing in front of him, mocking and badgering him appeared first. It was vivid, but not helpful. But moments later, his brain started to unwind and began to pan out the entire scene like a movie camera. The picture of what took place moments before total darkness enveloped the cave flashed before his eyes. He saw Abdullah and his men throwing Tania exasperated looks as they watched her berating him. In the shadows behind the four men forming a full circle around him, he could make out low hanging archways, evenly spaced around the church like standing guards. But in the end, it was the memory of the excruciating noise of rock grinding against rock that stirred his mind to reveal the location of the entrance to the tunnel.

With one hand running along the wall, he moved in the dark towards what he believed would lead to an escape route. He chose his steps carefully, unsure if his memory of the place had not left out any sinking hole or hidden stairs. It felt like an eternity had passed before he was able to reach the circular break in the wall. The entrance was blocked by a huge stone, which unlike the walls, felt rough and uneven to the touch. He tried pushing the massive rock out of the way with his shoulder by leaning against it. Nothing happened. He then lay down on his back, while pushing with all his might on the boulder with his feet. It did not work either. He needed at least a steel crow bar to wedge the stone gate. As a last attempt, he tried using his fingers to roll the huge millstone back to its original position on the side of the cavity. He pulled and pushed along the jagged edges of the heavy stone built like a wheel. His efforts were futile. All he got for his hard work were bloody fingers, blisters in his hands, a chest damp with perspiration, and a subterranean, bone-chilling cold running down along his spine.

He was trapped, buried alive, hundreds of feet below ground.

He grit his teeth and rose to his feet, not yet willing to give up. "There must be more than one way out of this hole," he cursed aloud. He then remembered the archways circling the church. *If they're like all the others in the communal caves, they must lead to other rooms and more passageways.*

It did not take him long to trace the first arched entryway. He stumbled on a fissure on the ground when he entered the first room and had to dampen his enthusiasm. He cautiously advanced in the dark, carefully feeling his way along the granular wall. The room was small, or so it felt to him after one complete tour around the four corners. One after the other, he entered every doorway, only to exit moments later even more disappointed. By now he had his routine down pat. Staying always on the perimeter, he would paw his hands along the walls until he could feel a cavity or large circular crack from the ground up. He would then attempt to clear an opening. But like the main tunnel entrance of the church, he found every passageway and stairway permanently sealed by immovable boulders or massive millstones.

The fifth room contained the only surprise of the day. No bigger than a monk cell, it also featured an unusually low vaulted ceiling. He bumped his head as he stepped in, and hesitated for a moment before releasing his hand from the wall to carefully move a safe distance away to where he thought the bowed peak of the ceiling would be at its highest. Almost immediately his foot hit a hard object and he fell over on his knees and hands. The hard object was, in fact, a pile of rocks the shape of an elongated oval mound of about five to six feet long and a little more than a foot high. The unexpected discovery shook him hard.

He had found the burial place where Martina—and most certainly her daughter—had been buried. The shock quickly turned to anger, and then a rush of sadness overcame him. He shut his eyes more as a way to ease the pain than out of a strong desire to offer a silent prayer to the dead, for he knew not the sacred words. He lowered his lips to kiss the stones, blessing the two harmless souls with a lasting farewell. And then he raised his head to stare at the empty darkness above him as it all came to him in wave after wave.

While he had faced, up to now, his demise with somewhat of a fatalistic mind-set, the surprising reappearance of ghosts from his past hit him hard. He was repulsed by the mere thought that the murder of his former colleague's wife and daughter would go unpunished. This was unforgivable, as far as he was concerned. He struggled with his breathing as he thought of the two innocent victims buried under a pile of rocks in this dark hole. *I must find a way to survive for their sake!*

Whereas he had been calm and serene about his prospects of finding a way out of this underground maze, from that moment on his mind was beginning to let self-doubt slowly trickle in. He began to worry about the amount of oxygen left in the cave, the lack of food and water, the length of time he would remain alert before his body would shrivel up to a slow and excruciating death. The possibility of failure was too much for him to bear.

It was not the outcome that he had envisioned when he caught the first flight from Paris to Istanbul. Even if nothing had gone his way, he nonetheless continued to forge ahead with his quest, convinced that the truth would wipe out all his past mistakes. A compelling premonition that rapidly turned into an unrelenting obsession, had driven him to this dreaded end. The journey had taken its toll and the burden of his past had consumed his last drop of energy. He felt weak, and a leaden fatigue suddenly crushed him into a restless sleep.

He was awakened by the sound of water dripping from the ceiling. He rubbed his eyes out of habit and shook his head like someone wanting to shake away a bad dream. Another drip of water echoed across the room like a door bell. He held his breath as long as possible, not daring to breathe or move, hoping that his mind was not playing tricks on him. And there was, at last, another drip—an unmistakable trickle of water somewhere in the dark recess of the room.

It's a rain drop, he thought immediately.

An odd mix of tension, elation, and hope ran through his mind. He waited with anticipation for another rain drop to trickle its way down to the ground. It would serve as his guide to where a passage leading back to the surface might exist.

The drop finally came, hitting the hard surface of the stone floor with a barely audible dribble. No matter, he had registered the faint spill in his head and zoned in on its location, crawling on all four like a hound. He brushed his hand on the wet spot on the floor, ran the tip of his fingers along the wall, and finally felt his way around the dampness to a small opening in the ceiling. No more than three to four inches square, he immediately recognized it for what it was—an air shaft built by the ancients for ventilation. A ray of hope swept across his face as he looked up through the tiny orifice to see if he could detect light at the very top. He was only to be disappointed by the ingenuity of the early settlers, for the pin hole was artfully built to avoid detection from the surface.

Not knowing what else to do, he began to scream for help until his throat was raw and hurt so much that he thought he had permanently lost his voice. He banged in frustration at the orifice with his fists, stopping only when his bloodied knuckles could no longer take the pain. Exhausted, he finally collapsed on the floor with the knowledge that his hope of finding an escape route was just a pipe dream.

An oppressing silence returned in the room as Eric's mind slowly descended into another nightmare.

He heard in his dream the millstone being whined out of its base. A slow, rasping grind shrieked loudly in his ears. He glanced up at the entrance of the tunnel and quickly shut his eyes tight. The faint glare of a lantern was too painful after the darkness he had endured. His body, slouched on the ground, felt heavy, not able to move, so weak were his limbs. He was a shadow of himself—his head pounding from the lack of food and water, his confused mind drifting in a fog of surreal images.

The nightmare got progressively worse until the time his mind caught a glimpse of hope. A brief moment where all seemed well, that somehow, someone had found out where his abductors had buried him, and that this person had come to his rescue and figured out a path down the maze of tunnels. And his nightmare would end.

It all made sense somehow when hope was the only thing worth hanging on to. Eric stirred in his semi-conscious state and greeted the approaching silhouette like the last wish of a dying man.

Then the dream took another turn.

CHAPTER 27

There were moments in Eric's life when the concept of time had lost all relevance. These extraordinary gaps in the time continuum were fashioned by the tug of war between the two opposite forces of nature that delineate the essence of our existence. They were brief intervals when time stood idle, as life hung on dearly to its last breath in the face of the inexorable pull of death. Such moments were rare, but would always be etched in Eric's consciousness to remind him of the precarious nature of our life.

And he certainly experienced one such moment when his very own life stood at a standstill some three years ago, as he was unceremoniously dumped overboard off the coast of Gibraltar. He quickly sank to the bottom of the Mediterranean, pulled down by the weight of the heavy chains that had been tightly wrapped around his entire body. His thoughts immediately went to the amount of time he could hold on without breathing before his lungs would collapse inside his chest for lack of oxygen. Gasping for air moments later, he saw glimpses of his life flash before him in a medley of images absent of any chronological or logical order. But he survived that horrific experience, rescued from drowning in the frigid water in the nick of time by a contingent of U.S. Special Forces.

Later when remembering the event, he often wondered about all the thoughts that went through his mind at the very instant the essence of his life started to slip away from him. Were they the products of a mind starving for oxygen, or something more profound, like a soul shedding off its last worldly baggage as it readied itself for the journey to the after world? As time wore on, so the memories of that horrifying experience moved on and eventually vanished out of his consciousness without explanation or further elucidation.

Yet again, three years later, the notion of time had once again lost all its raison d'être in the underground city of Cappadocia, where Eric had been buried alive. No daylight, no dawn, no dusk to toll the passage of time. Somehow, Eric's terrifying isolation had created a vacuum where time had lost its purpose. His mind drifted from one nightmare to another, often mixing the past with the present, interposing events and places with no regard to order or progression.

In the depth of the earth, time stopped one more time as life and death struggled for the possession of his soul.

And so, when the familiar silhouette of the agent from Interpol emerged from the darkness, he wondered whether the shadow he saw hovering over him was the cruel fruit of his imagination. His initial impulse was to reject the apparition as the creation of a demented mind hungry for food and water. Yet, the voice he heard was calm and soothing and the vision did not disappear from his psyche the way it did with his other ghostly apparitions.

"Eric, please open your eyes. It's me, Stephanie."

The voice echoed in his ears as more familiar feelings returned. He opened one eye but kept the other shut, not yet fully trusting himself. In the fog of his frenzied mind, he caught glimpses of many more eerie spirits hovering over him, and he recoiled back to a fetal position.

Stephanie poured water on a handkerchief and used it to clean his face and moisten his lips gently. She heard Eric mumble something. He was incoherent, but she took his grumbling as a good sign. She raised his head, holding his neck with one hand, and slightly pressed the water bottle on his mouth. Eric groaned and tried to pull his head away, but Stephanie held on firm. She titled the water bottle against his lips and water trickled down on both sides of his cheeks. She kept on pouring water until Eric started sucking on the bottle like a newborn.

"Please drink some more, Eric; it will do you some good."

Eric was starting to regain consciousness, and it did not take him long to gulp the water down his throat so fast that he almost ended up choking. He drank without stopping to breathe and in between two long coughing spats, he asked Stephanie if she had another bottle.

"Easy boy. Take it easy, we don't want you to drown yourself now that we have found you," Stephanie said teasingly as she pulled another bottle of mineral water from her knapsack.

Eric exhaled slowly. He had a million questions for her, but his mind was like mush. He felt weak and wobbly. Quenching his thirst was all he wanted to do for now. Food would come next, but that would have to be shared with his eagerness to find out how she had found him.

His first question came as a shock even to him. He was still having trouble organizing his thoughts in spite of the two bottles of mineral water and the chocolate power bar that he shoved down his throat in one bite.

"What time is it?" he asked while wiping his mouth with the back of his sleeve.

Stephanie looked at him in a funny way. "It's eight minutes past 11:00 a.m.; why do you want to know the time, may I ask?"

Eric did not have an answer. He was as confused as Stephanie that his first concern was to enquire about time. He thought about it a moment, then tried to correct himself.

"No, that's not what I meant to say," he said, his mind still in a haze. "How long have I been held prisoner in this hole, is what I want to know?"

"Oh, now I understand your question. Well, you left Istanbul four days ago. I imagine that they must have brought you here the next day, judging by your condition. So that would make three days that you have been left to die in this cave."

Eric wiped his face with his hands. He repeated the motion several times, like someone wanting to remove an invisible cobweb from the face. He rubbed his eyes, pressed his fingertips on his temples to help him regain his focus, and then gazed at the small lantern placed at his feet. *Get a grip, old boy.* He slid a sideways glance at the pack of power chocolate bars on the ground by his side and started to grin.

Stephanie watched Eric carefully. She thought his behavior odd. Uncertain about what to expect, she readied herself for a relapse. She was rewarded, instead, by an accusation.

"Tell me, Interpol agent extraordinaire, what took you so long to find me? I almost died in this shit hole, you know."

Stephanie burst out laughing. If she had harbored any fear about Eric's physical condition or his state of mind before, there was no longer any trace of it now. *The man is full of surprises.* She looked at him totally amazed at the speed of his recovery, and she could not help herself but laugh at his dry sense of humor. In a weird way, she liked that about him. But despite all her misgivings, she had also gained a new respect for Eric, as a man with great inner strength and the knack to surprise anyone at the most unexpected time. She looked him over one more time and decided that she was not going to let him off the hook so easily.

"Well for one, if you had told me where you were going when you left me in the hotel without forewarning, maybe, just maybe, I would have found you sooner. Maybe the courtesy of a note to let me know where you were headed would have been helpful. No? But of course you were in too much of a hurry to worry about such things. And do I dare say that you did not stop to think for one moment that I might be of some assistance to you? Or perhaps I'm totally wrong about your intentions. Yes, that's right come to think of it. I must be way off base. Let me tell you what I really believe you were doing. You wanted to protect me by keeping me in the dark. You wanted me out of harm's way. Now, I get it. My God, I owe you a big thank you, Eric. Don't I?"

"Touché," Eric replied.

He was pleased by her reaction. *That woman has lots of funk in her, I like that.*

"Please remind me to never taunt you again, or to underestimate you for that matter. And yes, I feel bad about the way I treated you in Istanbul. I thought I could handle it all by myself and I screwed up big time. There, I said it. And thank you, thank you, for saving my life."

Stephanie shrugged in response.

She was still mad at him for what he did. His lame excuses would not cut it as far as she was concerned. She could not forget that she had to endure Bartolli's wrath because of him. And if that were not enough, Aslan had given her an ultimatum. "Find him or we will find him for you, and I promise you, he will be spending the rest of his life in a Turkish jail," he had told her when she landed in Nevsehir.

"Can you walk?" she coldly said.

"I think so," Eric replied as he slowly got up on his feet.

"Good, follow me then." And she walked away without checking up on him.

As she made it to the entrance of the tunnel, two *Jandarmas* emerged from one of the adjoining rooms. They observed Eric for a moment, with stern expressions plastered on their faces, and without a word waved for him to step ahead. With Stephanie leading the way, the three men marched in a single file heading for the opening in the wall of the underground church. Eric did not remember the tunnel being so small. He watched Stephanie hunker down through the cramped orifice and waited for her to clear the passage before venturing his large frame in the confined space. She stayed posted near the exit at the other end of the tunnel with her flashlight pointing at the maddeningly low ceiling. As soon as Eric caught up with her, she turned her back and moved briskly, heading for another meandering passageway. She seemed to know her way around the maze of narrow and circuitous passages, as if a compass had been implanted in her head. Once in a while, without breaking stride, she would throw a glance behind to see if Eric was keeping pace. Otherwise, she kept her thoughts to herself, climbing out of the underground city as fast as possible.

When they finally reached the surface, the sun was nearing its zenith and the temperature had reached its peak for the day. Eric had a tough time adjusting to the sudden brightness. He was breathing hard and felt wobbly and light-headed. Yet, despite his poor physical condition, nothing seemed to be able to dampen his good spirit. He could stand tall without fear of hitting the top of his head and could freely stretch his arms in all directions. He was alive standing in the open air under an azure sky that stretched into infinity above him. And that was all that really mattered to him at this point in time.

The grounds were bustling with military police. They were folding down their camps and getting ready to board large transport vehicles parked near the entrance of the tunnel. The two policemen that had accompanied them in the underground labyrinths had already joined their comrades, and Stephanie and Eric were left standing alone as if they no longer mattered.

Eric had a smirk on his face that stretched from ear to ear."My God, are all these people here because of me?" he asked Stephanie.

"Don't flatter yourself. They did not come for you. They are here because they found a large terrorist camp a couple of kilometers away."

"A camp. You mean a farmhouse?"

"Yes, a farmhouse that hid a large network of tunnels and caves dug out inside the mountain."

"Great, so they got the bastards," enthused Eric.

Stephanie pursed her lips."I'm afraid not. They were long gone by the time we reached the encampment. We found the farmhouse where they must have held you captive, but nothing else except for a couple of sheep ruminating around, a dead dog, and lots of empty caves."

Eric could not hide his disappointment and kicked a stone with his left foot. It landed a few meters away where Aslan stood glaring with eyes that left no doubt about his hostility towards him. Stephanie's face hardened as she met Aslan's stare.

"Don't move, stay put," she ordered Eric. "He's still very angry with you for having disobeyed him. And now he must be mad as hell that the terrorists have slipped away. I would not be surprised at all if he is blaming you for it."

Stephanie approached Aslan with a smile that was borderline flirtatious. It had little apparent effect on the counter-terrorist officer. Aslan looked her over and then shoved his hand in his pocket, looking for his silver cigarette case. He pulled it out, taped the shiny metal case twice with his index finger, and then shoved it back in his pocket without opening it.

"So they did not kill the Canadian pest after all. I guess they wanted to give me that pleasure for dragging me to this hole in the middle of nowhere?"

"It's thanks to him that we found their hiding place. Let's not forget it," Stephanie shouted back.

"What good did that do us? Now they have gone deeper underground and we will never be able to find them again."

"Maybe so, but I'm sure he can tell us a lot about these men and help us identify their leaders. And who knows, they might even have bragged to him about their plans, thinking that no one would ever find him alive."

"Stephanie, you're a dreamer. These people have been at war for almost three decades. They did not survive that long by spitting out their secrets to anyone, and least of all to a man they want dead at all costs."

"Well, I don't agree with you. I have a lot of experience dealing with hostage situations and the need people have for boasting about their accomplishments, particularly when they believe they have outdone themselves. We shall see who is right after I have had the opportunity to drill Eric," she replied with more than a trace of sarcasm in her voice.

Aslan smirked.

"Let me give you one good piece of advice, Stephanie. I'm telling you this because I know a hell of a lot more about the Kurds than you will ever know. Don't pin your hopes too high on what you might find out. It will turn out to be useless in the end, even if Eric tells you something you might think is important."

He then paused to scrutinize her. He stared at her big green eyes, challenging him to tell her what most in the agency would consider classified information. He always disliked the lack of openness that was too often exhibited by his people towards allied intelligence organizations. It stifled progress, as far as he was concerned. And it did not help matters that he was in dire need of improving upon his success ratio. The counterintelligence business had not been kind to him of late. And this latest adventure had all the appearances of another fiasco.

After some hesitation, he finally decided that it was time for him to throw a bone at this agent from an Interpol. "Perhaps it's time for me to clue you in something else I know about this whole sordid affair," he said. "I'm afraid I have not been totally honest with you. The fact of the matter is that we were on to this terrorist cell long before Interpol contacted us. You see, ELINT—that's our electronic intelligence branch—has, in fact, been monitoring the activities of this particular terrorist group for almost two years. What initially intrigued my people was the sudden influx of money the group seemed to have come across. When the electronic intelligence agency dug further into their online activities, they were able to trace where some of the loot came from. But they could never figure out how the money was made or whether or not a foreign state or organization was in fact financing them. They knew cash was electronically transferred to them from all over the world, but they were mystified as to how they were able to raise so much money so fast. With the help of your agent, they finally got closer to finding some of the answers."

"You mean Jules Betton?"

"Yes, him. He's really good. With his help, my people were able to make incredible inroads into the terrorists' ways and means—that is until your friend over there poked his nose into something he had no business getting involved with. And now, it looks like all our hard work has gone down the drain."

"Wait a minute. I don't agree with you. Let's not forget that Eric is the one who first alerted us about their financial dealings. Without his data, Jules would not have been able to do what he did. And without Eric's help, you would never have been able to locate their center of operations in this farmhouse in the middle of nowhere, as you so aptly said."

"Well maybe so. But now they know we are on to them and they took off. I mean gone, really gone. I got a call moments ago from the director of MIT. He is the head of our national intelligence agency that oversees the Directorate of Electronic and Technical Intelligence. He told me that we have lost all electronic contacts. It looks like these guys have shut down their entire operation. Their IP addresses are duds. Nothing is going through anymore. They have vanished into thin air, Stephanie."

Stephanie stared hard. She was not convinced, and the way Aslan spoke to her annoyed her even more. That the Turkish counterintelligence agency had not been entirely forthright with Interpol did not come to her as a huge surprise. Unfortunately, she knew that in her line of business the practice was more prevalent than not. That was par for the course and would probably never change. What irritated her was Aslan's self-defeating attitude. This was not what she had expected from a seasoned counter-intelligence officer. And this was certainly not what she came here to do.

She briefly glanced back at Eric, who seemed to be biding his time a short distance away. He had not moved, but there was something about the way he looked at her that clinched it.

"I don't believe you really think that. These people would never walk away from a gold mine, just like that. If Eric is right, the algorithm is as good as money in the bank. They must be using different channels to funnel their funds," she said pointedly.

"Possibly," Aslan replied while turning his attention to what his men were doing.

"No, that's a certainty. I'm 100% convinced that's what they have done."

There was no reply at first. Instead, Aslan took time to take stock of what was going on around him. What he saw was the aftermath of a failed raid. He watched his men pack their gear without great enthusiasm. He noticed the way everyone seemed to be keeping busy. *A poor substitute for the high drama incursion they had trained for and been promised,* he thought. And then his emotions got the better of him.

"Just do me a favor, Stephanie. Get him out of my face before I kill him with my bare hands," he hollered out of sheer frustration.

"All right then, but please grant me one last favor. Let me hitch a ride to the closest airport in your helicopter."

The helicopter dropped altitude rapidly over the runway of Nevsehir airport. It landed moments later close to a twin engine Turkish airline jet waiting on the tarmac for the take-off signal from the control tower. Stephanie and Eric were hustled to their seats by a flight attendant who looked unhappy that her flight had been delayed. Eric's appearance did not go well with her either. She gave him the dirtiest look possible as she stared at his torn shirt, his bloodied hands, and his filthy pants. She left them immediately after, intending not to give them any further attention for the rest of the short haul to Istanbul.

Stephanie and Eric had not spoken to one another since the time they had boarded the helicopter some ten minutes ago. The recent events had left them both with many thoughts and concerns to ponder, process, and sort out in their minds. Stephanie, still reeling from her conversation with Aslan, could not help wondering whether Eric would be able to provide her with the kind of information she needed to steer the investigation in the right direction.

Meanwhile, in the seat next to her, Eric had one burning question in his mind, and he blurted it out as soon the plane reached its cruising altitude

"Tell me, Stephanie, how did you manage to find me in that maze?"

"Simplicity itself, my dear Eric. I just followed your feet."

"Enough with the teasing. I thought you had accepted my apologies earlier. Please tell me Stephanie, how did you do it?"

"Your feet led me to where they buried you," Stephanie replied then burst out in a loud and full throttle laughter. Still laughing, she gave Eric a gentle pat on the arm and whispered in his ear like a co-conspirator sharing an important secret:

"To be precise, my good friend, your right foot told me where to find you," she chuckled.

Eric gave her a dirty look that made her laugh even more. Feeling sorry for him, she finally clarified her last bit of information further. "I inserted a beacon in the heel of your right shoe that I bought before I picked you up from the hospital in Istanbul. There, now you know my secret."

"Great, so you knew where I was all this time and you let me waste away in that hellhole for 3 days!"

"With an attitude like, that maybe I should have let you die," Stephanie snapped back.

"OK sorry, but please start making sense."

"You think it was a walk in the park looking for you when you were buried hundreds of feet in the ground in the middle of a desert?" She said, trying to tame her flaring temper.

"I don't imagine for one instant that it was easy. But if I was carrying a tracking device on me, why could you not find me sooner?"

Stephanie considered what Eric had just said for a moment. She realized that she should stop teasing him if she wanted Eric's co-operation. *There is also the matter of what he could tell me about the terrorist group,* she reminded herself.

"You're right, you deserved to know. My turn to apologize," she said after an awkward pause.

Eric waved off the apology, and she took it as her cue to continue with the explanation.

"It all started with a tourist guide that spotted you in the valley. When Aslan told me what his local spy had said, I immediately flew over looking for you. Unfortunately, the beacon has only a four to five kilometer range. So I spent the next three days circling around in a helicopter hoping to catch a signal. It was not easy. There was a huge area to cover as you can well imagine. And the fact that you were hidden deep underground made the search even more challenging, to say the least. Luckily for you, once we located the signal, we had the tourist guide to help us find our way down into the underground labyrinth. That was a real challenge all by itself. What a web of caves and nonstop tunnels leading to who knows where. My God, they must have spent several lifetimes building that place. The truth of the matter is that you owe your life more to the guide than to the tracking device. He not only helped us narrow our search, but he also showed us an easier way to move that stone wheel than to dynamite it to pieces and risk the whole cave collapsing on you."

She paused for a beat, and then added, "Now you know everything. Are you satisfied?"

Eric just sat there, his expression knotted with uncertainty.

Stephanie did not wait for his response and wasted no time to broach the subject which had been on her mind since they boarded the plane.

"We have much to talk about, my dear Eric. Why don't you start by telling me what happened when they held you prisoner."

CHAPTER 28

KASIMPASA DISTRICT, ISTANBUL

"He escaped. Eric is here in Istanbul," Abdullah raged as he smashed the phone on the floor. Standing in a corner of the room, Karzan stepped back and pressed his hands against the wall behind him. He had never seen Abdullah so angry. Hagir lowered his eye, avoiding any eye contact with anyone. Tania stood still, staring ahead, her mind busy trying to make sense about what she had just heard.

"Impossible. It can't be Eric. There is no way he could have found his way out of this cave alive. No one has ever escaped from the underground city," Tania screeched.

"Well, the bastard did it somehow. And now he is free to tell all he knows about us. Why the hell did you have to tell him what we were about to do? Damn it Tania, why did you show him the computer algorithm? What were you thinking, for God's sakes!"

Tania ignored the accusations and stood her ground.

"Before you start blaming me for something that may be not true, can you tell me that you are 100% certain that it's Eric they saw, and not just someone who looks like him?"

"Tania. Yilmaz is the policeman who just called to let me know that he has just seen Eric at the airport. He has never failed me. It's the same man who caught sight of Eric catching a flight to Cappadocia earlier, remember! He certainly knows what Eric looks like. There's no mistake. It's definitely Eric."

Tania gave Abdullah a brooding look, the one she favored when something was deeply troubling her.

"If you are right about Eric, then we have an even more serious problem."

"What do you mean? Don't you think I know we are in deep shit, Tania?"

"Abdullah, you are missing the point."

"Speak up, Tania! Now is not the time to play mind games. Spit it out right now!"

"Alright, I will. But first let's calm down and think through this rationally. How could Eric have escaped?" she said pointing her chin at Abdullah. "How do you think he managed to get out from a cave hundreds of feet below ground, dislodge a one ton millstone in the process, and find his way out of this maze all by himself? Unless...."

"Unless what?......You can't be serious, Tania."

"I'm afraid this is the only logical explanation. That's right, someone must have helped him, and whomever got him out knew exactly where to find him. Yes Abdullah, you can't trust your men."

"What are you saying? I'm surrounded by spies and traitors?"

"Not necessarily traitors, but most probably at least one of your men must have helped him."

"No way. No fucking way. They have been loyal to me for far too long to betray me now. These men are like brothers to me. We've fought too many battles together, we've killed too many men together, we've taken care of one another in good and bad times, and above all, we all share the same dream for a Kurdish motherland. My men are dedicated to the cause. I'd trust my life with anyone of them."

"What about Celik?"

"Celik was not one of us. We used him when we needed him. He was an outsider, more like a mercenary."

"He must have had a partner on the inside."

"Why do you think that?"

"Because there's no way he could have known about Eric otherwise. How did he managed to trace Eric in Paris, you think?"

Tania paused for a moment while she watched Abdullah slowly absorb the implication of what she had just told him. She saw Abdullah coming to terms with the possibility that Celik had an accomplice. But she also noted that his eyes conveyed a different message. The look he gave her did not reassure her. Somehow she felt Abdullah no longer trusted her.

"Listen to me Abdullah," Tania said in a tone meant to reassure. "The news is not all bad. What are we faced with? First that Eric knows that we have the algorithm and knows that we're behind the high-speed stock trades. So what? He can't stop us from trading under different numbered companies. On the other hand, he may have led the police to the farmhouse, but we have nothing to fear from that either, since we cleaned up the place and shut down our online connections. That's the good news. The bad news is that Eric knows who we are, and if that alone does not spell enough big trouble for us, we also have a turncoat who may be on his way to the police as we speak."

Abdullah turned sharply to address Karzan standing close behind him. "Gather the men right now. We need to get hold of Eric right away and find out who's helping him."

Tania pulled Abdullah aside. She had recovered from her initial shock and her mind was working in overdrive, planning her next move. She was at least two steps ahead of Abdullah.

"Forget Eric for now. Get the woman married to the Greek professor," she whispered in his ear.

"What the hell for?"

"A trade, Abdullah. A life in exchange for a life."

"Why not just grab him?"

"You are not thinking straight, Abdullah. Do you really think Interpol is going to let him out of their sight while he's in Istanbul?"

Abdullah stared at his men for a beat, wrestling with Tania's suggestion."But what makes you so sure he will go for it?"

"I know that my credibility with you is at an all time low at the moment, but believe me when I tell you that I know Eric. His conscience must be burning him like a fire in hell. He blames himself for all the people who've died because of the algorithm. He thinks that he let them down—that it was all his fault. He will do all he can to save the life of his former girlfriend, especially after what he must have found in the underground church."

"Alright then. But if that does not work, we will kill them both and pack our bags immediately after."

Eric felt the full thrust of Stephanie's debriefing expertise. She bore into his mind with all the finesse of an inquisitor from the Middle Ages. She was thorough in her pursuit for information, tireless in her demand for the facts, and relentless in her need to know all the minute details. She made him describe the interior of the farmhouse five or six times at least. She drilled him over every room dug into the mountain, probing his memory of the place with a fine tooth comb. What was the function of each room, how many men were in there, what they looked like, what were they doing; she kept asking again and again until Eric almost exploded in exasperation. She wanted to know how many computers were stored in the large cave at the very back of the complex, how many computer analysts he saw in there, what they were working on, what they looked like, who were their leaders.

He told her about Tania, where they first met, what she was doing back in Casablanca, how she managed to not get caught on the boat that sank in the Mediterranean killing all the passengers on board, and how she ended up with the stolen algorithm. She asked him if Tania had changed much since Casablanca, if she had any particular mannerisms, what she told him about her role and activities in the group. She did not flinch when he told her about the enhancements she had made in the software program. But he was certain that he detected the faint trace of a smile on her face when he told her what Tania was planning to do with the redesigned financial model.

Her enquiries about Abdullah were particularly exhausting. She paid special attention to his description of the leader of the terrorist group, often making him repeat the same things twice or testing his memory of what he remembered of the terrorist by purposely mixing up key details about his facial features and other physical attributes. The only time she seemed to relent on her line of questioning was when he related his discovery of Martina's body and that of her little girl buried at her side. She kept quiet and looked away when he told her how much the murder of these two innocent victims was tearing him apart.

Thankfully, the grueling debriefing was interrupted by the musical ring tone of Stephanie's cell phone. She picked it up right away, listened to the caller for a second or two, and immediately handed over the phone to Eric.

Eric's heart froze when he heard the hollow metallic voice of the caller.

"Don't do anything stupid, just listen up," Abdullah said. "Laura is a pretty young woman, and we don't want anything to happen to her? Right?"

A ripple of fear swept across Eric's face as he listened to Abdullah's detailed instructions. Words like, *do not call the police, do precisely as you are told, and Laura will be fine,* were permanently etched on his mind.

"Are you going to do it or not, Eric?" Abdullah asked a second time.

Eric breathed deeply.

"Eric, are you there? Did you hear me?"

Eric nodded. Stephanie looked away. He swallowed hard, not able to speak. Laura's screams echoed on the phone and his jaw tightened so hard that he felt it would shatter into a thousand pieces.

"I heard you. I will do what you want," he finally stuttered with as much confidence in his voice that he could muster.

"Good. Very good. Now, please let me speak to the Interpol agent standing beside you."

Stephanie grabbed the phone from Eric's hand. She was all business, listening intently to what Abdullah was saying, keeping her emotions well in check. She scribbled a few notes on her notepad, hummed her understanding a few times, and shook her head when Abdullah finished telling her what he wanted her to do.

"What assurances do I have that you will not harm Laura?" she asked.

"None, really, except for the fact that you have my word."

"Your word is not good enough. You can do better than that."

"Listen and listen very carefully to what I'm going to tell you. I will not repeat myself. If you do what you're told and bring Eric to the rendezvous point, I will let Laura go safely. If you don't, you will have not one, but two dead bodies on your conscience and nothing to show for it. We will eventually catch up with Eric; it's only a matter of time. If you're the professional I know you are, you must have already figured this out. So let's not waste any more time. The exchange will take place in broad daylight at the Galata Bridge during rush hour, to avoid any misunderstandings. We will release Laura at one end of the bridge and at the same time, Eric will walk towards us from the opposite side. No tricks and everything will be fine. We are freedom fighters, not murderers. And lastly, no need to call the local police. That would be a fatal mistake."

Eric spent the next couple of hours avoiding Stephanie's stares. Twice she had asked him if he still wanted to go ahead with it. Each time he had answered her with a categorical YES. The relief he had felt when he emerged from the underground church was now replaced by a distressing mix of self-afflicted feelings—guilt over the tragedy of Ivan's family, responsibility for the death of David Luchatel, and remorse that he did not believe in Valerie's innocence, the love of his life. And now, the horrific feeling of culpability that once again, another innocent life was in danger because of him. "This must end right now," he yelled at Stephanie to shut her up.

Stephanie finally backed off and kept herself busy by checking on some handheld device that pinged every time she switched it on. She glanced at her watch a couple of times, and then let her gaze settle on Eric at the far end of the room.

"I understand that you want to go ahead with this crazy thing," she said, her voice solemn. "I will not stop you even if everything about it tells me this is wrong.

But I want you to know that I will use everything in my power to save your life."

Eric stared hard at her. He had an alarmed look on his face, not liking the sound of what he had heard.

"No, don't be afraid. I will not put Laura's life at risk," Stephanie reassured him quickly. "I can't share with you what I have in mind; you just have to trust me for now. Now let's get going; we don't want to be late for our rendezvous."

Rush hour was in full swing when Stephanie and Eric arrived on the European side of the Galata Bridge. They had parked their rental car under a large tree on a side street and walked the rest of the way to the ramp leading up to the upper deck of the bridge. They were on time. And not surprisingly, there was no sign of Laura or her captors anywhere. *They must be hiding, watching our every move from a safe distance,* she thought, knowing full well the time-proven procedures the terrorists must be following. She gazed silently at the immediate surroundings, sensing eyes prying on them, but made no mention of it to Eric. After a short pause, she signaled Eric it was time to get going.

Looking east across the Bosphorus to *Üsküdar* and Asia, Stephanie more closely scrutinized the full length of the upper deck of the bascule bridge that spanned the Golden Horn in Istanbul. There was a beehive of activity on the two sidewalks lining the deck on both sides. Fishermen, vendors, travelers, and commuters crowded the pedestrian paths along both sides of the bridge. Sandwiched in between the walkways, the six vehicular lanes running on opposite side of each other were also jam-packed. Traffic was moving at a snail's pace. A streetcar crawled by them carrying its heavy load of passengers across the Bosphorus. Stephanie gave the typical rush hour scene of the large cosmopolitan city an apprehensive look. The Galata Bridge was as promised—busy, crowded, and chaotic—the perfect cover for a discreet swap, offering little or no opportunity for a successful rescue raid.

She gave Eric a quick glance. He seemed calm and at peace with himself. He acknowledged her silent query with a nod of the head, and they both turned their attention to the small group standing at the far end of the bridge. Two men and two women were standing together, observing them from afar. They were only noticeable by their lack of interest in the scenery. No awe-gasping tourists for sure.

Eric recognized Laura immediately. She looked fragile, worried and frightened at the same time. A tall woman with her hair pulled back in a chignon held on to her arm. A man stood close behind her. From afar, one could have mistaken him for a protective lover. Standing slightly aside from the group, Abdullah stared in the direction of Stephanie, who raised her left hand in acknowledgement.

The signal had been given.

Eric did not wait for Stephanie's instructions to move ahead. He walked along the crowded sidewalk, not daring to look back. He kept a steady pace, breaking a path through the throngs of people blocking his way. He caught Laura stumbling through the crowd on the opposite walkway across the bridge. She looked distraught, on the verge of a massive nervous breakdown. But her tears had the opposite effect on Eric. It fueled his resolve to forge ahead. He was more determined than ever to put an end to her distress as quickly as possible.

They both reached the midpoint of the bridge at the same time. And they both stopped, overwhelmed by an irresistible impulse. They stared at each other across the six car lanes and one tram line for a few seconds that seemed to last an eternity. Laura wiped the tears off her face and yelled something at Eric.

Eric waved back.

Laura seemed agitated and kept motioning at Eric to turn back.

Eric blew her a kiss.

She grasped the meaning of the gesture and started to sob loudly. People stopped to stare at her, a handful seemed genuinely concerned, others unsure of what to do, but none attempted to console her. With time, her cries sounded more like groans than sobs. When she saw Eric wave goodbye at her for a second time, she started to run as fast as she could toward Stephanie who was waiting with open arms.

Eric watched the two women locked in a tight embrace, seeking comfort in one another. Body melted against body, not wanting to let go, as though entranced by the drumming of another human heartbeat. He could sense the intensity of their emotions. It reassured him.

Suddenly, the horn of a ship passing by deadened the noise of the crowd and the traffic. And in that instant, everything and everyone around him came to a stop, as if the whole world had been caught in some kind of suspended animation. He remained feet-rooted at the half way point of the bridge, his mind torn apart by the wrenching pull of two opposite and powerful forces. He contemplated the idea of making a run for it, and even perhaps—if he was lucky enough—managing a daring escape from the claws of his tormentors. But he quickly discarded that thought, fearing that Abdullah had planned for it and posted armed men at both ends of the bridge. There was only one absolute truth that really mattered to him at that point. He was prepared to sacrifice his life in order to save another innocent victim.

Eric noticed Tania glaring at him, her piercing eyes daring him at a distance to make a wrong move. He observed Abdullah who was standing impassive and expressionless at her side. Time was fast losing its elasticity, and he instinctively knew that he had to follow the path that had been set out for him. He slowly closed his mind to extinguish any lingering thoughts of Laura and Stephanie. And without further hesitation, he resumed his march to the east end entrance of the Galata Bridge. His final steps were the most gratifying, comforted by the feeling that his sacrifice had saved a life. Stephanie had already taken Laura away to a safe place.

As he approached Abdullah and Tania, three men suddenly emerged from the crowd and grabbed him from behind. They dragged him to a black SUV and shoved him inside the vehicle with a kick in the backside. Moments later, they were heading at high-speed for the Kasimpasa District of Istanbul. He heard the call to prayer from a mosque close by, as the SUV pulled over onto the side of the road and rolled along a small pebbled courtyard framed by thick walls and three small non-descript buildings. Two pairs of hands grabbed his arms and yanked him inside the building in the center of the courtyard. Six or seven men were waiting inside and immediately formed a tight circle around him as he was kicked to the ground. The men looked tense and fidgety, nervously holding on to their guns. Eric caught a few glances, surprisingly not directed at him, but at the other men standing in the room. The heavy footsteps of Abdullah as he marched in raised the tension inside the cramped room by at least three more notches. The men nervously tightened their grip on their guns.

"Who helped you to get out of the underground church?" Abdullah barked.

"I don't know what you mean. I got out all by myself."

"Don't you lie to me! You could not have done it alone. Give me the name of the man who helped you."

"No one."

"Alright, he is yours. Let's see how fast his memory will come back to him."

Two men stepped forward and grabbed Eric from behind. One man yanked his head back, pulling him by the hair, the other beating him with a black rubber baton. They would then take turns, but this time adding a few kicks in the groin to their repertoire. The intense beating must have lasted a good ten minutes. When they finally released him, he fell head first on the ground and made no attempt to get up.

"Is the man who helped you to escape in this room?" Abdullah hissed.

Eric did not answer.

" I see, you are being stubborn. Hit him some more, if that's what he wants."

"What's his name?"

Eric split blood from his mouth and raised his hand signaling that he wanted to talk.

"Who helped you?" screamed Abdullah.

"Machoose."

"Who?"

"Myyy… shooooose." Eric garbled, barely coherent.

"Enough with this nonsense. Karzan! Cut his fingers off. Start with his right hand and then his left and don't stop until he gives me the name."

Karzan drew his knife from its leather sheath and stepped forward with a wide grin on his face. He held on to Eric's wrist with his left hand and raised the long knife high in the air with the other. Eric shut his eyes tight and tried to mentally prepare himself for the pain. The knife sliced the air but nothing happened.

The walls in the room suddenly shook. The earth trembled, shaken by the roar of a loud blast. Karzan's feet wobbled. He had a hard time keeping his balance. Another loud explosion. Gunshots. Two more detonations, each one louder than the first one, followed by the rapid-fire of machine guns.

Karzan and Abdullah exchanged alarmed glances.

The men pulled their guns, and four of them rushed out with Abdullah leading the charge. Screams, more gunshots, and the distinct sound of a metallic canister rolling on the ground. Smoke was everywhere, and the acrid smell of fire burned Eric's eyes and throat. Two men dressed all in black, their head and face hidden under black balaclavas, stormed into the room. Gunshots. One, then two guards fell to the ground with blood gushing from the middle of their foreheads. A masked man hustled Eric out in the courtyard and shoved a gas mask on his face. They left him sprawled on the ground, wheezing, coughing blood from his mouth, and his eyes on fire.

"Mr. Martin. Mr. Martin can you hear me?"

Eric moaned in a semi-state of consciousness.

"The ambulance is on its way. Our finest physicians will soon take care of your wounds, rest assured," Aslan said in a voice that was meant to convey concern.

Eric groaned. A medic removed the rubber mask and wiped his eyes with a cold compress. His body stirred. The medic gave him something to smell.

Eric coughed and opened his eyes.

"Thank you," he nodded with a weak smile, his head was now feeling like lead.

"No Mr. Martin. I thank you. Without you we would never have gotten rid of that band of criminals," Aslan replied.

Eric coughed some more. He thought he was going to puke. He spat up blood and washed his mouth with the potion the medic had given him.

"I did not do it for you," he finally managed to blurt out.

"I know that. You're a very courageous man. I owe you an apology for treating you the way I did."

The medic raised his head and made him drink the rest of the potion. He spat more blood, coughed a couple of times, and glanced up and down, finally settling his gaze on Aslan.

"That won't be necessary. Just tell me what happened to the algorithm."

"I'm afraid they managed to blow up the place before we got to it. The building where they stored their computers was rigged with explosives. I lost three good men in that explosion."

The smelling salts were starting to clear Eric's mind. He held onto the medic's arm to steady himself. He flushed confusion from his head, and familiar faces returned.

"I'm sorry to hear that. But I hope that your men did not die in vain. Are you absolutely sure that the algo was totally destroyed."

"With this sort of thing, one cannot be absolutely certain. Even if the program was reduced to pieces in the blast, what guarantee do we have that copies were not made and stashed safely away somewhere?"

"But at the very least, can you reassure me of one thing. Did you get hold of Tania?"

"Yes. But I'm afraid not in time to get her to talk to us. We found her body in a pool of blood in a ground floor room. Someone had sliced her throat open."

Eric remained silent.

He found no joy or satisfaction in the death of his most vile enemy. Another chapter in this tragic saga had just ended. It began with an alluring invitation to join an investment boutique in Casablanca that turned into a trail of dead bodies leading up to Istanbul. Against all odds, he had escaped with his life for a second time. And now he had only one wish, one thought, one plea—the dire need to put closure to his nightmare once and for all.

Eric watched as two men wearing white gowns laid down a stretcher beside him. Stephanie had joined the group and was standing over him, holding a large shopping bag. When their eyes met, she shook her head as if to say, *it's beyond belief.*

"I brought you some fresh clothes. You will need them when they release you from the hospital, once again."

"Thank you, that was very thoughtful of you."

"Not so fast, my friend. You can have them under one condition."

"Oh I see. Let me guess. They are mine if I promise to fly back to Paris and mind my own business from now on."

"No. I want you to give me back the shoes that you're wearing."

EPILOGUE

*"Please give me the light of your wisdom
To dispel the darkness of my mind
And to heal my mental continuum."*

LIBERATING PRAYER
PRAISED TO BUDDHA SHAKYAMUNI

CHANIA, CRETE – EIGHT MONTHS LATER

"Mr. Martin, Mr. Martin"

"Yes Yannis. What is it?"

The young, good-looking boy with tight curly black hair and long eyelashes to match, caught up with Eric. He was slightly out of breath from his chase as he glanced up at Eric with his deep brown eyes.

"Mr. Martin," he repeated one more time.

"That's my name. Now please calm down and tell me what got you so excited."

"A beautiful lady is here to see you."

"Is that so? And does this beautiful lady have a name?"

"I don't know her name. She didn't give it to me, Mr. Martin. She just asked for you." Yannis paused for a second, unsure whether he should tell Eric what he had heard his aunt say about the visitor.

Eric quickly picked up on the boy's hesitation."What is it Yannis? What else do you want to tell me?"

Please Mr. Martin, don't tell anyone that I told you. I will get in trouble with my aunt if she finds out."

Another short pause. A deep sigh. And then Yannis blurted out."I heard aunt Laura tell uncle Alexis that she is definitely your type."

"What did you just say?"

Yannis looked slightly embarrassed. "That's all I know, I swear. Aunt Laura thinks that you will really like this woman. You should really meet her. Please Mr. Martin, come with me I will take you to her right now."

Eric burst out laughing. "So it's a conspiracy. Your aunt is trying to set me up on a blind date. Is that it? Tell me the truth young man."

"No. It's not it at all. This lady said that she is a friend and that she would really like to see you. Please Mr. Martin, let me take you to her."

"That won't be necessary. Just tell me where to find this beautiful friend of mine."

Eric caught the mischievous look on Yannis' face as the boy tried to hide away his glee by staring down at his well worn Nike sandals.

"What is it now, Yannis? Just tell me where I can find her. Don't worry about me, I won't get lost. I know my way around town."

"Alright, Mr. Martin. I guess it's alright if you go on your own. If you give me five euro I will tell you where you can meet her."

Yannis was no longer the shy and nervous-looking young boy he first appeared to be. He was staring at Eric with all the confidence of a shrewd operator who had just befuddled his victim and was about to reap the benefit of his scheme. The transformation was sudden and totally unexpected.

"Really. And why do you think I will give you such a generous reward?" Eric asked, slightly amused.

"Uncle Alexis said that you are an investment banker, so I figure that you should be able to easily afford to double the reward that the lady has already given me. Beside she is..."

"Beautiful, and she would fulfil all my dreams. You already told me that son." Eric appraised the young, enterprising boy with renewed interest and respect. He remembered what his father had told him when he was about Yannis' age. "My son, you'll never learn in business school what I'm about to tell you," his father confided one day after a particularly heated discussion they had about how to best ensure a successful transaction . "The fine art of winning negotiations does not lie in how badly you think the other party wants the deal, but in how much they think they will lose if you don't deal with them." That lesson had stuck in his mind throughout his career as an investment banker. It had helped him win many very lucrative deals. But somehow that lesson had slipped away when he switched careers at the bank. He had just been taken for a ride by a young Greek boy who obviously possessed all the attributes of a fine and promising businessman. It was the wakeup call he needed. Now was the time to go back to what he knew and did best.

"Let me tell you what I'm going to do for you, since you worked so hard looking for me. Here is one euro. If the woman is as beautiful as you said, I will give you another euro. If I fall in love with her, you will get another euro. And if I marry her, one more euro will come your way. Now tell me where she is and you will be able to add a whole new euro to your bank account right now. Otherwise, I'm going to tell your aunt that you spied on her. How does this sound? It's a good deal, don't think? "

The old town of Chania has, to a large extent, preserved the traditional architecture and distinctive charm of its Venetian and Turkish eras. Crisscrossed by narrow stone-paved alleys, picturesque taverns, ancient monuments, and old mansions that have seen better days, the old quarters were a delight for anyone looking for a memorable trip back in time. But to Eric the town had a déjà vu feeling to it. In many ways, it reminded him of many Spanish and Portuguese towns and villages which could be found cresting all along the Mediterranean coastline and where the strong influence of the Moorish invasion permeated every building and every archway.

After a good twenty minute walk, he had arrived at Kastelli, the central part of the old town, making his way on to the Venetian harbor and the main square where all the tourists usually gathered. His favorite tavern was situated slightly off to the west, and while it offered a magnificent view of the Aegean Sea and the old harbour's lighthouse, it was often missed by the horde of visitors that descended the hills every morning.

Stephanie gave him a shy smile as he made his way to her corner table. She seemed ill-at-ease in her white cotton dress. It was a kind of a revelation to see her conducting herself in this way, after being more accustomed to her usually defiant and proud demeanour. *Perhaps she does not feel comfortable wearing a dress,* he thought as he smiled back. But as he observed her from close, something else surprised him even more. Yannis had not lied. She was, indeed, a truly stunning woman. She had warm chestnut color hair and golden brown skin which made her deep green eyes stand out even more. She wore little make up. but the way her long eyelashes framed her eyes made it impossible for anyone to look away once you looked at her. With high cheekbones, full lips, and a body well honed from hours in the gym, she was not just perfect, she radiated an intelligent beauty. Eric could not believe his eyes and chided himself for not noticing her good looks earlier. But then again, other pressing matters were on his mind at the time.

The owner of the establishment immediately recognized Eric and grabbed a cold bottle of Mythos Hellenic lager from the fridge. Eric waved him a thank you and pulled out the empty chair in front of Stephanie. He had not said a word. His eyes seemed to be doing all the talking. Stephanie shifted her body in her chair and gave Eric a slight uncomfortable smirk.

"Well, hello stranger. Remember me? My name is Stephanie. You know—your guardian angel. You can stop staring at me like that now!"

"Yes of course. It's just that I'm so surprised to see you here. What a coincidence."

"Well, it's not exactly a coincidence. I knew you were in Crete."

"And you flew one thousand miles to come to see me?"

"That's also not exactly the reason why I'm here. I'm ashamed to admit it, but the truth is that Bartolli was fed up seeing me around the office. He ordered me to go on vacation."

"So you chose to spend your holiday in Crete because.....?"

"Laura invited me over. We have been keeping in touch from the time we met in Istanbul, and she has been bugging me to come visit her ever since. So, here I am. And yes, she also told me that you were here. Is your curiosity satisfied now?"

"Well, not entirely. But I'm glad to see you."

"It's good to see you too. I'm happy to see that most of your scars are gone."

"Now at last I know the real reason why you are here. You were concerned that I might have lost my good looks."

They both burst out laughing, truly enjoying their teasing acts.

"I always liked that about you."

"And what might that be?"

"Your weird sense of humor. But seriously, it's good to see you in good spirits, suntanned and relaxed. I'm glad to see that you have recovered so quickly."

"Thank you. You look great yourself."

"My turn to thank you for the compliment," she replied with a faint, blushing smile. "So, how long are you planning to stay in Crete?"

"I don't know. But long enough, I hope, to enjoy your company."

"Well, thank you. But I have to be honest with you. There's another reason why I made this trip to see you. Laura is very concerned about you lately. She is afraid you might end up like those beach bums that roam around town at night. She asked me to talk to you about what you're planning to do after your extended stay in Crete. For some reason, she thinks I've some influence over you." She smiled at her last remark and blinked her eyes a couple of times as if she was expecting some sort of affirmation.

"So now I have Laura to thank as well. Listen, I don't have a clue where I'm going to pitch my tent. At times, I think Australia might look like a good spot. Alain still wants me to join him down under. I don't understand why, after what I did to him. He said something about owing me big time for saving his career at the bank. I have no idea what he is talking about. In any event, the only thing I'm certain about is that I miss investment banking and all the wheeling and dealing that goes along in that crazy world of business. It took a young boy to remind me where I belong. So now that I know what I want to do for the rest of my life, the only question that needs to be sorted out is where I should go. Any suggestions?"

"Australia sounds like a good idea to me," Stephanie said. She studied Eric's face for some time, and then slowly shifted her gaze to the cubic-shaped structure sitting on the edge of the harbor. She tilted her head to the side to gain a better view of the large hemispherical dome connected to the main building by four stone arches. She then let her gaze glide down the archway facing the sea before turning her attention back to Eric.

"It's a beautiful mosque. Does it remind you of anything you have seen before?" she added after a long pensive pause.

"It's called the *Mosque Kioutsiouk Hassan;* it's a vestige of the Ottoman Empire. You will find many remnants of the Turkish occupation on the island."

Eric paused long enough to gaze into her eyes, and then continued with a smile. "Please don't take this the wrong way. I'm really looking forward to spending some time with you and getting to know you better. But I don't think you asked to see me today because you wanted to discuss architectural vestiges. What's really on your mind, Stephanie?"

"The high-frequency algorithmic trades have started again, you know," she said in one quick breath.

"Yes, I know."

Stephanie reached out across the table and let her hand rest on Eric's hand.

"And it does not bother you?"

Eric caressed Stephanie's hand and closed his eyes.

ACKNOWLEDGEMENTS

A large group of friends and acquaintances helped me shape this novel better during the research, writing, and editing of the manuscript. First, I must thank my critique groups at the Summer Literary Seminars (SLS) and Disquiet: Dzanc Books International Literary Program in Lisbon, who served as my test readers, initial editors, and who above all so generously shared their insights and their time with me while I was writing the novel. I'd also like to thank a number of friends and family members—Yvette Szmidt who let me borrow her office when I needed a hideaway, Sylviane de Roquebrune, Daniel Benay, Vesela Beleva, Mickhail Lossel, and Marek Birner—for their support, encouragement, and unbridled enthusiasm for my work.

I'm deeply grateful to my literary manager, Ken Atchity, for his guidance, patience and wise counsel. Ken shepherded the novel from its inception and worked tirelessly promoting the manuscript and on getting this book onto the shelves of bookstores. I owe you a big one, Ken.

Many thanks, too, to my fine editor and copyeditor, Christine Dixon and Maggie Smith, who somehow managed to produce a coherent piece of work out of my rough manuscript. Additionally, thanks to Indie Designz for the wonderful book cover design—without forgetting all the folks who had a hand in one way or another in the production of this book.

Many thanks to you all.

Nomad on the Run

GEORGES BENAY

AN ERIC MARTIN NOMAD SERIES

AVAILABLE NOW

PLEASE TURN THE PAGE FOR A PREVIEW OF
NOMAD ON THE RUN...

PROLOGUE

ROCK OF GIBRALTAR
MONDAY, OCTOBER 13, 2007

Paco gazed at the turn-of-the century building and struggled with his emotions. Soon he would lunge into action that, by some ironic twist, would change the lives of two men: a new beginning for him and a premature death for the foreigner.

His journey to Gibraltar had begun in a Spanish prison. There he had been introduced to the Brotherhood, more as a means of survival in a hostile environment than out of any true religious zeal. The voice of a shadowy bearded man came to him one day from the dark recesses of the cell opposite his own, and he had listened to that voice because of his passion for the history of his people. The man had told him of the great injustice and humiliation his people had endured over the centuries because of their religious beliefs. He was reminded of the glorious past of his ancestors, who had conquered half of the infidel world. At first, all he had done was listen to the voice. Until one night, when he had dreamed he would one day bring fame and honor to his family. And so, he finally spoke back to the man with the grey beard, who told him to wait for the call that would come one day. From that day forward, his fate was sealed.

Paco had left Madrid two days ago in the middle of the afternoon with two trusted companions. They traveled through the night and most of the following day in his old Renault. They lived on bitter coffee and dried dates for almost two days to reach their rendezvous before nightfall in Gibraltar. Standing under the canopy of a jewelry store, he surveyed his current surroundings, satisfied with his preparations. He set a safety perimeter around the hotel where they knew the stranger would soon check in. One man posted at each end of the street kept a watchful eye for unwanted onlookers. A distant cousin who cleaned rooms at the hotel would give them access to the garage in the basement. That same cousin had promised to leave the key to the stranger's room in an envelope inside a hamper full of dirty linen in the basement laundry just inside the stairwell.

Paco knew the importance of this mission and hoped it would be the first of many to come. Many years ago, Paco had escaped his village in the High Atlas Mountains of Morocco where his family lived in a "tighremt" with thick walls. The old patriarchal house stood in the middle of a small plot of land surrounded by gaunt peaks and the sparse field of barley, maize, and potatoes that grew under even the most unforgiving conditions. The middle child of a family of eight, he had decided at a young age to run away from the anonymous and poverty-stricken life of a shepherd that was predestined for a middle son by his father and the father of his father before him. He had arrived one bright afternoon in Casablanca looking for fortune and fame. There he met another young man, who told him that the West was where he would find the life he was looking for. But he found none of these things in Madrid. A life of drudgery, menial and shameful jobs, and in the end, petty thefts were all he could hope for to survive in that strange city. Those thefts had led him down a lonely road that ended in imprisonment. And he had sworn to himself the day he had walked out that he would never see such a place again. From the depths of that dusty hell, grand dreams of heroism were born.

He was near his goal, Paco thought now, a bitter irony. What he could not find in a land across the sea, a foreigner on the very edge of his homeland was about to deliver to him. They had been promised a very generous reward to kidnap the foreigner and deliver him, dead or alive, to the stranger he knew only as a voice on the phone. But to Paco, the wealth mattered little. He would gladly have given his share to his two comrades. He had a greater purpose on his mind when he had decided to join the war against the West.

Paco felt his cell phone vibrate in his right pocket and flipped it open. He listened to the man's voice on the phone reserved for incoming calls. The foreigner was on his way, he was told. He glanced at his companion beside him, who immediately understood the silent message and nodded. He had made it clear from the start: Speak only if danger arose.

They both watched the SUV emerge from the top of the hill, followed by a local police car. The two vehicles came to a stop a few yards away from their observation post and the foreigner walked into the hotel alone. Paco grinned, while his companion crushed his cigarette on the ground.

Their eyes focused on the third floor of the grey stone building. After several moments, a light flickered inside the room that had been reserved for the foreigner, and a mild trepidation filled their hearts. Paco left his vantage point and walked hurriedly up the street. In front of the hotel, he threw a quick glance at the window above without breaking stride. A closer look confirmed his initial assumption. The foreigner was settling down in his room. Satisfied, he pulled another cell phone from his left pocket, the one reserved for outgoing calls.

He spoke Arabic in a low voice.

"Everything is set. We will move in soon."

"May Allah be with you," the voice on the phone replied.

Paco, a.k.a. Rashid, checked his watch again. In a few hours it would be all over, he thought. His cousin had agreed to house them and their parcel for the night, for a small fee, of course. The final delivery and exchange would take place on a deserted stretch of road along the coastline. He tensed when the cell phone on his right side buzzed again. That was unexpected.

Paco closed his eyes.

His companions stared at his gaunt face, worried. With a sense of foreboding, he flipped the cell phone open and swallowed hard. The voice carried the harshness of someone used to giving orders.

"I want the man alive. I'll double the reward."

Paco shuddered at the venomous tone. He suddenly felt a stab of pity for the foreigner. Better for him if Paco had been forced to kill the man; the fate that awaited the infidel in the hands of his employer was not to be envied. His life would end all the same, but not before hours or days of torture.

It was mid-October, and an early fall chill was in the air. He raised his head and thought about kneeling down to the east to pray for the success of the mission. The look his comrades gave him convinced him that this was not the time.

Gazing at the third-floor window, Paco saw the light go out. At that instant, he suddenly knew in his heart that his destiny was linked with the foreigner in a dance of life and death. Dusk was settling in quickly over the Rock of Gibraltar, and Paco and his accomplices prepared to strike.

Georges Benay is a former international banker who is now working as a Toronto-based writer and award-winning photographer. He is the author of two novels, including *Nomad on the Run*, and a collection of short stories. His award winning pictures have been featured in several magazines and book covers.

Visit his websites at:

www.georgesbenay.com and www.georgesbenayphotoart.fototime.com

Made in the USA
Lexington, KY
17 June 2017